There were a thousan⟨ ⟩ her tongue, but no more than that made it past her lips.

Instead, Artemis gave in to her baser instincts, and lifting her hand to Ruth's cheek, her other now twining with Ruth's more intricately, she gently caressed the soft skin as she trailed her fingers down to Ruth's lips.

Ruth didn't move, she didn't shy or pull away, and Artemis watched as the dark gray turned to clear skies again. Clear skies, alight with the fire of desire. Slowly, giving her every opportunity to refuse, or move, Artemis leaned in, until their breaths were mingling, their lips but a hairsbreadth apart, every detail from the lightness at the ends of Ruth's eyelashes and the hairs on her cheek in clear focus.

And then, after a pause, seeing nothing but relinquishment and want in her eyes, Artemis surrendered to the moment, her own eyes drifting closed as she met Ruth's lips with hers.

Damn it.

It was too...good.

Too overwhelmingly perfect, and right.

Author Note

We must tell our tales when their time has come,
So it's been before; so it was with this.
For long I desired to pen a story
Set in theater, in some era long past,
My love for the art mighty, and steadfast.
Then grumpy Artemis and joyful Ruth
Introduced themselves to me, and I knew:
'Twas time to write the tale long in my heart.
Doubts assailed, as ever when embarking
On travels new, discov'ring as I did,
Not only more of myself, but as well,
Fascinating histories of worlds past.
Indeed, the 1830s were a most
Intriguing time in theater hist'ry,
Particularly in the British Isles;
Much innovation born of restriction.
Here, I should like to most ardently thank
Stephen Wickens, Dr. Ian Beavis,
For their gracious assistance with research
On local theatrical history.
It should be noted, too, for those intrigued by this,
The Amelia Scott's local studies room
In Tunbridge Wells was a most helpful space.
One should also be sure to look into
The life and journey of Sarah Baker.
I shall leave you now with this entreaty:
Should historical inaccuracies,
Or other such details sparking disbelief,
You find, I pray you forgive this humble writer.
I pray, too, above all, that you be swept
Away by the pure, immortal magic
Of theater; but most of all, of love.

A LIAISON WITH
HER LEADING LADY

LOTTE R. JAMES

HISTORICAL

Harlequin®
HISTORICAL

ISBN-13: 978-1-335-59621-5

A Liaison with Her Leading Lady

Recycling programs for this product may not exist in your area.

Harlequin Enterprises ULC
22 Adelaide St. West, 41st Floor
Toronto, Ontario M5H 4E3, Canada
www.Harlequin.com

Printed in U.S.A.

Lotte R. James trained as an actor and theater director but spent most of her life working day jobs crunching numbers while dreaming up stories of love and adventure. She's thrilled to finally be writing those stories, and when she's not scribbling on tiny pieces of paper, she can usually be found wandering the countryside for inspiration or nestling with coffee and a book.

Books by Lotte R. James

Harlequin Historical

Gentlemen of Mystery

The Housekeeper of Thornhallow Hall
The Marquess of Yew Park House
The Gentleman of Holly Street

The Viscount's Daring Miss
A Lady on the Edge of Ruin

Look out for more books from Lotte R. James coming soon.

To those who came before
and made this book possible.

To anyone needing the story,
and love, within these pages.

To all my friends, near and far, who've walked
with me along so many roads.

And always, to my mother, Brigitte.

ACT I

Chapter One

⌘

'Rejoice, my fellow devotees of thespian delights, for the law now permits us to enjoy the same amusements as those lucky inhabitants of London, Bath, Liverpool, Manchester, or Bristol! For naturally, in the past fifty years, we have not enjoyed any such entertainments in our great town on a regular basis, every June to October, Mondays, Wednesdays, Fridays, and Saturdays, at the hour of six o'clock.'

J.W.F. Hendon, *The Wells Chronicler*, 1788

Tunbridge Wells, May 1832

It should be raining. It felt…wrong for the sun to shine as brightly as it did, barely any clouds marring the pristine cerulean sky. It felt wrong for the temperature to be so perfect, neither too warm, nor too cold; a pleasant breeze carrying away any unpleasantness. Birds sang, trees rustled delicately all around them. Flowers popped up in bright swathes despite the care of the minders of this place to keep it somewhat reverently bleak.

It doesn't set the scene properly.

Ruth knew life wasn't… Well, that life didn't follow the rules, or precepts that ruled life *onstage*. She was a grown woman, not a girl—despite rarely truly feeling the former—though even as a girl, she'd known that much. Perhaps it was one of the first lessons life—*Father*—had taught her in fact.

Still, it felt…insulting, that on this day, of all days, Life, the Creator, the gods—whoever it was ruling the Universe—couldn't see to it that an exception was made. That there couldn't be a bit of atmosphere, a *scene set*, to honour a man whose entire life had been devoted to the theatre.

To any of us who have.

A scene such as this, a sad, sorry scene, full of grief, woe, and pain, should not be set to glorious sunshine and beauty. Ruth knew from experience such a scene should be set to shuddering thunder, and apocalyptic rain. It should be grey, and lamentable, and…*mournful*. In their world, anyone who attempted to discard such rules of dramaturgy would be ruthlessly mocked and summarily cast far from any place of theatrical endeavour.

Father would've laughed.

In fact, he would've been happy—*might be, up there, laughing at us all*—that it wasn't so sad, and sorry, but joyful. He would've said that he'd specifically asked for this to be a celebration of his life, not a sad goodbye, and the Heavens were merely granting his wish. Only, Ruth *wanted* a sad goodbye. She wanted the world—or at the very least, this corner of it—to feel as gloomy as she did. She wanted them to know today was a sad day, not a good day.

And not solely for me.

Lifting her head slightly, she cast her eyes around the gathered crowd—which couldn't even be considered a crowd, barely a *troupe*—all heads bowed in silent contemplation and prayer as the man dressed in black and white droned on with the words from his mighty book.

You'd think he'd know his lines better by now. He looks to be as old as this church.

That was another thing which sat uncomfortably with Ruth. Not the vicar's lack of memorisation, or even his generally bored and unemotive countenance, but the fact that there was a vicar involved to begin with. That they were in a churchyard, burying Father all *good and proper*, when his life had been anything but, and when her father hadn't even been a believer. In the One True God and all that. Her father, like her, and others of their ilk, was a pagan of sorts, who worshipped the old gods of theatre.

Yet apparently her father's wishes had been unmistakably clear on the matter. The note he'd scrawled in his final days, and slipped to his solicitor, had read something along the lines of:

> *Suppose 'tis better to be safe than sorry. I was baptised in the faith, and should therefore exit the world according to its rites—if only for poetic symmetry. Having my body interred beneath my theatre would be most inconvenient and impractical.*

Poetic symmetry indeed.
Hmph.

However, beyond the fact that she supposed there weren't many alternatives to this particular spectacle—*not like we could give him some Norse funeral*—it was what Father had wanted, and therefore Ruth was here, respecting his wishes. Father had always been a slightly incomprehensible man to her, and this all was just further fodder for *that* fire; but then on the other hand, Ruth knew that like most of those who chose a life such as they did, he danced to his own singular tune.

Even at the end it seems.

The others didn't seem so bothered by all this pomp and circumstance, so she supposed she shouldn't be either. Only it had taken half a lifetime for her and Father to become... father and daughter, therefore she couldn't really help feeling cheated in a sense, that this whole spectacle wasn't quite... *right*.

Glancing at the gathered bunch of them, she took some comfort and peace in their steady presence. Some years ago, or perhaps, if they'd been in London, there might've been more. Perhaps the church might've been full, and this graveyard too, but now...

There are only those few of us who remain.

Thomas, sweet, lovely Thomas; her best friend since childhood. Looking uncharacteristically sombre, his tall, lanky form bent over, as if folding itself into his ill-fitting suit— three inches too short on the sleeves and legs, having surely not worn it since his own mother's funeral many years ago.

Montague, in all his ghastly, sharp-featured, early middle-aged handsomeness, looking strangely at home in the graveyard.

Laurie, the Beau of the Boards as the papers—and audiences—sometimes called him, dashing as ever, his gaze seemingly worlds away as he stared into the trees across from her father's resting place.

St John, the tiny ferret of a fellow with a heart of pure gold, sliding his hands incessantly along the brim of his hat, looking the most uncomfortable. Still young—barely two years out of his apprenticeship—perhaps he'd been spared until now the grim realities of death, and grief.

Madeleine was here too, looking as a graceful, gorgeous widow might—though she wasn't anything of the sort. Well.

Graceful and gorgeous, yes, but a widow, she most certainly was not.

If anyone might lay claim to such a title in this case, it would be Rose, the theatre's seamstress and costumier, who had been Father's companion since his return from London some ten years ago. Rose had been a second mother to Ruth, and had the steely strength and beauty of an ancient chieftainess, but the softness and warmth of a bright summer's eve.

Guy was here too—their builder, effects genius, and painter extraordinaire—and Fanny, their stage manager. The apprentices, the workers, the musicians, the whole lot of them—which came to barely more than twenty, including Ruth. They ran a small, tight ship—*not that we have much choice*—but all of Father's true friends were here.

Which is all that matters, here, at the end.

Vaguely, Ruth registered the vicar's droning had ceased, and her eyes focused properly on the people she'd been examining. She found they were all staring at her expectantly, some offering encouraging smiles, and she realised this was…the moment.

It…hit her harder than she expected.

Glancing at her father's plain coffin, there, beside the hole in the earth which would hold him for ever, she felt…the weight of the grief. Of what her life would be without him.

The weight of the goodbye.

Pushing back tears, she glanced up at the vicar, and nodded.

Men came, and slowly lowered the coffin into the ground.

Rose sobbed.

The breeze felt colder, seeping through Ruth's threadbare gloves.

Thomas watched her.

Ruth kept her eyes on a robin perched on an ancient, leaning gravestone just behind the vicar's right arm. The robin quirked its head, and watched her, and Ruth felt…

Lost. Alone. Strange.

Her father lay at the bottom of his grave, and she took the first handful of dirt to toss upon him, and commit him to the earth.

The others followed suit, and she kept her distance from them, wondering why she did so. Not seeking Thomas's hand, or Rose's embrace. Even a pat on the head from Montague, or a cheeky smile from Laurie.

Instead she stood slightly apart from them whilst they too committed her father to the earth, and glanced down at the dirt marring her glove. She wondered if it would be disrespectful to wipe it off. To toss the glove. Perhaps she should've taken it off to begin with.

She glanced to the robin to see if he had any wisdom to share on the matter.

He didn't.

He did sing his little song before flying off, and Ruth stood there, in the sunshine, and perfect breeze which didn't suit the occasion, and quietly cursed Life, God, the Universe, or the gods for taking her father from her.

Then, she silently did as one was meant to do in such a place, on such an occasion.

Goodbye, Father. I love you.

Early June

Oh, Father, how could you do this to us? How could you not tell me? And how did you ever manage to hide this from me?

Objectively, Ruth supposed she shouldn't be so surprised. Not after the plans to buy a second theatre on the coast were abandoned the year before last. Not after the loss of some of their best touring engagements. Not after the loss of over half their company. Not considering she saw just as well as anyone else how many people came to watch their shows.

Still, she'd thought…

That all the reasons you gave me, Father, were true. That all these 'sacrifices' as you called them had been worth it.

Turns out, wrong is what you thought, Ruthie.

Sighing, she tried to expel some of the anger, and fear from herself, and it helped, *somewhat*. Well, not really, but then, right now, she doubted much would help unknot everything that had been knotted within her by the solicitor's words.

'Six weeks, Miss Connell. There will be nothing to hold the creditors back past then…'

Stomping her foot, and shaking her head, Ruth began walking away from the man's office, down through the whole of town, past the rocks, the common, the lodges and hotels, back to the theatre which lay just off the ever celebrated and famous Parade. Though she wished to walk briskly, to potentially expend some of the excess terror and frustration, she forced herself to walk calmly, lest she arrive too quickly, with no idea what to say to them all.

How do you tell your family something such as this? People who've shown loyalty, care, and friendship. Who have believed in your dream, that…

The dream might die a quick death all too soon.

Before the season even ends.

If she'd had it in her to cry any more, that thought might've brought more tears to her eyes, only she'd expended them all since Father had slipped away to his next life. Losing him had been hard enough, but she'd consoled herself in some way with the idea that he would always live on in the theatre he'd built. He'd live on through what they'd all create together, only now, that too, that last vestige of him, her heritage, their somewhat guaranteed livelihoods, their haven…it would be taken from her—*them all*—too.

How do I tell them?

How could you not tell me, Father, that things were so dire? We'd have found a solution together...

Perhaps the most frightening thought of all was that Ruth didn't think she had it in her. The strength, the intelligence, the...wherewithal to do what it would take to save their apparently crumbling little enterprise. She'd thought... Father had trusted her more these past years. He'd taken time to teach her so much, and yet now, she realised, she'd never fully carried any weight. She had no actual idea of what... saving the theatre would take. In that moment, she felt as if she'd learned nothing at all.

In what world am I, Ruth Connell, a theatre manager?

All she could truly say that she *did* know with any certainty right then, was that saving the theatre would take more than what they were already doing—*obviously*—because this theatre was all they had. Those few local businesses who were their patrons...had already given what they would; even if they could be called upon to contribute further, it would never be enough to save them. Besides, she couldn't rightly go to them, and in essence, ask them to invest further in an enterprise which was apparently so indebted. She might not know much, but she knew that wasn't very good business.

So no, there was nothing else, no other way to find such funds as she now required. No homes, no art, no money, merely that last building, and their craft, so they needed something new, and exciting, to bring in those audiences, again, and again, and—

Blast.

Walking slowly had not prevented her from arriving back at the theatre too quickly.

There it stood in all its...subdued, if not glory, then steadiness. Unassuming though it might be from here—plain white stone, squat somewhat, four stories, with large ground-level windows behind and beside a simple oak door—fading into its surroundings, all neatly renovated and unified nearly two centuries before, it was…

Like the thieves' den in *Ali Baba*. Full of treasure, and wonders, hidden behind plainness, which one could access with the magic words; in this case: *one ticket, please*.

Ruth stood before it, the sight, the welcome of it, and the potential hidden inside, swelling and twisting within her, inspiring yet terrifying at once.

I can't lose it.

I can't lose what family I have left, and if the theatre closes, they will scatter in the wind.

Even Thomas.

And I…

Have no idea what or who I'll become, but I don't think it will be…me.

Bittersweetness invading her heart and veins, Ruth pondered for a moment walking further, perhaps going up to the common to properly take some time to think this all through, but instead, she forced herself to head around the building towards the stage door.

It might hurt to have to tell the others everything, but perhaps they could help. Perhaps they could help her unknot this. Perhaps they could think of some clever solution or perhaps…

They will abandon me. Leave now, to find something surer.

Go to join the hungry wolves who have been circling us for…some time.

One of the other companies in the environs, such as Mr Warlington's, who'd been trying to get their hands on the licence to perform here for years.

I have to risk it.

A large portion of the anger she now felt towards Father was born from the fact that he'd kept their dire situation from her. That he'd purported to be sharing everything with her, including how to run the theatre in time, but never mentioned anything about debts this significant, or the *true* scale of the dwindling receipts. The few occasions she'd tried to question him on their rather small audiences, and waning bookings of other entertainment—famous singers, composers, dance troupes, even jugglers, or contortionists and so on— he'd shrugged, and pushed away her concerns, saying everything was *just fine*.

That they were *just fine*. Even just before he became ill, she'd questioned their schedule for this summer season, and wondered at how they'd manage, and he'd just said: *'It will be fine.'*

Well, it isn't fine, is it?

Why couldn't you tell me, Father? Why...?

It was the question which had been running incessantly through her head since the solicitor had told her of the situation, and which continued to plague her as she made her way into the building, and through the dark, sparse, empty labyrinth of tiny corridors towards the stage. Most everyone would be there, rehearsing and preparing for their summer programme, set to open at the end of the week. Typically, they would've rehearsed, and finished everything by now, however, because of Father's illness and passing, there had been some delays.

The loss of their captain, so to speak, had left Ruth at the helm, and though others, stronger of mind and heart might've continued on without flinching, Ruth had taken some time to...find her sea legs.

I am still unsteady upon them even now.

Though recently, Ruth had to admit she had been finding work to be most distracting and useful, and would've much preferred to be—as she would normally—rehearsing with them, and not at the damned solicitor's meeting.

It is done. Now you must find a solution.

Right.

Like a prisoner being led to the gallows, Ruth made her way up the steps leading backstage, nodding at the one or two workers and apprentices, buzzing about as they tried to finish the sets, props, effects, and everything else.

Reaching the wings, she concealed herself in the darkness for a moment, leaning against the thick, dusty red curtain hovering hidden at the edge of the proscenium arch.

Taking a breath, and trying to screw her courage tight, she watched them all. Her friends, all the family she had left, making their way through scenes in little groups—far downstage so as not to hamper the others' work—as behind and around them, the sets were assembled, final painting was done, rigging was adjusted, and props were taken or given. It was a cacophony of noise and rhythm, of industry, and if not creativity, then passion.

Their main new play for the season was *The Revenge of Captain Marshall*, written by a talented, but derivative writer whose name, truth be told, Ruth couldn't even recall. It was the best of the stack of 'new' plays Father had brought back from London on his last trip before his illness—their licence here only permitting performances of what was or would be produced at one of the licensed or patent theatres in Westminster, unless of course, they wished to submit something to the Lord Chamberlain.

Ha. That'll be the day.

So yes, they were left with whatever they could find which trickled down from the *legitimate* houses. It wasn't all bad, but neither was it…

New. Exciting. Challenging. Intriguing.

The Revenge, for instance, wasn't terrible. There were some good things hidden within the sentiment, and cheap spectacle, really, there were. Only, it wasn't…

Anything which will keep people coming.

Even the *cheap spectacle* and *sentiment* weren't quite enough to truly capture the audience's fancy. It was the sort of play which reinforced people's thoughts that theatre—at least in this country—had lost its…soul, heart, and beauty. That all which remained now—because of the assault and rise of *illegitimate* theatre and the utter demise of morals and taste—was vulgar, cheap, and unnoteworthy. Usually derived from those *lesser* artists on the Continent, according to some.

Yet vulgar, cheap, and unnoteworthy is found first and foremost in those seemingly grand houses now; true innovation remains the province of those on the fringes…

Not that they could afford to risk such innovation here—whether by law, or lest they risk their audience, who always wanted *the latest from London*.

That wasn't to say *all* they could *potentially* perform was unnoteworthy, that there truly *was* no good theatre left in Britain as some posited—even be it adaptations of Continental work or great novels—only that… Well, on top of all the rest, if there was something truly good, and interesting, and noteworthy—at least in Ruth's opinion—some other company managed to snatch it up before they did. And Father would never deign to—or now Ruth wondered, *risk*—putting on what another company within fifty miles was.

So it was such as *The Revenge* for them. Its pairing with *Lady Lily's Lesson*, and *The Black Beast's Return*, along with the usual light entertainments—songs, dances, and music, all provided by themselves, since anyone else worth booking was, according to Father, *otherwise engaged*—was solid enough, but it wouldn't…excite anyone.

What Ruth wouldn't give to be able to produce something…

Extraordinary.

Really, she just wanted to be able to *produce* something. Something new, and challenging, which reflected the tumultuous and changing times they were living in. She wanted to be able to engage a dramatist, and *create*, not just reproduce or emulate or borrow.

Hell, at this point she'd even settle for a Shakespeare, or a Molière, which they themselves could properly play with.

Though truthfully, no one here wants Shakespeare or Molière, unless it's a star of the London stage playing Hamlet or Tartuffe or Lady Macbeth...

And unfortunately, such stars were certainly out of Ruth's reach.

Even further out of reach than those in the Heavens.

As so much seems out of our reach just now.

A sense of deep melancholy and uncertainty filled her heart as she continued watching them all onstage for a time, their business somewhat soothing. Until finally, her heart twisted with a pang of sudden, sharp grief, as on came the man who'd taken over the patriarch's role usually played by her father—William, a retired London actor, and old friend of Father's who had retired to Sevenoaks, but happily agreed to grace the boards again, his time, as he put it, *not quite over yet.*

And neither is ours.

Resignation more than courage pushing her onwards, she stepped into the light, and made her way downstage, so she could face all those gathered. She might've called them to attention, but instead she just stood there, as everyone slowly halted their work, and turned to face her.

Many she knew, could see the grimness in her; though she was onstage, she wasn't acting, and even if she'd tried to, she wouldn't have had the heart to be any good. They gathered around her, tension in them from whatever terrible news she would bring, assembling in a close, but not tight half-circle—Fanny behind in the pit, leaning on the stage.

Drawing in a breath, she made to open her mouth, however both her courage and her voice deserted her suddenly, even though her mind raced.

Something new.

Something good.

Something exciting.

Something unmissable.

A rousing, popular and critical success.

The thing actors' dreams are made of.

Actors...

William...the retired actor living nearby...

A star of the London stage...

'As you all know, I've just had my meeting with Father's solicitor,' she said, her attention on those present slipping, as her mind began to form, if not a plan, then...*an idea.* 'Apparently...there are debts.' Everyone's faces fell, some nodding, some shaking their head, as the meaning of what she'd said took no time to solidify in them. 'We have six weeks before the theatre is lost. *But,*' she added, before the open mouths of some could produce sound, objections, questions, or anger. 'I have a plan. If you all... If you stay, I will save this place. I promise.'

Questions, objections, anger, confusion, and exclamations sounded at once then, any restraint gone.

Yet they seemed to fade away, merely music to underscore the moment, as Ruth stood there, smiling, confidence trickling into her heart. She met Thomas's eyes, and the smile in them boosted it even further.

I can save it. I will.

Because if nothing else, a solemn oath proclaimed on the boards, before her family, her gods, and the ghosts living here—could not be undone.

I have a plan.

Chapter Two

The scissors snipped with a satisfying click and swoosh as they made their way through the newspaper, and Artemis smiled to herself. She also took a moment to congratulate herself silently on how far she'd come, as she continued to cut the page in her hands into tiny little pieces, with all the care and tranquillity in the world.

Three years ago, she would've been raging, crying, tearing the dashed thing to pieces with her own bare hands, and now, here she was, not tearing, but cutting. Not crying, or raging, but sitting quietly and peacefully.

Progress and growth indeed.

Someday, perhaps, she might no longer need to indulge in destroying every printed piece of proof of *their* triumph. Their success, their…everything, born of their betrayal of her. Someday perhaps, she might not find it so cathartic, and liberating, *exorcising*, to wreak some sort of havoc on their… *achievements*. Someday perhaps, she might be happy in some measure, that they'd found what they were so desperately looking for. Someday, she might…forgive them. Move on.

Artemis paused, considering that for a moment, then began laughing with uncontrollable mirth.

'That'll bloody be the day,' she murmured a few, long minutes later, when she'd calmed again, then resumed her work.

A better person, perhaps, might truly achieve something such as that.

Forgiveness.

Only Artemis knew herself well enough to know that she

wasn't so...*good*. Even good *enough*. Her bitterness had settled nicely upon her shoulders like a delightful, well-worn coat, or beloved blanket. It comforted her as such items would, keeping her safe from that which lay beneath the now mostly worn-out rage, and hurt.

It protected her from the utter desolation which was far beyond pain, and sadness; kept the emptiness, the void of all she'd been, the hollowness, at bay. It lurked still, beneath the veneer of stilled comfort, she knew that, but being wrapped in bitterness made each day bearable.

Just as destroying the papers lauding her former partner—in every way—and former friend's shared supposed *triumph*, helped keep the void at bay.

Artemis resumed her little ritual, shaking the echoes of desolation away. Thinking on it...brought it dangerously close to the forefront. Which wouldn't do. So on she cut, until she had a very neat, and satisfying pile of nigh-on perfect squares of paper, and then she set aside the scissors, gathered up the pile in her hands, and knelt before the roaring fire beside her. Moving aside the screen, she slowly sprinkled the pieces into the flames, taking time to warm her chilled hands as she watched the shreds of words combust and dance to an inaudible tune.

That of my broken heart perhaps.

Once she'd finished, she rose, setting the screen back into place, and rubbing her hands as she pondered the question of what she would do next to fill her day. Glancing over her shoulder at the window—not that she needed to, considering the sounds filling the air were enough to tell her the state of the world outside just now—she saw only the dark gloom brought on by the storm which lashed at the diamond-shaped panes of glass, thick rivulets washing down them as more drops were hurled at it with the fierce wind that shook the surrounding trees.

A grim day, some might say, but the sort of day Artemis loved for it matched her…countenance now. The sort of day which forced isolation, and made her feel less as though she was…missing out on something, out there, in the wide, wide world.

But there is nothing out there for you. Nothing worthwhile. You know that well enough.

Quite.

Unfortunately, days such as this limited her choices for activities to keep her mind and body busy. Certainly, she would cook later—it being only barely ten in the morning—and perhaps even make some preserves from the strawberries she'd harvested yesterday.

Making preserves. Artemis Goode. Who would've imagined.

Shaking off the annoying thoughts, Artemis returned to her chair to enjoy the cosy comfort of the room whilst she made her plan for the day. Cooking meals and preserve-making would take up a good portion of it. There would be no gardening—something else she'd never thought she'd do, and it had taken some time to learn—no walks through the surrounding woods, nor even a venturing to the shops in the village a mile away. Cleaning…she'd done that yesterday, along with the laundry.

There was a myriad of other things she could do—there was some mending to be done for instance, and perhaps embroidery too—but she thought she might just sit here, in the lovely warm gloom of this room, and read.

No greater pastime than reading by the warmth of a good fire whilst a storm rages beyond.

An entirely honest sentiment, yet the lurking thoughts and grimness pushed to the forefront again. The thing was… reading by firelight, curled up in a magnificently cosy chair, whilst a storm raged outside, *was* one of life's greatest pleasures. And reading all manner of books was one of Artemis's greatest passions. It stimulated her mind and soul in ways not easily expressed, inspired her, and—

There.

That, *right there*, was the crux of the thing.

It used to inspire her. Used to fill her with passion, ideas, and joy, but now...

It keeps me occupied.

Oh, she still got swept away to distant, imaginary vistas, or learned new things about the world, but the words... The words didn't move her in the same manner any more. They'd become *solely* an escape from her life, rather than *sometimes* an escape, and not truly any more, a new road into and about her life, and self. Books filled her days, which were altogether too empty to even remotely be considered *fulfilling*.

Retiring away from the world and her previous life had sounded—and been for a time—all well and good, however now that she'd settled into this new life, Artemis couldn't deny at times how sorely she felt the lack of...*everything*. She kept herself as busy as she could so as not to feel it, but she felt a passionless spectre, repeating cyclical days, her soul gone.

Captured, by the villain of this tale, and the evil enchantress by his side.

That helped too, to view them thus. Killian, the man with whom she'd spent half a lifetime, built so much, shared so much, and who she'd believed would be her partner...for ever. And Winnie, the woman who'd been a friend once, before replacing Artemis in Killian's eye.

A tale as old as time—thus deserving of pathetic and tired stock characters.

How melodramatic you're being, Artemis. Perhaps you should find some reading to suit this mood of yours. Some sad and sorry tale of a young fool, wandering about stormy

moors, finding her way to some ominous ruin of a house,
inhabited by the seemingly handsome, but secretly dark,
haunted, and twisted lord...

Come to think of it, perhaps that was exactly what she
needed. Something pathetic, yet entertainingly lurid and cathartic.

Artemis rose, intent on finding such a book in the not in-
significant collection upon her shelves to pass the morning,
and even considered making some tea to go with it, but only
made it as far as a couple steps.

Someone was banging very insistently on her door.

Bothersome.

Yet at the same time... I find myself welcoming a minute
of distraction and unexpected disturbance to the monotony
of my life.

Let's go see who this is, then.

Who this was, then turned out to be no one Artemis
knew—not that she knew many hereabouts, nor expected
visitors from further afield. She supposed some of the latter could surely find her if they tried, though she hadn't told
anyone where she was retiring to—not that she'd known
where she was going when she jumped onto the first coach
available the day she'd packed her things, and disappeared
from London.

As for the former—people *hereabouts*—Artemis kept to
herself as a general rule, and after a time, people nearby—
including the postman, her only regular *visitor*—ceased trying to make a friend, or even friendly neighbour out of her.
Which suited her just fine.

In any case, she didn't recall even glimpsing the drenched
mouse on her doorstep on her occasional social interactions
in the vicinity, and even drenched as she was, Artemis knew
she would remember the woman's pretty face.

I may be a hermit and thoroughly through with love but I can still appreciate beauty.

Soft, classically rounded and symmetrical features. A straight, but proportional nose which didn't quite qualify—as the fashion named it—as a *button*. Generous lips that—beyond looking absolutely rosy and scrumptious—were painted on with all the illustrative dips and curves. Thick—oddly thick—perfectly arched brows. Eyes...

Big, rounded eyes the colour of silver clouds.

As for the rest of her...

Beneath a rather worn and masculine hat, what looked to be thick brown hair—soaked, like the rest of her, and plastered against her face and delicate neck. Not much of her form was hidden beneath the thin, water-saturated light brown cotton gown; she was rather tiny—the top of her head barely reaching Artemis's nose—and had a static grace to her, with discreet, yet bountiful curves.

There was an agelessness to her—at first glimpse, from a distance, Artemis might've guessed her to be a child, but then looking at her closely, it appeared as though the woman wasn't much younger than Artemis's old age of five and thirty.

There were little lines, little crinkles, that Artemis felt the urge to decipher the origins of, and to—

'Atchoo!' the intruder sneezed, thankfully both covering her face, and tearing Artemis from her useless stream of appreciative and desire-laden thoughts.

Right. Intruder. Pretty or not—get rid of her.

'I've no need to hear the message of the Lord, nor His Son,' she stated flatly, straightening. 'And there is no charity to be found here. The village is just a mile that way,' she told the drenched mouse—*yes, drenched mouse, not beautiful woman*—gesturing south. 'You'll find both the good word, and charity there.'

Determined, and slightly…*unsettled* by the sudden rise of a desire she'd thought long extinguished by betrayal, Artemis made to shut the door in the stranger's face, but was halted by the woman's next words.

'Artemis Goode?' Artemis considered denying the charge, but instead merely stood there, and raised an expectant brow. 'My name is Ruth Connell,' the mouse continued as silence reigned, fighting through chattering. If Artemis had been a better person, she might've invited the woman in, but the sheer fact that this Ruth knew who she was, and sought her out, meant whatever this was… Artemis already knew she would want no part of it. 'I'm Toby Connell's daughter.'

A pang of wicked nostalgia twisted Artemis's heart at the mention of the man who had once…

Opened the door to my life, and my soul.

Still, she pushed it back. Three years she'd been here, ridding herself of everything of that former life, and of its ghosts, and the very last thing she needed was some pretty little reminder of it, to send her back into the depths of desolation.

Steeling herself against such dangers, she tightened her grip on the door, glaring with as much *unwelcome* as she could manage.

'And?'

The mouse's eyes flicked over Artemis's shoulder, seeking out the promised warmth and dryness of *inside*.

Artemis didn't move, though she felt the urge the other woman did—standing here, even with the shelter of the tiny portico, she was getting wet and chilled as the rain blew in sideways.

Finally understanding that she would receive no quarter, Ruth sighed, rubbing her hands, and nodding.

'It's a long story,' she said with a resignation and wry sorrow that echoed within Artemis to an uncomfortable degree.

'The short of it is, my father is dead. And I will lose the theatre he built, and called home these past ten years unless I can put on a show which will have everyone talking. A new play by Artemis Goode would do that.'

Snorting at the insanity, the *nerve* of the little mouse, Artemis shook her head.

'I'm retired.'

'Then come out of retirement. Surely after everything—'

'Who do you think you are, coming here, demanding I write you a play, you impudent little mite?' Artemis exclaimed, taking a step forth—though to her credit Ruth didn't move. 'I'm. *Retired*. I left the theatre. I no longer act, I no longer write—in fact I made a vow never to write another damned play in my life. Were I ever to go back on such decisions and promises, it would certainly *never* be for some desperate stranger, begging on my doorstep. Now go away, and never darken that very doorstep again.'

'I am desperate,' Ruth said, as she turned away, swallowing emotion that Artemis did feel *slightly* guilty for provoking. Though she didn't move, merely kept the woman at her back as she clutched the door, ready to close it in her face. 'I will lose everything—my family, my home, my livelihood—if I am forced to sell my father's theatre. I... I know you suffered disappointment in London, and came here to...whatever you came here to do. Still, I came to you, because my father... He used to tell such tales of you.' Artemis clenched her teeth, ignoring how well the other woman's arrows struck. 'How you lived and breathed this extraordinary thing called *theatre*. I mistakenly thought... I don't know what I thought,' Ruth chuckled bitterly, and that chafed more than desperation.

Because a woman such as her should never know bitterness.

'But since I am desperate, I will say this. Once, my father gave you a chance. He gave you the first opportunity of your career. I would say, a debt is owed. So I don't know what vows, or promises you made, but I don't really care either. I've come to collect on his behalf.'

Artemis did slam the door in Ruth's face then.

Not without second thought, and not without remorse, but without the ability to do anything save for that. She needed... to get away. From the woman, from her words, all she brought with her—*a challenge, a debt to be paid, the past*—before...

Well, before *what*, she wasn't entirely sure, but she did know it wouldn't be good.

So she slammed the door in the woman's face, and listened as Ruth swore her way off her land, and then she went to her chair by the fire, and stared into it, promising herself that she absolutely, certainly, would never agree to this.

Certainly not.

A couple of hours later, well stymied by a good amount of local cider, Artemis found herself doing what she hadn't in a very long time. What she knew was the worst idea she'd had in a very long time. She found herself looking in *the chest*.

It had begun as a desperate attempt to rid herself of the guilt in her heart which had grown, festering and feeding itself as she'd stared into the fire after kicking the mouse off her land.

Guilt, regarding Toby Connell.

She'd told herself that to look through the chest—to confront some portion of her past—was to reassure herself that...

It was all best left behind.

That there was a *very* good reason she'd made her vow—beyond the simple fact that it had been an easy one to make considering the words...were gone. Considering they'd abandoned her in her darkest hour, and therefore it was no great feat to, in turn, forsake them for ever.

Surely there had to be something more to it than that, however; more to her decision to come here, and not hide but... *retire*, and if she remembered it, she would be secure in the knowledge that...she owed the Connells nothing.

Certainly.

However, before such a thing could be remembered, Artemis had required a new bottle of cider, because even just *thinking* on how the words had abandoned her... That seemingly simple and succinct reminder of losing that part of herself—something beyond her voice, a true piece of her soul and identity—was altogether worse than anything else.

When Killian and Winnie had cast her away like some piece of rubbish to be used and discarded... They'd well and truly broken her in a way she'd never expected. In a way she could never forgive herself for, because like as she might to blame *them*, she knew very well it was her own weak heart and mind that had cast the final, terrible blow. It was her own weakness which had extinguished the flame alive in her since...birth perhaps. Childhood definitely.

For as long as she could remember, she'd had these... voices in her head. As if there were hundreds of people—not all at once, though sometimes too many to hear properly— telling her their stories. Who they were, what they liked, who they were hurt by, what they wanted most from life...

They were her friends. Imaginary friends, yes, but whom she brought to life by first telling their garbled stories to other children or her parents, then by drawing them—etching little figures in dirt and fences, whatever she could find. Then, once she'd learned to read and write—despite her rather meagre upbringing, her parents believed that much gave a measure of freedom over one's destiny—she'd begun writing those tales on what blank spaces she could. Once she had, the voices, those friends, would fade away, satisfied their story had been told, and new friends would come along to share theirs.

They had always been with her. Through good times, and bad. Through harsh winters when food was scarce on the table. Through her father's sudden death on the wharf where he worked, then some years later, her mother's illness and death. They'd been with her as she made her way from singing in the streets for coin, to singing in taverns, to…

Gracing the stage of some of the most reputed theatres in London.

Even as a celebrated actress, the words had been there, her imaginary friends whispering to her whenever…she wasn't onstage, begging to be scribbled onto sheaves of paper. Then, with her name established, she'd been able to leverage her popularity to have those words brought to life by actors like herself.

All thanks to Toby Connell.

Artemis glanced over into *the chest* as though it was full of vipers rather than a hodgepodge of old journals, newspaper clippings, mementos… All that remained of her old life; all she hadn't been able to bring herself to burn no matter how sorely she'd wished to…

Many times.

Taking a hefty swig of cider, she extracted the old, and beautiful leather-bound collection of Shakespeare, and ran her fingers gently across the embossed cover. She'd bought it herself. Saved up for two years, limiting herself on everything else, because she'd known…to become a serious, and respected actress, she needed to know the Bard.

It hadn't ever been her dream to act—she'd never really known what her dream was, though she'd always known… there was a desperate desire within her to do something *different*. She'd always had this sense, that there was something beyond life, beyond mundanity; another world, of beauty, and feeling, and mystery, that only a few could see.

When Papa had died, and the odd jobs she and Mama both worked hadn't been enough for them to survive on alone, she'd taken to singing, and acting out comedic bits she devised herself on the street. She'd seen enough others scraping a living doing such, and she'd known…perhaps it was a way out of her own life. Off the path of her prescribed destiny as a child of Shadwell. Mama had been doubtful, urging her to find better work—until Artemis began bringing home more coin than she might've working a shop, or the factories.

So Artemis had persevered, sometimes working bits with others, or getting jobs in the little plays or puppet shows they put on in people's front rooms or taverns. Over the years, she'd been told often that she was pretty enough, sang well enough, and was overall magnetic enough, to be a proper favourite on the boards. And she'd seen enough to know, those women who made it and became the darlings of the town, had…power. Sway. Money.

Thus the dream of becoming a *proper* actress was born.

Artemis told herself she'd become big enough to never worry about another meal, and perhaps, someday, to become a playwright. And so, she had.

All thanks to Toby Connell.

Setting the thick volume on her lap, Artemis set the cider aside, and slowly opened the pages, the book itself opening to what it knew she wished to reveal. She might've thought it some sign or portent, had the size of what was tucked between the pages not made it a natural thing for the book to open on it. Taking a deep breath, Artemis gathered it up gingerly, cradling the dried rose in her palm, stroking it as though it were a fragile, newborn animal.

Tears pricked her eyes, and she swiped at her lashes, banishing them away angrily as memories assailed her. This dried-up rose…

Toby Connell had given it to her after her first performance at his theatre twenty years ago. She'd played the innocent young heroine in some gothic melodrama she couldn't even recall the name of.

Lies, you know very well it was The Widow of Grimstone Tower.

Yes, she remembered the name. In fact, she remembered almost every moment of that night. The thrill. The pounding heart. The gasps of the audience. The smell of her musty costume, and of the actor playing her lover's breath. She recalled the stuffy heat, and the otherworldliness of it all.

And she recalled Toby Connell greeting her after the bows, standing in the darkness of the wings, this rose outstretched. He hadn't said anything. Merely smiled, a twinkle, and a knowing look in his eyes.

When she'd left him some two years later to go off with Killian—an actor himself still, though he already fancied himself an *impresario* who would secure Artemis the very best engagements, and some day, have his own theatre— Toby Connell had only nodded, and told her he'd known that first night she would leave to conquer the world someday. That he'd known from the very first that she was made for this strange world of theirs. Destined to be not only part of it, but a beacon of it.

Of course he'd also cautioned her against putting too much trust into Killian, but then what heed did young lovestruck girls give to wise men's warnings?

None.

'I should've listened to you, Mr Connell,' she murmured, placing the rose back where it belonged, and closing the volume again.

She wouldn't have *not* followed Killian, but perhaps, she would've guarded herself, her life, and her future a bit better.

Too late for that now.

Sighing, Artemis sat there, staring into the box, a sum total of her achievements. Her life. Her career. Everything except…

Another reason to my leaving it all behind.

Yes, there was heartbreak, anger, resentment, humiliation, annoyance at the ways things worked in theatre even, but the only thing which had truly sent her running, had been the knowledge that she could never…live up to her own reputation again. She would never be Artemis Goode again, rebuild herself, because the words had abandoned her.

And I am the words, as they are me.

Still, despite all of that, dread filled her heart, because she knew that unfortunately, there was one thing she wouldn't be able to live with on top of the rest.

The guilt of leaving her debt to Toby Connell unpaid.

I'll write her a play, old man.

I don't know how—and I do know it will be…the worst thing I've ever written, that will likely ruin us both, but I will write her a play.

The world will see what Artemis Goode has become, and then perhaps it will let me retire in peace.

Chapter Three

'I don't know *what* I was thinking,' Ruth whined, shaking her head as she stared into the cup of ale before her despondently. Thomas said nothing—he hadn't since he'd found her shivering on the pavement outside the theatre, staring up at it, tears running down her face. He'd said nothing as he'd tucked her arm into his, and led her here, to their local drinking establishment—luckily one with a wonderful, roaring fire she could sit beside to dry and warm herself.

Unfortunately, though the cold in her limbs had waned as her clothes turned from wet to damp, the cold in her heart hadn't lessened.

Though at least she wasn't crying any longer. That had stopped at ale number…three?

Sometime after the kidney pie.

In some way, she missed the tears. The woeful pain. Because now…

I'm merely defeated. Resigned to our inevitable fate.

She'd thought…

Well, that was the problem, wasn't it? She'd thought she'd had a stroke of brilliance to save them.

Recalling that the great and illustrious Artemis Goode had retired from her career in London and come to live but three and a half miles from Tunbridge Wells, she'd thought she'd found the answer to their problems. William had come out of retirement for her father, and for himself, having missed theatre so much—or so he was wont to tell them—so surely

Artemis Goode, after three years away from it all, might feel the same.

So their theatre was nothing grand. So the world of theatre in the countryside was nothing like it was in London, all excitement, and glorious chaos, and innovation—or so she imagined it to be, for Father never let her go, even with him, and Ruth…had never had it in her to disobey, and displease him no matter how she longed to experience the city.

No… I had disappointed him quite enough in other ways…

Regardless, Ruth had recognised all that—about what she offered being nothing like the life Artemis had once surely known—still, as she'd walked all the way to her door, she'd told herself that it didn't matter. An opportunity was an opportunity, and yes, she'd believed some kind remembrance of Toby Connell would help sway the woman.

Then it had gone so very wrong.

The storm had descended when Ruth was already halfway there, and she hadn't been about to turn back. It had thrown her slightly, as, to be entirely honest, the woman herself had.

Her father had always told these stories of Artemis Goode—so much so that for years she'd been jealous of the woman who seemed to have a dearer place in her father's heart than his own daughter—and Ruth had heard enough otherwise to know the woman was not only beautiful, but had something…*more*. Everyone said she was electric, magnetic. Alluring.

So she was, and *that* had…thrown Ruth off balance momentarily.

Severely.

Tall, long-limbed, with lean grace and strength, and gentle curves hidden beneath the rather dowdy-looking dark grey gown she'd sported, the woman moved—even just *stood* there—with feline ease and fierceness. Dark brown—nearly black—thick curls had framed her face, escaping the seemingly simple but elegant chignon. An oval face, soft, sloping features. Thin dark brows—which had been incessantly imperiously arched—a straight nose, wide mouth with the fullest, most tempting lips Ruth had ever seen—a delicate cherry blossom colouring, just like her cheeks—and even though it had been set in a disapproving, disdainful way, Ruth had somehow known the woman would undoubtedly have a brilliant, and hypnotic smile.

Hypnotic, like her eyes. Hooded, almond-shaped eyes, of a strange colour, somewhere between grey and honey. They shone with intelligence, and verve, and that magnetic quality which had likely made her who she was.

It was terribly annoying that even now Ruth felt the gentle tingling of desire and interest coursing through her—despite *everything*.

It was terribly annoying that she'd felt it even then, as she'd tried to find her words, and *not* beg to go inside into the warmth to make her case properly, and that she'd felt it even as she'd felt desperation clawing at her heart, whilst she continued tripping over her words as she had.

It was terribly annoying that she'd felt it even as the woman said *no*, and even as Ruth's heart had fallen at the realisation her miracle would not materialise. Even as she'd spat that idiotic challenge about *debts* at the woman—she'd bloody well felt it.

Infuriating.

Sad.

She was about to lose everything—she'd been owner and manager for…days, and was about to lose it all already—and she was *still* thinking of how beautiful, and striking, the woman was. Well, she was thinking about how horrid she'd been too, but somehow it wasn't nearly as consuming.

Perhaps this is what happened when one faced inevitable defeat.

One focused on nonsense.

Beautiful, striking, tempting nonsense.

'That's it?' Thomas said, tearing her from her thoughts. She glanced over at him, lounging back in his chair against the wall beside the hearth. 'I thought you were going to talk about whatever happened.'

Ruth pondered keeping silent, but he'd have the truth of it eventually, and besides, she needed…

Help. That's the word.

Help.

'My great, ridiculous plan was foiled,' she muttered, twisting the ale in her hand, and sighing heavily. 'I went to see Artemis Goode.' Out of the corner of her eye, she spotted Thomas's brows shoot up in surprise. 'I know… Like I said. *Ridiculous.*'

'It wasn't ridiculous, Ruthie. Your father knew her, yes?' Ruth nodded. 'And she's highly celebrated. A new play from her might've been just the thing.'

'Might've been,' she grumbled mutinously.

'Was she very horrible?'

'Yes. But also… I don't know. I didn't think it would be easy to convince her to help us.' Ruth shrugged, sipping her ale distractedly. 'I know she was… I knew it would be like asking Hrotsvitha or Sarah Siddons or Aphra Behn to come help, to come write for the little country theatre, but at the same time… I suppose I saw the hand of fate in her presence so near, and her connection to Father. And then, when I saw her… I made a complete muck of it, yet I also… I don't know how to explain it. I felt almost as if she was…tempted. Even beneath the *unwelcome* attitude, she seemed, bitter in her retirement.'

'I mean, even down here we heard the rumours,' Thomas pointed out, drinking from his own cup thoughtfully, his eyes dancing across the patrons behind and around them. Something Ruth typically did too—a great way to find inspiration for characters—but today she hadn't the heart. And she had the feeling she wouldn't see much beyond grey honey eyes and dark brown curls. 'Regardless, some people just like to fester in their own disappointments. But that is not what we shall do, is it?'

Thomas grinned, setting down his cup, and straightening to lean on the table, fingers steepled beneath his chin—a perfect pose of *reflection*.

'What else is there to do?' Ruth grumbled back at his efforts to liven her spirits.

As he always did, and which truly, she did appreciate. Couldn't live without, really.

Thomas and she had grown up together, just up the road towards Tonbridge. He was a farmer's son, and his family worked the land upon which sat the cottage Ruth's mother had rented. They were the same age—both four when Ruth and her mother had come here from Hastings, to be closer to London, and Father.

Father, who had included Thomas in the few outings he took Ruth on whenever he came down—usually to shows, or the common to practise their Shakespeare or Sheridan. Mother had always accused him of trying to mould both Ruth and Thomas into smaller versions of himself, but all he'd ever said was: *'One must nurture young talent.'* So he had.

By the time Mother died, and Father returned to settle here, and bought the theatre, though both working other jobs—Ruth, in a shop, Thomas, at the farm—both of them were ready to try their luck on the boards, and well-versed in what it took to be *actors*. So their new lives had begun, together.

For a time, they'd been more than friends, but then slowly that had returned to friendship, neither of them feeling that for ever, marriage—at least together—was what they wanted.

So yes, she was lucky to have Thomas in her life, but at the same time, the fact that he knew her so well was…

Infuriating.

'Come now, Ruthie,' he coaxed, jostling her shoulder slightly, proving her point about *infuriating*. She narrowed her eyes, but he wiggled his brows in a way that never failed to make her smile. Even if only a little. *Clown, indeed.* 'We can figure this out. We can't have *Connell's Castle* closing. So, what shall we do?'

'Thomas,' Ruth said sadly, her smile not waning, but dimming. 'We need a success. A *lasting* one. This isn't about merely keeping creditors at bay, month after month. We won't survive long that way, especially not through the winter. We both know *The Revenge* won't fill the theatre, and even were it to cover the debts by some miracle, no one will engage us once we finish the summer if we don't have something better to offer. They might give us a chance out of respect to my father, but such demonstrations of loyalty won't last. And what then, next summer, when comes time to petition for the licence here? Do you think they'll grant it to us out of loyalty? Or shall it go to Warlington instead?'

'I think you're getting ahead of yourself, Ruthie. I understand, and appreciate all you're saying, but right now, we need to pay back those debts, and keep the castle walls standing.' Ruth nodded numbly. 'Then we can worry about Warlington and the rest. Though we'll not let him have Tunbridge Wells without a fight, be sure of that. He's got enough as it is with Rochester, and Canterbury, and the rest of them.'

'So you've a plan then?' Ruth asked, unimpressed, doom still in her heart.

'We've got a few we could put back on,' Thomas offered, patently ignoring her mood. 'Like that one we did two years ago. What was it? *The Red Hand of Farrell's Ghost*?'

'*The Red Mist of Farrell's Ghost Ship.*'

'That's the one! Everyone loved it! Put together a few like that, and they'll come!'

'They *won't*, Thomas. They've seen it. Here, and much of the same elsewhere. We need to do something that will have them coming for miles. From London even. Revivals of prior successes, even anything we could get from London now… won't save us from doom.'

'Doom. Now that's rather glum. We needn't think of it thus,' Thomas declared seriously. 'We are actors. We are people of the stage, descended from a long line of travelling artists, and fireside storytellers,' he continued, his voice rising as he did, addressing the whole room as though this were some great speech of Hamlet's. 'We have been run from towns, and thrown in gaol for practising our craft unlawfully. We have been called rogues, vagabonds, thieves, and mountebanks. We have starved, and we have sweat, and we have bled all to make people laugh, and cry! Debts are not doom! There is no doom for artists such as we, merely the truth and wonder of *theatre*!'

A roar erupted in the small, but relatively quiet inn, whistles and cheers and applause filling it to the rafters, and Ruth grinned as Thomas took a bow.

She had to admit, though some would call it overly sentimental and trite, Thomas's speech had buoyed her.

We are the minstrels, the saltimbanques, the clowns and the storytellers of every age.

As Thomas settled back in his seat, and his impromptu audience settled down, Ruth found the fire which had been slowly dying inside her since her father's death, being rekindled. She still felt tired, weak, and just *sad*, but she also felt as if the fight was returning to her.

Though she knew it was improbable now that they could in fact save the theatre, she also knew that whatever may come, she would meet it. She would find a way to continue her father's dream, and her own, another way, if it came to that.

I will not let us be scattered to the wind.

Ruth was smiling from ear to ear by the time Thomas focused his attention back on her, with a wink, and smile of his own.

'There,' he said, chuckling. 'I see I've made my point. So shall we make a plan, which is likely to fail miserably, but of which we shall enjoy every second?'

'If I may,' another voice said from behind Ruth.

Her eyes widened, for though she shouldn't have known it so well, she felt as if she knew it *very well* already indeed. Thomas and she both turned to look at the newcomer, Thomas's eyes growing round like saucers when he realised who this must be.

Artemis Goode.

And it was her, though Ruth didn't quite believe her eyes either. She was—if possible—even more alluring because of the strange and endearing version of overly confident hesitancy about her. Their eyes met, and Ruth felt...

Everything will be well in the end.

In this moment... I'm inexplicably certain of it.

'Might I suggest this plan of yours include a new work by Artemis Goode?' the woman said, boldly, yet with a sort of plea in her gaze too.

'I thought you were retired. Made a vow to never write another play.'

Artemis squirmed slightly, and though in some measure, Ruth wished to...well, to make the other woman grovel slightly considering her earlier behaviour, as she'd said, she was desperate, and so best not to look gift horses in the mouth and all that.

Which also meant that even though she was intensely curious about this whole *vow* business, she wouldn't ask, and tempt the woman to change her mind.

If she wanted to break vows she'd made, that was her choice, and Ruth certainly wouldn't stop her.

Nor feel guilty.

'I…'

'I won't reject your offer,' Ruth said gently, and Artemis relaxed. 'You know our circumstances, so despite our previous meeting, I won't refuse your help. Though I am curious, as to what changed your mind, when you were so adamant before. I suppose I need some reassurance you won't change it again.'

'You were right,' Artemis sighed, as though the words were being pulled from her. 'I owe your father a debt. I shall see it paid.'

'Very well then.' Ruth nodded.

'May I ask…how you were planning to get approval for this new work of mine?'

'I don't think I'd quite got as far as that,' she admitted sheepishly, not even daring to glance at Thomas, who might find the lack of planning which went into her *great plan* thoroughly amusing. 'I suppose I thought I'd send it to The Examiner.'

'I thought you might,' Artemis sighed, clenching her jaw, and shaking her head, and Ruth's sheepishness—*embarrassment*—increased, confronted with her own ill planning, and apparent foolishness. *She must think me a right ninny.* 'I may have another way,' she continued, once again sounding as though she was being poked and prodded by invisible demons to pronounce these words. 'You'd be lucky for the Examiner to read the play, let alone approve it, whether or not my name be on it. However… There may be a deal to be made, with an old acquaintance of mine who manages *The Agora.* Were *he* to send it to be approved, there would be a better chance for it. Of course, it would need to be performed there as well.'

'A London theatre performing a show of ours…' Ruth grinned, overwhelmingly grateful for Artemis's—albeit reluctant—*help.* Slightly dazed too, by not only the woman, but the possibilities she was offering; the doors opening ever so slightly to a world Ruth had only ever dreamt of. 'That would be quite a change. I think I can live with that. Shall we properly discuss terms then?'

'Indeed.'

'This is Thomas, by the way,' she said, gesturing for Artemis to sit. 'One of our company. Typically the good-natured, comical and friendly servant, he is also a talented clown, and funambulist. Thomas, I'm certain you've realised this is Ms Artemis Goode.'

The two nodded to each other as Artemis rounded the table, taking a chair from nearby, and settling at it, if not awkwardly, then stiffly.

'I'll get Ms Goode a drink then,' he said, grinning, a twinkle in his eye as he rose which gave Ruth pause. 'What's your preference?'

'Cider, please.'

Thomas nodded, then wandered off, leaving the two of them alone for a moment.

Straightening, now fully awake and sobered, Ruth studied… her new dramatist, she supposed, for a moment.

'I am sorry for your father,' Artemis said, and Ruth nodded, glancing back down at her drink. *Much safer.* 'He was… A good man.'

'That he was.' Ruth smiled wanly.

There was…so much to say, and yet Ruth couldn't quite find it in her then.

No matter, there will be time for it all, later.

Thomas returned, setting Artemis's drink before her, and the three lifted their glasses, and drank to Toby Connell.

And then, they began to speak terms; they began to speak of how to save Toby Connell's legacy.

For we shall.

Chapter Four

'It isn't much,' Ruth said, inadequacy in her tone, though she did try to conceal it with false enthusiasm, a tight smile on her lips as she stood in the middle of the room in the eaves. Her shrug, and dispirited outstretching of the arms however, gave her away. Artemis had to admit, the woman wasn't wrong. It wasn't much.

As she supposed the other spaces were up here, it was primarily used for storage—though one of the larger rooms, nearly half of the attic space, had been transformed into a costuming workshop which Artemis had to wonder the wisdom of, considering the woman apparently in charge of that, Rose or something, looked far too aged to be ascending and descending the four stories with any ease.

It was low-ceilinged, rather cramped, with bare, rough walls, exposed beams, and only one small skylight which, to be fair, did a good enough job of illuminating the dusty space. Trunks and crates had been piled along the wall closest to the door, and much, Artemis could tell from the tracks on the floor, taken away to be shoved elsewhere.

At the far-right corner, a surprisingly large and comfortable-looking bed, nightstand, dresser, washbowl and pitcher beside a screen, and to the left, beneath the skylight, a desk and chair. On the desk, sheaves of paper, pens, ink, even old quills, and a bunch of daisies in a tiny crystal vase. The bed looked to have been here some time, but the desk, that was new she could tell—though if anyone were to ask how, she would be at a loss.

So this is where I'm to spend the next month.

Part of their agreement, that Artemis would lodge at the theatre until her new work opened. She could've very well made the walk to and from the cottage every day—it was only a little over an hour—or even merely written in the comfort of her own home, but in a sense… Well, when Ruth had offered, Artemis had accepted, citing the *ease* of it, but in truth…

In truth she didn't think she would be able to work in the cottage, considering there was too much…of everything there. This task, which Heavens only knew why she'd agreed to it—*to pay your debt*—would be difficult enough, so she had to give herself the best chance of completing it speedily. A new writing space, untainted by the past, in the *midst of it all*, well, that would give her a better chance than home comforts would.

Anything to get this done…

Artemis focused her attention on Ruth again, noticing two things.

One, in the soft light filtering into the dust mote strewn room, she looked even more beautiful, and enticing, like some sprite born of light. Artemis reassured herself that it was only because she wasn't as bedraggled as she'd been at their first meeting, nor even at their second, when passion, drink, and warmth had tinted the woman's cheeks pink, and brought fire to her gaze. She only seemed softer, because she wasn't being as challenging as she'd been at *both* meetings, concealed strength bubbling up like some miniature warrior queen—not that Artemis minded. Quite the opposite.

Yet all that was irrelevant, really. It didn't matter that the woman was beautiful, or enticing, or that she provoked long-lost desires. Artemis was here to do a job, do it quickly, and be done with all this, so she could return to her hole, and continue her exile.

The second thing which Artemis noted, was that there was fear in Ruth's eyes, blooming with every passing second of silence from that hesitancy she'd first spied.

It chafed Artemis, in the same manner her bitterness had.

'It's perfect,' she said, not *gently* or *kindly*, or anything so trite and uncomfortable, but without venom. Ruth stared at her, slightly wide-eyed, those thick brows darting up comically. Artemis wondered vaguely how the woman could be an actress when she wore her emotions on her sleeve every second. 'Don't look so surprised,' Artemis sighed, wandering further into the room, trying to avoid…staring at her to see what endearing quirks or expressions she might discover. 'I might've lived very comfortably when my success solidified, but it wasn't always so, and I'm not so foolish as to forget my own beginnings.'

A glance back told her Ruth wished to ask more, but instead she merely nodded, the smile which followed relieved, and…

Certainly not addictive.

'Well, if you need anything, please don't hesitate to ask. Any of us.' Ruth smiled broadly, while Artemis resumed her wandering. 'I've moved into my father's room, just through his office on the ground floor.'

'This was your room?' Artemis asked, ignoring the queer buzz which shot through at the thought of living in a space which Ruth had once inhabited.

Whatever nonsense will you think of next?

Intimacy as there existed among those in the theatre—sharing rooms, dressing rooms, complicity, friendship, lacking any inhibition sometimes… She'd forgotten it.

For a reason.

And she would do well to remember it was something she'd relinquished when she'd left that world, and cared little to revisit. She simply wasn't built for it, and this was just…

Business.

'Since my father bought this place, yes. This was my room.'

'It doesn't bother you, moving into his?'

Not that Artemis had ever experienced such a thing, but for months after Papa had died, her mother had opted to sleep in a rickety old chair by the fire, rather than sleep in what had been their bed, alone.

Risking another glance at Ruth, Artemis found her pondering the question seriously, the fresh grief darkening her gaze, and her...energy.

'It did.' Ruth nodded, and when their gazes met properly, Artemis witnessed an openness in her she hadn't really seen in anyone before. An unguarded vulnerability which was fascinating, yet innately dangerous. 'But if I'm to be...the manager of this house... I need to find my place, in every way. Besides, it will be nice to be surrounded by his things. Though sometime soon, I know I'll... I'll need be rid of them.'

Artemis nodded, turning away, and resisting the urge to...

Comfort her. As though that is something you do.

Reaching the desk, she let her fingers dance lightly over the writing materials... Things she hadn't touched in years, but to write what little correspondence she had. Gentle footsteps sounded behind her, and a moment later, she felt Ruth's presence, even caught a hint of her warmly citrusy scent.

Delicious.

'I know writers are particular creatures,' Ruth chuckled. 'So if you've need of anything specific, just say so.'

'Particular creatures we may be,' Artemis said, raising a wry brow as she lifted an old quill into the air. 'But did you truly think I wrote with these antiques?'

Ruth laughed, and Artemis smiled, despite herself, broader than she had...

In years.

'Father told me of a writer once who would only work in charcoal.' Ruth shrugged, and Artemis shook her head. 'Luckily, he allowed the stage manager to make actors' copies in pen and ink once he'd written it, if not it's doubtful that script would've survived. Though Father purported that wouldn't have been a bad thing.'

'Indeed.'

They drifted gently into silence, which felt…uniquely comfortable, gazing at each other for long enough a moment that Artemis was able to note the tiny streak of grey hairs in Ruth's left eyebrow, and the nearly invisible freckles across her nose.

How very useful.

Clearing her throat, she turned back to the desk—not that the sight of the blank pages thereupon was any more…any safer.

'Thomas should be up shortly with your things,' Ruth said lightly, stepping back slightly, sensing…something. *My need for space, for time, to not be here at all, doing that which I vowed never to do again.* 'I need to get to rehearsal. I'll leave you some time to settle in, but then perhaps if you'd like to come down in about an hour? You could watch for a time, see how everyone works, and then we can introduce you to the company.' Artemis nodded. 'The papers will be running the announcement tomorrow. Unless…you think you might need more time? We can't delay much longer, but ten days is a bit…fast, if you've not…written for a while.'

Unless you've changed your mind, Ruth left unsaid, though Artemis heard it nonetheless in the woman's gentle prodding.

'I've written more complex things in less time,' she said, not harsher than she meant to, for she meant it to be harsh, and for it to chase Ruth away, but with a harshness that felt, ill-fitting now. 'It'll be fine. The question will be whether you can do it justice. I'll be down in a while,' she added, only slightly gentler.

'Very well then,' Ruth said, with that false joviality again. 'I'll see you shortly.'

Artemis nodded distractedly, turning away as if to explore the sleeping area.

Ruth's footsteps stopped short, and before she left the room, she uttered words which pierced harder than Artemis expected, in a tone so...heartfelt it was nearly revolting.

'Thank you.'

Don't thank me yet, little mouse, Artemis thought grimly as the woman finally left.

For with every passing second, I feel less and less capable of fulfilling this promise.

Chapter Five

'Is it just me, or does Ms Goode seem...out of sorts?'
Thomas asked quietly, as they stood in the wings, waiting
for their next entrance. Rehearsals were going well—inordinately so—everyone seemingly buoyed by the news Ruth
had brought them yesterday morning.

Ruth had been buoyed by it too, her emotions soaring to
the Heavens after having dredged into, if not the deepest
depths, then rather low. She'd been a jumping ball of energy,
such momentum and hope coursing through her veins, she'd
thought she could conquer the world.

After agreeing terms with Artemis at the inn, she and
Thomas had bid their new dramatist farewell, leaving her
to pen a note to her acquaintance at *The Agora*, Mr Kit
Laughton. Then, despite both being dazed—in a spectacular way—they had celebrated well into the night. The following morning, they'd announced the news to everyone,
before informing them of the new schedule.

They hadn't really discussed any particulars of the new
pieces with Artemis—Ruth trusting her to work her magic.
All Artemis had decreed was that any music played during
the evening *must* be new, and that she would also be writing
the lighter accompaniment piece for the evening. Apparently,
Ms Goode didn't wish this new play of hers to be tainted by
a sub-par programme of reused and tired material. It seemed
ambitious, but again, Ruth trusted her, and if she was honest, thrilled to have such...help. With all of it.

In any case, yes, in four weeks' time, hopefully, they would open this new programme.

Hopefully, not because they couldn't mount everything in such time—in fact, what time they had was rather a luxury. It was *hopefully* since they had to get the new pieces to Artemis's man at *The Agora* with enough time for him to read it, hopefully like it, then get it to the Examiner—who hopefully would approve it without any or too many changes—at the very latest a fortnight before opening, which made it a *very* tight schedule indeed. And that was even *if* this Mr Laughton agreed to a partnership of sorts to begin with—they should be hearing back soon, but until then, they were working on faith.

Let us pray this friend is still a friend after all these years...

Let us pray it is approved, and let us pray...for many things.

All of it was a gamble. So many things could go wrong, at every step of this journey; still, Ruth knew, it wasn't as if they had any other choice.

Even if I'm not entirely sure of the wisdom of gambling when one is under a mountain of debt, with all manner of wolves howling and circling...

Despite her doubts, Ruth, like the others, was nonetheless determined to hope. The others, who had been ecstatic, and just as sure as Ruth was that *this* was the answer. What would help them not only save their beloved theatre, but also, become... something more. Something special, and in time, secure perhaps better opportunities. After all, the tight rein, monopoly, and reputation of the legitimate houses was dwindling with every passing year; so much so that there was now more than merely *talk* of *reform*, there were also exciting moves being made to incite proper change.

So Ruth couldn't deny that it felt as if yes, doors were opening along many future paths.

She'd slept like a babe last night—well, apart from some very interesting dreams featuring Ms Goode—and been at the local paper's offices first thing this morning, badgering one of her father's old friends to feature the news of their new, upcoming, as-of-yet untitled production by the great Ms Artemis Goode.

In all fairness, it hadn't taken much to convince him.

Buoyed by that too, Ruth had returned here, and ensured her old room was as tidy, ready, welcoming, and *something*, as could be for Artemis's arrival. She'd not really processed that she was moving into her father's old room, nor even that she would be having someone else sharing this…home with her.

Not that she'd had time yet, though Artemis's pointed question had…discombobulated her somewhat. In all the excitement, she'd let herself forget those things, and in that moment, realising it… It had been unexpected, that was all. She could deal with the emotional ramifications of it later. Right now…in all her waking hours, actually, she needed to ensure that everyone else was well, and doing their jobs, and that everything was as it should be.

Running smoothly.

Which Ruth was increasingly beginning to believe would be anything but an easy task.

Not that it ever was in their world. It was part of the joy, the intrinsic beauty of it. Its unpredictability. Its *realness*; its…existence and limitation in the present moment. It was part of what Ruth loved about theatre—the seemingly dis-organised chaos, the excitement of those final days before a show opened, when nothing appeared as though it would go right—yet somehow, this feeling now brewing in her heart, a sort of...dread, well it suggested the *not so smooth* road ahead, wouldn't be that same sort of excitement and...chaos.

It almost felt like she'd made a mistake, calling on Artemis for this, but that...

Is just your worry speaking.

Right. Of course it was.

After Artemis's original rejection, and even that meeting at the inn, did she honestly expect the woman to be overjoyed and excited to be working with them?

No.

Thoughts of that vow she'd mentioned popped in her head again, but Ruth mentally swatted them away.

Only, Thomas was right. There was something about Artemis which seemed...odd.

All artists—all people—were odd in their own ways, yes, except this was something different.

More.

Perhaps it was how taciturn the woman was. One moment, being kind, and sweet, reassuring her that the room was fine—which Ruth had thought it to be, until the great Ms Artemis Goode stood within it, and she saw it through the eyes of a celebrated, successful actress and playwright—and the next moment, being rather...vicious about Ruth's company being the ones more likely to ruin this whole endeavour.

One moment they were laughing, complicitly, something in the air between them Ruth...couldn't indulge in, and the next, Artemis looked so lost, and bereft, staring down at the writing implements on the desk...

Ruth couldn't quite figure her out.

And you don't have to.

Entirely true. She didn't need to know her for them to achieve what they needed to. Except that her heart niggled inside her chest, like a restless little caterpillar, seeking out the sun, proclaiming she sorely *wished* to know Ms Artemis Goode.

In every way...

'She's been removed from this world for three years, Thomas,' Ruth said, cutting off her own distracting and frankly useless thoughts. 'It's likely just…a bit much.'

Glancing over, she found him nodding thoughtfully, his eyes on those rehearsing, but his attention obviously elsewhere.

'At least she's been more civil than she was when you first went to her.'

'I don't think she meant to be horrid.' Ruth shrugged. 'I wasn't exactly myself either. I think… I don't know. I get this sense she's…lost. I feel the horridness is, as it so often is, a way to keep people away, and not show them our suffering.'

Thomas's attention turned to her, and she herself felt *exposed* then.

'You like her,' he said, grinning, a brow raising.

If not for the darkness in the wings, he would've surely seen her flaming cheeks.

'What's not to like?' Ruth said nonchalantly, side-stepping Thomas's meaning. 'She's a talented, beautiful woman, who's going to help us save Father's theatre.'

'You always have had a tendency to become besotted with gorgeous, ambitious, and successful people, Ruthie,' Thomas laughed, shaking his head. 'And know, yes, I'm including myself in that description. Ow!' he exclaimed when she swatted his arm with the Bible she was holding.

Montague glared at them from onstage, despite being in the middle of a very dramatic scene where he threatened the hero and heroine as they trembled upon dark cliffs.

'I'm not besotted,' Ruth hissed after a moment. 'I've only known the woman for a couple of days.'

'Just, be careful, Ruthie,' Thomas said softly. 'You've also a tendency to only see the best in people, and go into things with all your heart. To…give all your affection, and attention to them, yet to forget yourself. In many ways, it makes you a wonderful person, but also liable to put too much trust in the wrong people, and to lessen your own needs.'

With that, he strode onstage, rushing to help the hero—Laurie, naturally.

A few seconds too late, Ruth followed, nearly missing her entrance, her mind now battling with a choice few of Thomas's words.

I've not put my trust in the wrong person. Artemis will come through.

I know it.

Artemis had to admit, they weren't half bad. Not that she'd expected anything less from Toby Connell's people, but then, one never knew. It wouldn't have been the first time someone left London for the country, only to settle for lesser standards.

It wasn't that she thought London produced the best theatre in the country—she'd seen incredible things performed out of carts in market towns like in the days of the mystery plays—*however*, perhaps because of the inherent competition and constant demand which existed in the capital, those terrible creations people came up with sometimes had less of a chance of…surviving very long.

Fine, so perhaps she was a bit…*partial* to London's offerings. Or at least, always had been, to some extent. Yes, there were terrible plays, and terrible actors—she'd seen enough to know—there too. But people came to London, sought success in London, not just because of the popularity one could gain, but the prestige. One didn't *succeed* elsewhere as one did in London—even if yes, often popularity was less about talent, and more about…wooing the crowds and people in power. There was…hypocrisy to it all. Much to be loathed for its inherent injustice, yet in London…

There was also a sort of rebellious spirit. A spirit determined not to be quashed by law or whatever morality was in fashion that day. There was innovation, and fierceness, and defiance, and…

All things which are not part of your life any more.

Regardless, it wasn't that Artemis had thought she would find…*bumpkins* here, but she'd thought she might find…less to work with. She's already been pleasantly surprised by the theatre itself when she'd peeked in, searching for Ruth before finding her at the inn—not that she'd stayed long, since, as now, it felt…disquieting to be within such a space again—and now she was pleasantly surprised by the people, and talent which had obviously gone into the sets and costuming.

I should never have expected less, Mr Connell. You'd never have settled for less. Nor do I think your daughter would.

Not for the first time since meeting her—having heard much about her in the few years she'd worked with Toby, not that she'd recalled any of it until the woman had appeared on her doorstep—Artemis wondered…what the story was there. Why Toby had left London, come here, rather than bring his family to London.

Perhaps because London would've eaten Ruth alive.

Not that it matters, nor is any of your business.

Obviously.

Though it was becoming increasingly difficult to remember that the past, people's private lives, anything *but* work, didn't matter. The very last thing Artemis needed was to get *personal* in any way—that had cost her enough before. In fact, if she could've avoided it, she would've just remained up in that room until she had a couple bloody plays written—which, why she'd volunteered to write an accompaniment piece, only ineffable powers knew—and spoken to no one, unfortunately…she did need to know what she was working with.

So she'd descended, and now here she was, lurking in a darkened box, watching the company perform the most dramatic, convoluted second act in the history of theatre.

Well, perhaps a slight exaggeration.

Artemis's attention strayed slowly to Ruth, acting, as she'd said, the dutiful friend to the heroine—though there wasn't much comedy to be had in this moment, merely pathos and sympathy—and found… Well, it fit her, in some way, and yet in another, it didn't quite—and that had nothing to do with Ruth's talent.

Quirking her head, Artemis felt herself being drawn in by the observation, and leaned onto the box's edge to better see.

It feels too small, too restrictive, like an ill-fitting corset. I wonder…

Before Artemis could finish her *wondering* however, she realised the entire company had frozen onstage, having not only finished their scene, but apparently, noticed her.

Fantastic.

'Artemis!' Ruth called excitedly, waving as though they were old friends crossing in the street. *Lord, that woman is… bright and eager.* 'Join us!'

Forcing a smile, Artemis signalled that she would indeed do that, having the grace at least—which she applauded herself for—to wait until she'd turned, and was out of sight, before rolling her eyes, and shaking her head.

Feeling as though she was marching herself to the gallows, Artemis made her way downstairs, opting to go through the auditorium, rather than backstage. Once she had, she found herself rethinking that choice, for it was rather a long way to walk—when there was an entire company onstage, watching you with rapt attention.

Once, she'd enjoyed seizing people's attention, but somehow…this felt different. She felt as though she were some peculiar creature being studied before being pinned to a board, and exhibited in a museum. She didn't feel…adored, appreciated, *unknown* by those admiring her—as she'd always felt before. Instead, she rather felt they were all too excited, too welcoming, too…*observant*. In those long moments it took her to arrive at the stage, it felt that they saw her for what she was.

A failure. No longer Artemis Goode, but just…Artemis, a hollow husk.

Nonsense. Even if that were true you could…act.

'Good morning, everyone,' Artemis greeted with, if not her most convincing smile, then at least one which was… *acceptable.*

Polite enough.

Though they were all smiling, her greeting appeared to disquiet them, slight frowns appearing between the brows of a few.

See? They know you are not…congenial.

Still, you should say something more.

Such as…?

'So here we are,' Ruth said brightly, saving her from the awkwardness any longer. 'Thomas, you know, though I did fail to mention he's also one of our pianists. And this is William,' she continued, making her way around the half-circle they'd all formed, gazing down at Artemis from above. 'Our new resident parental figure, wise clergyman or sailor and so on. William also plays the fiddle.'

Artemis nodded, and William bowed his head in greeting, a small smile on his lips.

'We um…do as much of the music and other entertainments as we can,' Ruth added, answering the unspoken question, almost shamefully, which Artemis understood, though she hated it.

I've seen greater shows performed with less means.

'Though we do have other musicians join us to form our little orchestra. You'll meet them later. For now, we also have Laurie, our resident hero, a talented flautist, acrobat, and Harlequin,' Ruth said, moving on quickly, and Artemis was met with a florid bow, and bright smile some women might swoon over. 'And Madeleine, our gentle, innocent heroine, with the voice of a nightingale.'

Nearly snorting at that—the woman looked anything *but* innocent and gentle, though Artemis could see how audiences would favour the cold beauty, Artemis nodded.

The *heroine* of the bunch raised a brow, then smiled too sweetly for it to be genuine, and nodded back.

'Montague, our villain, naturally, who also plays the piano, and is an accomplished juggler,' Ruth informed her, gesturing at the ghastly, but handsome man with gentle eyes, who did some sort of salute. 'And St John, his dastardly accomplice, also an accomplished juggler, pianist and percussionist, and who, with Montague, writes our music for us.' She grinned, waving at the small fellow, who looked far too young to play *dastardly* in any convincing manner—yet having seen him just moments ago, Artemis knew that was far from the truth. 'Fanny, our stage manager,' she said of the wispy-looking battle-axe. 'Guy, our talented scene painter and builder,' of the man who doffed his cap, and looked as many were, and had been for generations in this sort of a work, an ex-sailor. 'Rose,' she continued, with an exceptionally fond smile for the woman. 'Our seamstress, mender, costumier extraordinaire—even though we don't usually have much call for new things, with what we've collected over the years. The apprentices, and our other helpers, I'm sure you'll get to know in time.'

There were nods, shy waves, and *hullos*, from the collection of souls gathered behind the main players and makers, caps rolling in hands, or heads peeking out from the wings shyly.

Though not entirely sure of how well in fact she *would* get to know them—*any of them*—she attempted another smile and nod nonetheless. She didn't...

That is, Artemis had never been...never thought herself better, or different, or...better left alone from those she worked with. She wasn't a naturally antipathetic or curmudgeonly person, and she had nothing against any of them, specifically, and it wasn't that she didn't *want* to be here, it was merely that...

I don't want to be here. Among them, with them...

I'm only here to pay a debt.

So she would be as...amicable as was required to be civil, but that is where it would end—no matter what Miss Ruth Connell's smile and annoying bonhomie were trying to entice her to.

'Well, I've a better idea of what I'm working with now,' Artemis said, the energy in the space chilling and stilling at once. 'I should get to it. Good day,' she added, as she turned to *not* flee, merely *return* from whence she'd come, Ruth's obvious protestations hanging in her surprised, gaping mouth.

We'll all be better off if you just...leave me be.

ACT II

Chapter Six

〜〜〜

'If pity is all I can ask for, and all you can give, I shall take it, for I've nothing left but desolation, and death to return to. I ask for no kindness, no warmth, only shelter from the hounds of Hell nipping at my heels.'

The Widow of Windswept Moor, A. Goode, 1832

I'm blaming this on you, Artemis Goode, Ruth thought mutinously, casting back the blanket she'd thrown over herself, and rising from the surprisingly comfortable leather chair, sliding on her slippers and dressing gown. Sleep, no matter how truly exhausted she was from the day, would not come, and Ruth knew only one remedy for it. There was only ever one remedy for it in her experience.

Not even bothering to light a candle, she made her way into the theatre—she could find her way in the dark, which she proved, by doing just that. Throwing open the doors with enough alacrity to wake any ghosts who may, unlike her, be slumbering, she went inside, immediately feeling more at peace as the smells, and dim light of the gas lamps enveloped her. Breathing in deeply, she paused for a moment, before wandering about the pit, slowly, gently, making her way towards the stage.

Though in her heart Ruth knew her emotional turmoil was her own heart and mind's doing, she continued to mentally chastise Artemis for it.

Firstly, if the woman hadn't seen fit to interrogate her on sleeping in her father's room, she might've—*surely would have*—been able to do so with more ease and tranquillity. After the day she'd had—rehearsals, accounting, overseeing the final work for *The Revenge* and other assorted offerings, and so on, not to mention managing everyone else's thoughts and feelings—all she'd wanted to do was curl up in a warm bed, and *sleep*.

Yet with the first step she took into her father's room, she froze, paralysed by an enormous wave of grief. It wasn't that she hadn't expected it to be...*something*, but she'd thought... fresh as it was, that she had a handle on her grief. That it wouldn't possess her so strongly; that each passing day, industry, *life*, would not lessen the wound, but lessen its impact on her life.

She hadn't counted on the way his room *smelled* of him. The way...everything had been just as he'd left it—as had the office, but they'd always worked together there, with no true set space within it for either of them, and so it wasn't quite the same.

It felt as though he'd left his room, intending to return, momentarily interrupted by illness, though she knew very well he hadn't. It had been his choice to spend his final days in the doctor's home up on the hill—a home which had been turned into a place offering those who could afford it day and night care. Not that she'd known they *couldn't* afford it, but regardless, Father had explicitly stated he didn't want to die in his own theatre. He didn't want the sadness of his final days to permeate its walls.

But have you returned to us now, Father? Has your ghost returned home?

I hoped it might, yet I cannot feel you here...

Perhaps part of the reason entering his room, what had once been his unalienable sanctum, had...wounded her so. She hadn't felt his presence since he'd left this world, yet stepping into that room...she had. Seeing his shirt cast over the chair he'd sit in to put on his shoes, or his comb with some bristly grey hairs still entangled in it. Stacks of plays with notes and marked pages piled up in every corner, and the pair of boots by the door, waiting at attention.

Not to mention his smell, which still lingered, and which she found herself unwilling to...contaminate in a sense, with her own. Oh, she'd changed the sheets when he'd left for the doctor's, but she'd done it as if an automaton, not processing what she would lose until she'd already bundled them, and thrown them into the theatre's laundry pile. His things, mementos from his life, they would linger, but she knew all too well how quickly his particular scent would fade, never to be found nor replicated again.

It had been thus with her mother. All had been thus with her mother, and so she should know better, know grief well enough to navigate it without losing herself, and yet...

It was also so different. She'd had time with her mother all her life until she passed. Her mother had been her rock, steadfast, ever-present, and loving. And Father had been there when she'd passed, and together they'd charted the troubled waters of loss. Now...

Ruth knew she had Thomas and the others, but the loss, it was too dissimilar to its predecessor. She hadn't had her father her whole life. For so long, he'd been this figure, mythical almost, a returning hero who appeared every so often and then disappeared again, seeking out another quest. Until the day the hero returned home; Odysseus returning to Ithaca, to remain evermore.

Only like Telemachus, she hadn't known him. Learning to know each other again, to trust, and be…family, it had taken a long time, and she'd thought they'd have so much more of it, except they hadn't. And the truth was, she wasn't entirely sure how to grieve a man she felt she only knew pieces of, yet loved with all her heart nonetheless.

Sighing, she ascended the few steps onstage, and sat on the edge, beside the glowing row of gas lamps.

All your fault, Artemis Goode.

Had you not questioned me on the subject I might've merely…done, and lived, and not…become so affected.

Which Ruth knew likely wouldn't have been entirely healthy either, but then it certainly would've been easier. Allowed her to function properly. At least a little longer. Until everything was sorted, and they were all safe, and she had…time to…unknot things.

Which will be soon. Very soon.

Yes. It would. Wouldn't it?

'Will it?' she whispered to the air, and the ghosts filling it.

Nothing.

She couldn't even feel them tonight. Perhaps they too were grieving the loss of her father. Or perhaps they simply didn't believe her worthy of their company and comfort.

Some might think her mad, to truly believe ghosts roamed within these walls, but Ruth didn't care. Whether merely out of tradition, superstition, habit, or true belief, she believed. Felt them. Never spied them, but *felt* them. As did many others.

Except for tonight, when I need you perhaps most.

Doubts washed into her heart, ebbing and flowing like

the tide, as they had all day. She'd tried to convince herself that all would be well—that Artemis was here, and would save them—but after that appearance she'd made at rehearsal today...

Thomas was right. She was out of sorts. There was a lack of confidence, hidden behind a veneer of defensive aloofness, and it made Ruth doubt that *all would be well soon.*

It made her wonder if she'd made a mistake—

Ruth whirled around at the sound of footsteps, her heart leaping to her throat even as she half prayed one of the ghosts had in fact decided to grace her with a true apparition. Flickering light in the wings made her heart beat with hope, and yes, some trepidation, until she spied the figure emerging, lit by a shielded candle, and she breathed out a relieved sigh, even as the figure jumped in surprise.

My thoughts conjured someone, though not a ghost...

'Hello, Artemis,' Ruth said wryly, but with a measure of shyness.

It wasn't that she'd forgotten they were, in effect, sharing quarters, but she hadn't expected...midnight meetings either.

Nor did you expect to find her even lovelier in gauzy nightclothes and lit by fire and gaslight all at once.

'I...uh...hadn't expected anyone.' Artemis shrugged awkwardly. 'I'm sorry, I just needed...'

'I understand,' Ruth said, before the woman could injure herself trying to find the words to describe a feeling she knew well. 'I often come here to think, or when I cannot sleep.'

'I'll leave you to it, then.'

'You could...stay,' Ruth offered as Artemis turned to leave. 'It's a small stage, but not so small as that.'

Artemis hesitated for a moment, before coming to sit beside her, if not awkwardly, then stiffly, setting the candle at her side, before thinking better of it, and blowing it out.

Just in case.

They sat in companionable enough silence for a few moments, before Ruth gave in to both her instinct, and need, to try and get to know the woman.

Perhaps if I open the door, she might open herself.
And then, I can help her fix whatever is ailing her.

'I couldn't find sleep in my father's room in the end,' Ruth said quietly, swinging her legs over the orchestra pit, and looking down at her hands to avoid…*being tempted to gaze.* And in a sense, also, to avoid…overwhelming Artemis with an intimacy, or complicity, she most obviously did not wish for. 'I hadn't thought much of it, yet being surrounded by his things, his scent… It seemed to tear the wound wide open again, even though when I lost him, it didn't feel as though it gaped quite so wide.'

'We can switch rooms if you prefer.'

'Thank you. I don't think avoiding the issue will help me solve it however.'

'Unfortunately,' Artemis chuckled.

'Yes, how much easier life might be if that were so.' Ruth grinned back, daring to glance at her, though she knew it was a mistake as soon as she did, for as she'd known, when the woman smiled, *truly*, it was…*something extraordinary.* The dim, ghastly light, far from diminishing its power, seemed to make it even more otherworldly, and enchanting. 'Though some, I'm sure, do just that, and manage very well indeed. Perhaps that's the great trick to life no one wishes to admit to.'

'Perhaps… Grief is a strange beast, and I wonder if anyone has found the key to grappling with it. You must've loved him very much.'

'I did. Though some days I wonder if I loved a man of my own creation.' Artemis's gaze met hers, questioning, and Ruth shook her head, staring out into the safer, empty space ahead. 'Father's greatest, and truest love was theatre. He met my mother in Hastings one summer, and…then I arrived the following spring. He did right by her as people are wont to say—married her, kept us in comfort, visited us…sometimes. When I was four, my mother moved us here, and his visits increased, but we were never… We never lived as a family, all together. It wasn't until Mama died that he moved here— she made him promise not to raise me in London—and he tried to…become what he'd never been before, but, as with most things *family*, it is complicated. I envied you for many years,' she added quietly. 'Not only for the time you had with him, but for all he adored you. Speaking of you nearly every time we saw each other.'

Ruth shrugged, smiling a wan, dismissive smile which said more, she was sure, than words ever could.

Or perhaps merely more than she was ready to articulate just then.

You would've made a worthier daughter for Toby Connell than I ever could've despite how hard I tried.

'I don't know whether… Well, you should know,' Artemis said, after a moment long enough to suggest she wouldn't say anything. 'You should know that your father spoke of you ceaselessly when I knew him. He was always so very proud of you, even the smallest achievements your mother would send news of in letters. He would always say that we would get along famously.'

Her heart clenching with touching, but wrenching pain, Artemis's words a greater gift than she could've ever asked for, Ruth turned to find her smiling yet another brilliant smile, this one full of humour.

'Toby Connell used to always think he was right about everything.' Ruth grinned, nodding as she understood where the amusement stemmed from. 'It's always nice to be reminded he didn't actually know anything as well as he thought he did. Though there's time, perhaps we'll prove him right in the end.'

'Perhaps…'

'What about you, Artemis?' Ruth asked, feeling bolder, for the lessening of the gulf between them. 'What's keeping you awake?'

You, for one, Artemis was strangely tempted to say, lulled by the peaceful liminality of this encounter, the shadows, and Ruth's ethereal beauty and gentleness. It felt as if she were a shade—not an ancient goddess, or fae, but the purest remnants of a mortal life—come to welcome and guide Artemis on her forthcoming journey.

Into the afterlife of my…previous lives.

Already, Ruth had beckoned her down here; well, perhaps *beckoned* was the opposite of what had happened.

Artemis had been right before, something of Ruth remained in her room—fragments of her scent, or merely her comforting energy… Whatever it was, it had kept her awake, tossing and turning, though in another life she *would've* found it comforting, rather than…troubling.

Yet as sorely as she wished to—for it would be infinitely easier—Artemis couldn't rightly blame her sleeplessness entirely on Ruth's…intriguing charm. It was her own mind, her own heart, her own doubts, guilt, fear, and self-loathing, which kept her awake. Her own frustration at having spent hours in front of her desk, staring at those blank pages, unable to write a single word upon them.

Not even a bloody title.

More than once throughout the day, she'd risen, fully intent on packing her things away again, and charging downstairs, to tell them all this had been a mistake, and she couldn't help them, and *farewell*.

Every time, she'd stopped at the door, her hand hovering

upon the handle, her heart beating so frantically, lungs not filling with air properly, in a strange state of...not pause, but paralysis almost. Being unable to stay or go.

Each time, she'd try to force herself out the door, and each time, it was as if a hundred sets of hands held her back, whispering in tones and languages she could neither hear nor understand no matter how hard she wished to.

Only one, could she hear, and it was the ghost of the man who'd brought her here to begin with. If only he'd hurled accusations at her, pleas to help his daughter, or threats to drag her to the depths of Hell himself should she not pay her debt...she might've been able to live with that. Instead, the ghost of Toby Connell merely whispered: *this is your last chance to find your soul again.*

And so, half believing that promise, she would turn from the door, and settle back at the desk; the process repeating itself for hours. Until all she'd achieved today was to eat a bit of cheese and bread from the trays left at her door—by whom, was a mystery—for which she was grateful, considering otherwise she might've forgotten to eat altogether.

Tomorrow, she'd promised herself, thinking of that adage about Rome not being built in a day. *Go to bed early, spend some time thinking of a story. You cannot write words without having a story*, she'd reminded herself, before attempting to do just that.

Unsuccessfully, obviously.

But all was quiet by then, and she'd finally managed to leave her room—though only because she wasn't attempting escape she knew. She'd wandered about everywhere, discovering the place, with more ease and tranquillity thanks to her solitude. It was peaceful, and restorative, and slightly less jarring to return to this world...without anyone in it.

Or so she'd thought.

Now, she was thinking she should've run, escaped *back* to her room when she'd had the chance.

Artemis didn't do well…with these sorts of conversations generally, or more aptly, *before her retirement*. It wasn't that she wasn't interested in others' lives, or that she felt awkward if they spoke of personal and intimate things—quite the contrary. She'd loved all that before, learned more about the human condition, and admittedly, got many ideas and inspiration from such times. Thing was…

She'd never been good, nor keen, to…*give* as well as take, she supposed, unless it was ideas about art or philosophy or politics. And people had never—or only very rarely—seemed to care, to ask, to truly wish for her to give as much as they did. To share as they did. When they did ask for it, well, Artemis had developed many ways of circumventing such requests.

And that was before she spent three years in near total isolation.

Now, it wasn't only that she wasn't used to sharing such intimate things with other…humans, it was also that even if she had been accustomed to it—*wanted* it, which she didn't particularly—she would've lost whatever ease she might've once had.

So, what Artemis *really* wanted to do was get up, say *good night*, extinguish all potential of further conversations, and try to find sleep again. Yet again, she couldn't, not because of a hundred hands holding her back this time, but because of soft grey eyes, flickering in gaslight. Because of Ruth, tender, sweetly beckoning, coaxing, and…

A desire to know this woman in a way I haven't wished to know anyone for a long time.

Though Artemis wasn't quite ready, nor able to…share everything, so she settled, as had always been her habit, on a slice of the truth.

'I haven't worked in three years, Ruth,' she admitted, as sincerely, yet nonchalantly as she could. Vaguely, she wondered how it was they'd so quickly gone to using each other's given names—but then she reminded herself that was often the way in their world. Not for lack of respect, but because of that same sudden, and natural move towards comfortable familiarity. Though this felt like something else entirely... *No.* 'I also haven't been around people, been in this world, in a long time. I left it for a reason, and coming back... It isn't so simple.'

'I never meant... Well, that's a lie,' Ruth chuckled, shrugging bashfully. 'I suppose I did mean to drag you here by whatever means possible, but in truth... I would never force a choice upon you, which you didn't want to make. If you wish to go home in the morning, forget any of this ever happened... I won't hold it against you. That is, I might, but I will understand.'

Artemis studied her for a long moment, not as appreciative as she might've otherwise been in such close quarters, but rather, trying to determine if Ruth truly meant what she said, and if...

Well, if she wanted to just up and leave tomorrow morning, leave all this behind.

Surely, if Toby Connell's daughter said, *you may go, no debt will be held against you*, then Artemis could live on without guilt in her heart.

And without your soul, the man's voice whispered, taunting, his ghastly breath nearly tangible on her neck.

'Thank you, Ruth,' Artemis said, shaking off her newfound ghostly conscience, resisting the urge to place her hand on Ruth's to...underscore her reassurance. 'I appreciate the offer, and perhaps a day ago, I might've taken it. However... I said I would write you a play—well, two now—and so I shall. I'm a woman of my word.'

Except when it comes to vows I make to myself...

A weight seemed to lift instantly from Ruth's shoulders, and Artemis wildly thought that she would do anything to ease her way until Kingdom come if she had the chance.

Absolute balderdash. You should run while you can.

Yes, she probably should. But in a very real way, Artemis felt that beyond guilt, debts, and ghostly consciences, the real reason she couldn't leave, the true meaning of the ghost's words, was that…she needed to do this. Not for anyone but herself.

Too long she'd been content in her own misery, accepting her fate as a writer without words. Now, she'd been given—*forced to accept*—a chance to conquer that loss, and something told her that if she didn't, she'd regret *that* until her dying day.

No matter how disastrous this ends up being...

Ruth had the grace not to comment, nor press further on Artemis's reasons for staying—though it was impossible not to see that the woman sorely wished to.

'Why did you leave London?' Ruth asked instead, which wasn't *at all, in any way*, preferable. Artemis felt tension invade her body, but rather than back away, as others might, Ruth instead leaned closer, her small smile coaxing even more. 'I heard… I think many heard the rumours. Still, you might've stayed, gone out on your own, found success elsewhere.'

'You've never had your heart broken, have you?' she asked, her intended harshness disappeared under a thick layer of admirative envy.

'By something other than grief? No, I haven't. But then I've never loved anyone enough to give them all my heart.'

'Not even Thomas?' Artemis asked, unable to help herself, having seen well the way the two moved and spoke to each other.

'No, not even Thomas.' Taking a breath, Ruth stared out into the dark void beyond the stage, and Artemis waited. 'I loved him, *love* him, and he is perhaps the closest I've ever come to loving…as we imagine romantic love to be. As we show it to be onstage, or in the pages of books, the greatest lines of poetry. But I think I came closest with him, merely because I've known him nearly my whole life, and he is my very best friend. I like to think, someday, I will find my great love, but… Another part of me thinks I'm *too* romantic, believing it will just happen. Wonders if I rely too much on belief, and not enough on…working to make love grow in places I'd perhaps not expect it. If I move on too quickly, not allowing time for something to bloom. And… I've always had this feeling I wasn't grown enough to love like that. That there is some fault within me, preventing me from relinquishing too much of myself.'

'That isn't a fault. Far from it, and I envy you for it. I've felt different variations of love, for many different people, and yes, love *can* be cultivated, but sometimes, it also just happens. Though that doesn't mean it doesn't require…commitment, and work. When I met Killian… It was the stuff of poetry, and books, and fairy tales, or so I thought. I launched myself recklessly into the endeavour of loving, and giving myself, but I took no care nor caution, and… Well, the rumours are true, if you must know,' Artemis sighed. Ruth nodded vaguely, turning back to look at her, with an envious sympathy Artemis found…rather hilarious in its sadness. 'The person I thought would be my partner for ever…cast me away for another. A tale as boring, and old as time. Yet still, it broke my heart in a way I…wasn't ready for.'

'I'm sorry.'

'It's life.' Artemis shrugged dismissively. 'As for leaving London… My thoroughly broken heart prevented me from playing my cards properly. Killian took advantage of my…

distraction, spread rumours I had no time nor energy to dispel, and many doors were closed to me, whilst he rose onwards to where he'd always wanted to be. I might've...fought, and scraped my way to some manner of return, however, I felt retirement was the best option.'

The only option, for I couldn't write a single word...

Amusingly enough, ironically enough, or perhaps tragically enough, that hadn't even been one of the rumours Killian had thought to spread. He'd instead concentrated on belittling her talent, purporting it had been he who had carried her to greater heights with his knowledge and influence. He'd focused on spreading rumours of her pretentiousness, and rupturing what few true friendships she had with lies of supposed underhanded deeds and gossip she'd indulged in.

Kit Laughton...he'd been one of the only ones who'd told her what was happening whilst she could do nothing but cry, and mourn, and rage at the loss of Killian. One of the only ones to stand by her, encouraging her to fight, trying to support her, and...

So I hope you will still remember me fondly, Kit.

And give me this chance I never thought I'd ask for.

'Perhaps this will be your...triumphant return.' Ruth smiled, with hope, and a conviction that might've swayed even the most doubtful cynic.

'Perhaps...' Artemis smiled sadly, not able to *entirely* kill the other woman's spirits.

Nor my own—though I do not wish to...return.

'Well, I should at least attempt to find sleep again,' she added after far too long a moment merely watching every flicker of emotion on Ruth's face, appreciatively admiring. 'Much work to be done tomorrow.'

'Of course.'

They both rose, Artemis the quickest, offering her hand to Ruth distractedly as she also gathered up the lifeless candle.

Though she didn't remain distracted long as Ruth took the proffered hand, and delicious, snaking warmth travelled up her arm, into her chest. All throughout the rest of her body, down to her toes, as she mindlessly pulled Ruth in ever so slightly, and the woman leant in too, tipping her head up, eyes searching, her scent filling Artemis's nose, and—

Stop it.

The very last thing you need.

'Good night,' she said flatly, dropping Ruth's hand, and stepping—*not fleeing*—away; though yes, the sudden chill she felt at the loss made her regret the choice somewhat.

'Good night, Artemis,' Ruth's voice called, seemingly chasing, echoing into the furthest, darkest corners of the theatre, and Artemis, though it was barely a whisper.

Very last thing indeed.

Chapter Seven

Whether it was the peaceful interlude in the quiet theatre, or the conversation with Artemis, in the end, Ruth
had slept, and slept well. So, she'd done it in the chairs in
the office, pulled together to form some version of a chaise
rather than settling for just one; still, it was more than she'd
expected to manage.

Just as that conversation with Artemis was…more than
she'd expected.

In fact, given their few interactions thus far, Ruth had fully
expected Artemis to either give her some non-committal answer such as *I'm not sleeping because I'm not in my own bed*,
or adversely, merely get up, and walk away, so when she'd
done neither, and instead…opened up, to a degree, and with
a sort of reluctance which reminded Ruth of a sugar-locked
jar being prised open, well. She'd been…pleasantly surprised.

Yes, let's call it that.

Certainly, she wouldn't admit to how it *actually* made
her feel.

Warm, and fuzzy, and…hopeful. The hopeful aspect wasn't
so…dangerous to admit. Because the hope was entirely—
mostly—tied to the professional side of things. Artemis may
not *want* to be here, but she would remain, and her opening
up in some way reassured Ruth that it was merely as she'd
said. An adjustment after a period of retirement. That Ruth's
and Thomas's concerns about her unease and general reluctance were, if not unfounded, then to be dismissed. As for
the warm and fuzzy side of things…

Well, it was best left *unadmitted* because that tied into the instant desire she'd felt for Artemis, and the slow softening of her heart which had followed. Her…*partialness* to the woman, which Thomas had of course noted, annoyingly perceptive in all things *Ruthie* as he was.

There was nothing wrong with blending personal and professional. Many did, in any world, and so Ruth had on occasion. So it wasn't so much that which held her back from admitting she was very quickly becoming…*besotted* by her new playwright. It was in a sense, tied to what she'd admitted to Artemis last night. That she'd never felt grown enough to be in love. To love, and be loved, as a true grown woman might. Learning about her father's debts, about all he *hadn't* shared with her, about all the burdens he'd not taught her to carry… In a sense it made her feel even less…capable. Less knowledgeable of what *responsibility* was.

It was tied to the fact that even *if* she wished to…cultivate love, she had no idea *how to.* Father and Rose had perhaps been some example, but the example he'd been with her mother, not so much. Yes, Ruth saw love in many places, but not for long enough a time to…study it, she supposed. To learn about how it worked.

Most of all, it was tied to the fact that she was grieving, and had a whole mess of things more important to think of right now—*saving Father's theatre, taking care of everyone*—than…well, selfish *feelings.* The beginnings of feelings. Desire.

Whatever it was.

A big mess.

Just like this paperwork was.

Heaving a great sigh, Ruth rubbed her eyes, and tried to focus on the enormous pile of work before her. It wasn't anything new—apart from the *very* suggestive letters from the houses they toured to in winter and spring, *heavily* implying amidst placid condolences that as she'd suspected, loyalty would only go so far, and they would need proof of her ability to fill a theatre before continuing to engage her company.

I will have a success for you.

I think.

I know.

The rest was bills, invoices, scheduling requests, orders, ledgers, and so on—but it had piled up since Father died, and to boot, well, he wasn't here to help sort it out. Yes, Ruth had had a hand in it, but the final payments, and filing and so on, that had always been Father.

Likely to hide how bad things were...

'Only now I see, Father,' she muttered angrily, trying to sort things needing paying into an order of urgency. 'Now I see, and I wonder how you kept it going this long.'

It seemed to be the literal definition of *robbing Peter to pay Paul*.

Taking with one hand to give to another.

And that was even without the papers the solicitor had forwarded, and which included details of the debts due in six weeks lest the theatre be forfeit—all which had served to pay the proverbial Paul in the past years.

Not even weeks, or months, but years.

Pay was safe, and Ruth could stretch what little money she had to cover what she would need to get this show open and running. The next, and any after that...

We'll need make a fortune from Artemis's play, and have packed houses for...months.

'Come in,' she said when a knock sounded on her door, not bothering to hide her despondency, thinking it was surely one of the company coming for...

Something I will add to my list of concerns—ever growing now...

Unfortunately, a moment later, she wished she'd done a

better job of doing her other job—*acting.* For it wasn't someone from her company; instead, it was Mr Grant Dempsey.

Vulture extraordinaire.

Though he didn't look like one, which was annoying in that there were times in life—her father's funeral for instance—when a little bit of theatrical simplicity, such as having a villain look like a villain, was welcome.

Not that Dempsey was a villain. Still, his handsome charm was infuriating to Ruth, though it likely aided in his success. In his mid to late forties presumably—all dashing silver-black hair, and squared, sharp features—Mr Dempsey had made quite a name, and built up quite a business for himself over the years.

His focus? Buying and renovating properties to aid in the town's *development,* and to *bring it into the future,* by ensuring *everyone had the services they required and desired.* He was a shrewd man, and not a terrible man, though his presence wasn't welcome, for what Ruth already knew he'd come to say.

Offer—for he was one of those many wolves circling and howling outside her door.

Straightening, and attempting to instil a bit more unconcerned verve about her—but not too quickly lest it be too obvious—Ruth forced a smile on her face as she set her pen down, and rose to greet the man.

'Good morning, Mr Dempsey, what a pleasant surprise,' she said lightly, offering out her hand, which he took, not missing the papers strewn about on the desk.

Surprise indeed. Perhaps I should begin locking doors. Especially if creditors will soon be knocking...

'What can I do for you this morning?'

Ruth didn't offer him a seat, though he took one nonetheless—not that she was surprised in any way.

Settling back in her own chair, she ensured she was giving as much of an air of *power* and *control* as she could.

'Firstly,' Dempsey said, in his gratingly lovely voice. 'I wanted to express my condolences on the loss of your father. Toby Connell was a great man, and a great entertainer.'

'Thank you.'

Dempsey inclined his head, and Ruth readied herself for the next part.

'I won't insult you, Miss Connell, by beating about the proverbial bush,' he continued.

And here it comes.

'I have connections. I'm not unaware of the financial precarity you find yourself in, in fact I discussed the matter with your father some months ago.'

More things you hid from me, Father.

How many more are there?

'I appreciate that, Mr Dempsey.'

'In plain terms, I would like to buy this theatre,' he said, and though she knew it was coming, Ruth still felt her heart twist in revolt. 'The sale would not only cover your debts, but be enough to see you set yourself up in comfort elsewhere. I'm certain it would be no struggle to obtain a licence such as you have here; your father had many friends across these counties, and I'm sure there are places which would be happy to be able to host your artistic offerings.'

'Are you implying there will be a struggle for me to obtain the licence here in future?' Ruth asked with too much panic in her voice to seem *unconcerned*.

Only she was trying to wrap her mind around it all— business divagations weren't her strong suit—and a bolt of fear shot through her at his words.

Note to self, go visit the mayor and magistrates and justices right away.

In her haste to solve the *debt* problem, she had let the other aspects—*maintaining friends in this town*—slip through the cracks.

So very much to do, and I seem to have no handle on the half of it.

'I imply nothing of the sort,' Dempsey reassured her gently, which helped, though she found it insufferable too. 'Mr Warlington is attempting to make himself known again, however that is not the way I do things. I only meant to say, this town is not your only option.'

Ruth nodded gratefully.

'Your offer is very generous, I'm sure, Mr Dempsey. I wonder, since you know my situation, why you wouldn't simply wait to buy it when it is forfeit for those debts in a few weeks.'

'That isn't how I do business either. And others might… beat me to it.'

'What a shame that would be,' Ruth agreed, not half-heartedly. 'May I ask what you plan to do with this building, should I agree?'

'This town is growing, changing, Miss Connell, you know that as well as anyone. It has been evolving since the spring attracted its first visitors, but now, we are entering a new era. I want to help build this place into all it can be.'

'And the Parade is key, with most valuable assets.' Dempsey inclined his head in agreement, a small smile on his lips, which seemed to acknowledge her minimum of brains. 'I think you already know my answer, Mr Dempsey, for you would've heard it from my father's lips.'

'I believe I do, Miss Connell,' he agreed, with no resentment, or disappointment. It was…altogether more frightening, and chilling, than any attempt at intimidation or convincing might've been. 'Though you should know, my offer doesn't merely stand today. It will remain open indefinitely.' Ruth nodded, and Dempsey rose. She followed suit, but said nothing, knowing he had more to say. 'I applaud you for your resourcefulness.' He smiled, pulling the day's newspaper from his jacket, and setting it on her desk.

It was open to the front page, which read: *'Celebrated dramatist and leading lady Artemis Goode to write for* Connell's Castle*!'*

Ruth smiled, overwhelmed by that one thing—having never expected the front page.

Her father's friend had more than come through—if this didn't get people flocking, she didn't know what would.

Though of course it is only the first step.

'I will be first in line to buy a ticket,' Dempsey continued. 'Be sure of that. However… You are treading water, Miss Connell. Even with a success… You and I both know you might rest for a while, but eventually, you'll end up merely treading water again, waiting for that great wave to pull you under. I don't believe anyone enjoys that sort of uncertainty, and I would urge you to consider not only the near future, but the long-term future as well. As I said, my offer will remain open indefinitely.'

'I appreciate your visit, and your words, Mr Dempsey,' she said sincerely, offering out her hand again. 'Rest assured, I will give them due consideration.'

'Good day, Miss Connell.'

'Good day, Mr Dempsey.'

The man let himself out, and Ruth sank back into her chair.

Glancing out the window, she watched him pass by it, seemingly unconcerned, and confident.

That at the very least would make me consider your offer, Mr Dempsey.

A life free of concern and insecurity.

Hours later, and Ruth was still pondering what such a life would look, and feel like—not that she hadn't achieved anything else throughout the day. She'd got through most of the lingering paperwork, responded to the letters from the houses they toured to, made some sort of a plan for all her payments, and made list upon list of all which needed to be achieved, checked, sorted, organised, etc., etc. for the next few weeks.

She'd also spent a couple hours visiting those supporters and *friends* of the theatre, ensuring relationships were solid, been at rehearsal, and fielded the enquiries of the first few visitors who'd descended to see if it was true about Artemis Goode, and was she anywhere nearby so they could meet her.

Yes, and no, being the answers to those respectively, and the latter not solely because Ruth wouldn't drag Artemis from her work to come meet admirers—though she did need to speak to her about perhaps making some version of a public appearance to truly get the word out, and people excited. *Eventually*, she'd promised herself.

But no, it wasn't solely because Ruth wouldn't do that that the answer was *no*, it was also because truth be told, she wasn't entirely sure Artemis *was* nearby. They all presumed she was in her room, writing away, and considering the tray Montague had brought her up—as he had yesterday—at nuncheon *had* been touched, it was likely she was ensconced in there. Working. Even though no one had seen nor heard her all day.

She's in there. Working. Likely. Hopefully.

So yes, Ruth had achieved much today, for which she was quite pleased with herself. Still, despite all the business, all she'd had to keep her mind occupied, and distracted, at regular intervals, those thoughts of a carefree, stable life, with no financial worries—that life Dempsey offered her—well, those thoughts returned.

And it wasn't solely herself she was thinking of either. It was everyone else too.

Their world, their chosen professions…weren't, and hadn't

been since time immemorial, what could be considered *stable*. Secure. There was an inherent risk attached to living the life of an artist. Renown, yes, brought some safety, but then, in a sense, Artemis herself was living proof that no matter how successful you were, doors could still be closed to you.

Ruth had never really minded the uncertainty of it. The lack of monotony which went along with it was actually part of what she liked. She enjoyed life slightly on the fringes of society—in fact she didn't think she would do so well living a *normal*, *stable*, *proper* life. She hadn't done very well—in her soul, and heart—the first time she'd tried.

That being said…not having to worry about money for a long time, finding a place where they could settle—as Father had believed they could here—well, that would be nice too. It would be relaxing after treading water for…*a long time*.

Are you truly considering selling Father's theatre?

Was she?

Truth be told, she wasn't quite sure.

Perhaps…not refusing to consider it outright, no matter how painful it would be.

Another knock at the door pulled her from the murky depths of her thoughts, though this time she knew it to be one of the company.

At least, at this hour, I dread to imagine anything else…

'Come in.'

Montague entered a moment later, finding her as Dempsey had—though likely more outwardly exhausted and dishevelled.

She smiled nonetheless, always happy to see him. Montague was a kind soul, and though quiet, and seemingly aloof, he was a clever, passionate, and talented man, who, when he did share his thoughts, was someone to be heeded.

He didn't fully enter, merely hung at the open door, debating his words, tapping the door frame lightly as his eyes took in the room, and Ruth almost feared what might come out of his mouth tonight.

'I've left her another tray,' he said after a long moment, and Ruth expelled a relieved breath. 'And I am off, so if you'd like to lock up…'

'Of course.' Ruth nodded, rising, and following him out to the front. At this time of night, it was easier for people to leave that way. 'Thank you for feeding our new guest. I don't think I'd have it in me to handle that too.'

Montague nodded, though he paused when they reached the door.

'You shouldn't sleep in the office again,' he said plainly, not looking at her, and she didn't even bother to ask how he knew. It was all part of his strange power. 'And finding another spot in this place won't help you either. I can stay, if you want help making his room your own.'

'I'll be all right, but thank you, Montague,' she said quietly, letting the blow she'd known he would mete out travel through her entire heart and body. 'I'll see you in the morning.'

He gave her a piercing, but quick study, then disappeared into the twilit, busy streets beyond.

For a moment, Ruth pondered going upstairs to check on Artemis. To see that she was still alive, and yes, in some measure perhaps, to check on the work. To even get some notion of what the work was. Very soon, she would have to, if they were to discuss sets, and costumes, even advertising…

But not now. That would be avoiding what you know needs doing.

Groaning a pitiful noise halfway between a moan and the beginnings of a child's tantrum, Ruth turned on her heel, and returned to her Father's—to *her*—quarters. Readying herself for the imaginary battle ahead, she lit a candle from the lamp in the office, and opened the door to Fa—*her*— room, and then…

Froze.

On the threshold.

Again.

Another pathetic noise escaped her. If Ruth had to name it, she would've called it *avoidance.*

Perhaps she should've asked Montague to stay, and help. When Mama died, she'd had Father, and they'd waited a while, though, come to think of it actually, not really that much longer than it had now been since Father had died.

It doesn't mean you're throwing away his memory, or casting him from this theatre.

Merely…claiming this space as your own, and putting order into what memories you'll keep.

Exactly.

Right.

Move.

Do it.

'Blast and damnation,' Ruth muttered, stomping her foot, thoroughly like an indignant child now.

'Cursing suits you,' a voice said wryly, making Ruth start.

Artemis.

Ruth turned to find her at the office door, arms crossed and a gently mocking smile on her face.

'Did you need something?'

'No,' Artemis lied, though Ruth wouldn't have been able to say how she knew that. 'Seems as though you might, however,' she added, gesturing at the room beyond.

It would be best to refuse, just as she had with Montague; Ruth knew that much very well.

However.

'Well, if you've nothing better to do, then yes. I would appreciate the company, I think.'

They exchanged small smiles, which felt anything *but* small, and a look filled with a promise Ruth wasn't sure she was ready to ever see fulfilled.

Yet as Artemis stepped forward, and they both entered the room together, she couldn't help but think that perhaps, she had no say in this matter, whatsoever.

Chapter Eight

Artemis wasn't entirely sure who it was she was becoming under this roof—under Ruth's pernicious influence—but she liked to tell herself that she didn't, in no way whatsoever, appreciate *who* it was. Someone who told personal things about themselves, and offered to help with sentimental tasks.

Someone who was *nice*.

Not that she'd ever been intentionally *unkind*, but she did tend to keep her distance.

And truthfully, even in her closest relationships—including with Killian—she'd never…quite been *effusive*. Demonstrative. Never really known instinctually what someone else needed— or perhaps, refusing to see because of her own selfishness— one of Killian's many reasons, in his own words, for straying, despite her trying for years to *correct that fault* as he called it.

Seeing Ruth standing there, frozen at the threshold of her father's room, cursing—*utterly adorable*—and making funny little noises, however, Artemis had known what she needed. For once, she was, if not *entirely* willing, then *able* to give it.

And here. She was here, so might as well.

Yes, might as well.

Though she wasn't entirely sure *why* she had come down from her lofty prison—*room, workspace, not prison*—to begin with, beyond that she felt she might go mad if she remained there a moment longer, re-examining the past for the millionth time, staring at pages of nonsense and pathetic scribbles. She'd come down…

To ask for help, if she was being honest.

Come down to ask for Ruth's help in finding a story.

Only when Ruth asked, and she might've done just that…
she couldn't quite bring herself to. It was one thing knowing
you were a failure yourself, when everyone else saw *genius*;
it was another entirely telling someone that you weren't as
great as they thought you were, and there was a strong likelihood you wouldn't be able to save them. *Help* them.

Especially if it was Ruth Connell, whom Artemis, in some
visceral, yet inexplicable way, wanted to…

Like me?

*Though our first meeting suggested that would be unlikely,
now I find myself wanting her to think…well of me.*

Another—likely *the grand*—reason why Artemis was
now sitting on Ruth's bed, folding clothes, and helping her
separate them, and everything else which had once belonged
to Toby Connell, into neat piles.

Keep or give away. Keep or give away…

At least, so far, Ruth hadn't dissolved into a puddle of
tears, because if she did…

Artemis wasn't entirely sure what she would do then.

'What was your family like?' Ruth asked suddenly, running her fingers tenderly along the cuffs of one of her father's
shirts. 'I mean, I've heard the stories of course, but then there
were so many—including ones which said you arrived on the
banks of the Thames like Moses in his basket. Sent down by
the gods to thrill us with your words and beauty.'

Artemis laughed.

She'd forgotten that one, and all the others—each more
incongruous than the next.

'I always enjoyed the one which told of my childhood in
the frozen, barren wastelands of Russia, learning my craft
with bears and wolves.'

It was Ruth's turn to laugh, and yet again Artemis found
herself thinking it was one of the best sounds in the world.

'That is a good one. If it were true, you'd have done well in Shakespeare's time, and perhaps he might've written more bears into his plays.'

'Perhaps.' Artemis smiled. 'Those stories… I'm not quite sure how they came about. Killian always said they…enhanced the myth of me, and I often wondered if he'd put them about, or at least added to them.'

'And you didn't mind?'

'I… At first, I think I did. I wanted… If anything, I would've wanted the truth of my life to be known so that perhaps it might inspire others to rise up, and question what they were told life could offer. But I was young, and Killian said there was no room for truth in our business. That it was all about artifice, and illusion. *Acting.*' She threw Ruth a small smile, and shrugged. 'We disagreed on that point, and many others, rather a lot over the years.'

Such as…the point of their careers.

For Artemis, it had been about…*creating*. Giving life to her imaginary friends, yes, but also, challenging the world. Offering truth, but also questioning it. Interrogating the status quo—whether it be in terms of politics or form.

For Killian, it had always been about money, and status. About legitimacy and patronage, power, and spectacle.

Artemis's success, and favour with the crowds—from washerwomen to royalty—had never quite sat well with him in fact. So much so, that after a time, she'd had to think very carefully before accepting any engagement, lest Killian…not agree.

Stop thinking on all that. Focus on Ruth, who is here, now.

Ruth, who nodded, handing Artemis the shirt she'd been holding, gesturing to the *give away* pile.

Silence reigned for a time, and Artemis glanced down as she folded the shirt. Ink stains marred the cuffs, and she smiled absently, brushing them with her own fingers lightly.

Once, she'd thought that when she died, such stains would be found not only on her person, but on every item of clothing she owned. She had this image of herself, an old, wrinkled, wizened crone, passing into the next world with her fingers clutching a pen—ink still drying on the pages before her. Her immortality, still drying.

She imagined friends, perhaps a lover, going through her clothes as Ruth did now with her father's, and finding ink stains everywhere—the marks of not only her profession, but her *raison d'être*. Her reason for being, for living, for having been created.

She'd always worn those ink stains with pride, and imagined doing so unto death, a mark—not like that of Cain, but not unlike it either—signifying her earthly deeds. She imagined that ink soaking up through the tips of her fingers into her bones until she quite literally would bleed black.

A fanciful image, and one which now…she doubted.

The words had abandoned her, and though she might scribble out something onto pages for Ruth… It wouldn't be the same. The words wouldn't be born of…her. She didn't feel them, emerging from the marrow of her bones and her soul all at once any more, merely felt them pouring—or trickling painfully—from her mind.

And after this was over, it was back to retirement, therefore…

My clothes will not bear these marks, nor shall I, and that foolish, ghoulish dream is now ended.

'My father was a lighterman,' she finally said, casting away the morbid thoughts, and feeling the need to…*answer the original question, that is all.* Ruth started slightly, but promptly turned back to the wardrobe to hide her surprise at Artemis's offering. *Which lights her eyes so wondrously…* 'My mother a publican's daughter, who worked every sort of job you can imagine—from the kilns to selling posies. They lived, met, died, and I was born in Shadwell. Lived there all my life until your father found me.'

'Was your life happy?'

'Yes.' Artemis smiled, not surprised at the question, but unexpectedly touched. 'It was a hard life, but a good one. My parents loved me, and each other, and that's something not everyone is lucky enough to have. Even when my father died—an accident on the wharves—Mama made certain I always knew we had each other. And our neighbours, our community... Despite what you hear, we were surrounded by good people.'

Smiling gently, Ruth took all Artemis gave, and nodded, handing her more clothes for the *give away* pile.

'Where did your love of theatre come from?' Ruth asked after a while, the wardrobe slowly emptying itself, the pain in her eyes diminishing with every increase in space therein. 'Your parents?'

'I suppose so.' Artemis shrugged, rising to begin putting the pile of clothes to be donated into an old travelling bag they'd already decided to let go, the question unsettling in all it forced her to think on. Still, she forced herself to both consider it, and answer honestly.

Burying the past is...useless.

'I remember... I don't know how old I was, but I must not have been more than perhaps four? Papa brought me to see this group of Italians, and their puppets, performing at market out of a cart. And I remember, growing up, he'd bring me to any amusement or entertainment he could find such as that. Songs, dances, plays in people's front rooms for a ha'penny. I don't...know why,' she frowned. 'I think he liked them as much as anyone, yet I always had this sense it was more than that. Perhaps it's just a nostalgic fancy. Still, I think it was like... teaching me to read. Making sure I knew there was more to life than just...what we were told there was, and we could have.'

'Explains why you would want your own story to be known.'

'I suppose it does.' She smiled, receiving a brilliant one back from Ruth that made her…feel better. 'What of you? Have we solely Toby Connell to blame for your choice of profession?'

'Yes,' Ruth said, kneeling down to begin on the man's small collection of shoes and other things gathered at the bottom of the wardrobe. 'Mother… Well, Mother met him when he was performing in Hastings—she went to see his show with friends. And she told me when they…spent time together, he took her to see many things. But then, I think… The reality of a life such as his… It wasn't something she ever wanted, nor could understand. Mother wanted to settle down, live a…normal life, I suppose you would say.'

'Then why marry him? Start a family?'

'Ah yes, well, that would be my fault,' Ruth chuckled wryly.

Oh, well done there, Artemis.

It shouldn't bother her any more, nor at all, really, to think about it—it didn't in any way change the fact that she *existed*—still, in truth, it did bother Ruth. Somewhat. Had, for as long as she'd known the truth, and been able to comprehend it—so say about twenty years give or take. It bothered her in an irrational way, to know that she hadn't been…*a chosen child*. A wanted child.

At least at the moment of her conception. Her parents had both always wanted children, though neither of them had *wanted* a child when they'd given in to their baser urges one sunny summer eve by the seaside. They were knowing and consenting adults, and might've given *some* thought to the possible consequences of their intimacy, but then that was a story told the world over, for all of history, wasn't it? And Ruth didn't judge them, or anyone else, for such accidental conceptions; however, she did feel the fact that her parents had married, and given birth to her, because they believed that to be their only choice. That had her accidental conception not occurred, they might've gone their separate ways, and lived very different, potentially happier, lives.

Perhaps it was her own parents' resentment and regret over how things *had* turned out, which coloured her own view of the situation, and herself in some sense. They hadn't ever set out to make her feel guilty or responsible for their own choices, yet still, she'd felt it. Because of the words they whispered or shouted to each other; because of the way they spoke of each other when they were apart. She hadn't been *made* to feel unwanted, yet she had felt it nonetheless.

Felt it still, a dull ache somewhere between her left ribs, tugging, and twisting regularly. Amplified by the fact that her father had chosen to live apart from them—from *her*—most of her life; that he'd returned out of…duty. Not love.

Even though I know he loved me.

Yes, Ruth did know. For all his other ills, Toby Connell—and her mother for that matter—had never made her feel unloved. Quite the contrary.

Which is why it was even more troubling that what Artemis said about her own family, made her…jealous. Just a slight pang of it, though it vied for attention with difficulty considering everything else Artemis said—and the sheer fact she said it, and was…letting Ruth know her again—which made her feel…glad, and hopeful, and giddy again.

Still, yes, she felt slightly jealous when Artemis described her own family, its solidarity, and cohesiveness, and happiness. The love within it. Ruth hadn't been miserable, unlucky, or cast away, yet in some way—though strangely she never really wanted such a thing for herself—she wondered what growing up in the sort of family Artemis had would've been like. How being part of a…settled family, would've changed her.

As useless as crying over spilt milk.

Glancing over her shoulder, she shook her head, smiling reassuringly at Artemis.

The poor woman looks at a loss for words.

'It's all right,' Ruth said gently, because despite her thoughts and feelings on the subject, the truth was, she was *all right*.

Even considering their current occupation—which was not turning out to be quite as emotionally upheaving as she'd expected it to be.

Perhaps because you are not alone to do it...

'My parents loved me very much,' she told her, turning back to finish with this wardrobe. 'And I had a good, happy life, if slightly unconventional. They loved each other too, I think,' she added quietly, trying to remember the good times, or even when Father had returned when her mother passed. *He'd missed her.* 'In their own way. Perhaps it was more respect, and care, but despite their...tugging at the reins of their own marriage, I think there was an appreciation of it. Its...promises.'

'An interesting choice of metaphor,' Artemis commented, and Ruth chuckled slightly, shrugging. 'Is that how you see marriage, Ruth?'

Ruth paused for a long moment, pondering not only the question, but also how much she wished to reveal.

And not in a small measure, *why* Artemis was asking.

'In some way, I suppose so,' she admitted finally, not daring to look back at her. 'Perhaps I only view it thus because of my parents' experience with it. But ever since I was a child... I never imagined myself as a bride. Marrying, having children. A partner... I always thought that would be nice. Which I suppose is what marriage is meant to be. And love. I think...despite not feeling entirely ready for it, I've always wished to know that kind of love. To feel it, and to give it.

Why did you never marry him?' she asked after a moment, daring to be...bold.

'Killian said we never needed such as the *little people* do,' Artemis sighed. 'That our lives weren't ruled by convention, and also that should anyone find out it would tarnish my image, as it might've if Elizabeth herself had.'

'Did you want to?'

'For what it represents, I think, yes, I did. But I would just as soon have made vows before God without all the other nonsense.'

'You're a believer then?'

'In a loose way,' Artemis said quietly, and Ruth heard the smile, as her fingers touched upon a tin box, and she took it onto her lap. 'I have reservations about many things, but I do find comfort in the idea of some...great force, beyond our understanding. Not controlling our lives, dictating them, but... Well, I suppose I find some idea of a grand plan, and something beyond this world, reassuring, as I know many do.'

'I wish I had such faith,' Ruth admitted softly, her fingers toying with the slight embossing on the characters dancing in metal on her lap. 'My faith is in the gods who rule here, in such houses as this one. Gods of comedy, and humanity, and joy, and luck. A man came by today,' she continued after a moment, glancing up at Artemis, who was studying her carefully, though she didn't find it quite so disconcerting now. It wasn't like her to...share her burdens thus, but she wouldn't talk to any of the company about it, and Artemis *was* here. 'He offered to buy this place. Offered me enough to make a proper start of it elsewhere. And I cannot help but wonder if I'm making a mistake, refusing. Clinging to my father's theatre, to what it represents, rather than...starting anew. I wonder if I'm being selfish, making it harder on everyone else. Which choice is part of the grand design, I wonder?'

'Both?' Artemis offered, before grinning widely.

Ruth shook her head, laughing quietly.

'Very useful, thank you...'

'You are most welcome.'

But then, from all she knew of religion, and faith, in a way, Artemis spoke the truth.

Focusing instead on the tin box in her hand, rather than philosophical and theological debates, Ruth pried it open, and found...

'These are...yours,' she breathed, fingers slowly fanning through the assorted pamphlets, articles, tickets, and programmes.

'What?' Artemis asked, before coming to kneel beside her.

'These are all from your shows,' Ruth said, dazed, pulling out one of the programmes, and laughing as she saw her father had scribbled notes on it, though still, she felt... oddly emotional about this find, in a way she couldn't quite describe. *Not quite jealousy nor envy, but something akin to it. Regret, for not being...but second best still.* '"*Artemis was tired it seemed this evening, however revived by the final act, and did a commendable job of keeping Horace in check,*"' she read, glancing up to Artemis.

Stunned, she laughed distractedly though she took the programme, carefully, and almost scared, when Ruth offered it out to her.

'I remember that one... It was one of the first after I left with Killian. He got me an engagement at some new theatre on the South Bank, not too far from the one your father managed. Horace Houghty was playing my kindly uncle, yet at every turn he would try to pinch my bottom—or something equally as despicable. I had to work with him for three weeks before Killian finally agreed to ensure he was fired,' she sighed, shaking her head as she handed the programme back.

'"*Artemis has found her place, and her calling. Her words*

*are as vibrant as she is, and hold a depth not many others
can claim to possess.'"*

'From my first play,' Artemis said quietly, taking hold
of the new programme. '*The Adventures of Laney Grace.*'

'A young orphan from the East End finds love and meaning on the high seas after many trials and tribulations.'

'A fanciful bit of nonsense,' Artemis countered, handing
her back the offending programme. 'A ridiculous aqua drama
that can barely be called a play in fact.'

Ruth…wasn't quite sure what to say, to lessen the turmoil
in Artemis's now shuttered gaze and countenance.

But then she herself was distracted when Artemis extracted
another tin box from the corner closest to her, and opened it.

'These are yours.' She smiled, brightness returning to her,
as Ruth's own heart soared slightly. *Why? You know he loved
you. You know you were his daughter.* 'And you've not escaped Toby Connell's notes either. *"Ruth will need to learn
to cease wandering about the stage on the balls of her feet.
Otherwise, exceptional energy and voice."'*

'With the amount of notes he gave otherwise, I wonder
at his keeping…these,' Ruth said, and Artemis held up the
programme she'd read from. 'Ah, yes. One of my firsts. *The
Lighthouse on Greenside Island.*'

'Why do any of us keep what we do for mementos?'

'Quite,' Ruth agreed, with a wan smile. Closing the box
on her lap, she offered it to Artemis, who did the same. 'I
suppose we should carry on,' she said, setting her box to the
side. 'If you're still happy to continue helping.'

With a soft, tempting smile, Artemis nodded, and before
she could do anything rash, or ill-advised, Ruth returned to
their work.

Wondering…many things.

None of which she quite had the heart to wonder about
fully just then.

Chapter Nine

It was late when they finally finished clearing Toby Connell's room, transforming it piece by piece, into Ruth Connell's. Ruth kept a fair few mementos, including a select few items of clothing—why those, Artemis didn't ask for fear of…things becoming any more personal than they had already—and emptied Ruth's own trunk of clothes and assorted possessions.

Learning all she had about Ruth, expressing all she had about herself, Artemis felt… At once out of her depth, in an unknown foreign land, and yet, at the same time, as the night before, both freer, lighter, and more at ease than she had been in a very long time.

It tempted her to dream of silly things, such as wishing for the rest of her life to be led in that room, with Ruth. Without the world, the past, the uncertain, opaque future, or…

Life. Choices. Fear.

Silly dreams and wishes indeed.

She knew it was merely her years of isolation, pain, and regret talking, whispering such nonsense to her. It certainly wasn't her heart, for that was shrivelled, and destroyed, thanks to Killian. Ruth was merely a kind, intelligent, beautiful woman, and after years of…if not loneliness then yes, isolation, she provided pleasant company.

Precisely.

And now… It was time to leave that pleasant company, and get to her own room, and rest, and think—no, not think, *sleep*, and rest, to be ready for the new day, and all she still had to achieve.

Yet I find I cannot think of anything less appealing just now.

It wasn't merely her reluctance to write, to resume real life, and face its vicissitudes again, either; though Artemis would've liked to be able to convince herself otherwise. It was a reluctance to leave... Ruth.

The attraction which flowed between them, undeniable, and yet at odds with the desire Artemis had felt for others by the ease and comfort which flowed alongside it, had simmered all night. Not bubbling, and brewing into something more, by one's fixation on it, or rather, on the other person— on how their brows lifted and fell comically, or the grey of their eyes changed into the silver of stars when they were happy—but instead, solidifying into the wholeness it already was. Becoming more apparent—or merely more undeniable.

Artemis had tried to deny it. All evening.

Tried to dismiss, and counter it in every reasonable way.

She had even tried walking away from it—hence her presence *not* in Ruth's room, but rather in the tiny office, on her way out.

Saying good night.

Not focusing on how Ruth again glowed in the dim lamplight, or how the rumpled skirts, and hair in disarray, were charming, and...

'Good night, Ruth,' she said most decidedly, still not moving an inch.

Leave. Now. Before...

'Thank you,' Ruth whispered. 'It was...good to have a friend to help tonight.'

'So we are friends now?'

Artemis had meant to be challenging, but she hadn't quite

meant to catch Ruth so off-guard, that her mouth was now opening and closing as she searched for words.

Nor had she meant to provoke the injury she saw in those now dark grey depths before Ruth turned away wordlessly.

Damn it.

Without force nor much strength, Artemis reached out, grabbing hold of Ruth's arm before she could move out of reach. Ruth stopped, looking down at the offending append-age, which Artemis merely slid down, until she could hold her hand.

Gently tugging, she silently asked Ruth to turn back to her, and after a moment's hesitation, and a sigh which bore in it as much recognition of all they would both be admitting as there was in Artemis's heart, she did so, stepping in even closer, and looking up with a silent plea Artemis wasn't en-tirely sure was for her to walk away, or do what she sorely wished to.

Perhaps both, as my own heart prompts me to do.

'I…'

There were a thousand words on the tip of her tongue, but no more than that made it past her lips.

Instead, Artemis gave in to her baser instincts, and lifting her hand to Ruth's cheek, her other now twining with Ruth's more intricately, she gently caressed the soft skin, trailing her fingers down to Ruth's lips.

Ruth didn't move; she didn't shy, nor pull away, and Ar-temis watched as the dark grey turned to clear skies again. Clear skies, alight with the fire of desire. Slowly, giving her every opportunity to refuse, or move, Artemis leaned in, until their breaths were mingling, their lips but a hairs-breadth apart, every detail from the lightness at the end of Ruth's eyelashes, and the hairs on her cheek, in clear focus.

And then, after a pause, seeing nothing but relinquish-ment, and want in her eyes, Artemis surrendered to the moment, her own eyes drifting closed as she met Ruth's lips with hers.

Damn it.

It was too...*good.*

Too overwhelmingly perfect, and right. Artemis had just meant to—well, she wasn't entirely sure *what* she meant to do, but she was sure it resembled something such as *satisfy a craving or curiosity.* Instead, she found Ruth's lips to be as delectable, as tempting, as addictive as they'd seemed at first glance, and what should've been a mere quick satisfaction, ignited an insatiable hunger she doubted she could ever satisfy.

What should've been a mere *sampling*, rapidly devolved into the best kiss of her life, she was sure.

Without any grace, planning, or forethought, she found herself cradling Ruth's face in both hands, pulling her closer—not that she'd have thought it possible before—as the other woman's hands snaked to her waist, and held her tight.

They opened themselves to each other in unison, little moans escaping them both as their tongues met and twirled, as they delved into each other's heat, and—at least in Artemis's opinion—delectable taste and scent.

Ripe blueberries, clove, the briny freshness of summer seaside breezes, and...

Something which was the very essence of Ruth, but impossible to name, for it was...a sensation no other could feel or provoke. A mystery wrapped up in sensation the best Artemis could find to quantify as *perfection.* The Word, the origin of all things, which couldn't be quantified or defined by mortal man's words.

And there was a softness, a tenderness, to Ruth's touch, which was tied to her soul, and heart. Which nearly made Artemis baulk, but for the newfound need she had of it; a need to fall into it, and lose herself completely. It was beyond terrifying, beyond dangerous, and some part of Artemis knew that, yet still, she couldn't pull away.

Instead, she succumbed to it, to the need, letting her body follow its instincts. First, delving as far, as deeply, and profoundly as possible into all the corners of Ruth's mouth, finding hidden divots, bumps, and tastes. Using her tongue, her lips, her teeth, to trace, memorise, and experience every new sensation, every new discovery, from the thrilling sharpness of Ruth's teeth beneath the bottom of her tongue, to the stark but fascinating line between the smoothness of her bottom lip, and the downy softness of the skin just beneath it.

Then, not satisfied, nor finished in her explorations, but needing *more*, she began peppering kisses along Ruth's jaw, cheeks, brows… Along her hairline, now dotted with beads of sweat; along that little gap between her jaw and her ear, down the column of her neck—tight, her pulse pounding against the barest veil of skin. Further, her eyes occasionally drifting open just ever so slightly to map the path with the freckles and spots marking the way. Down to where neck met shoulder, along the line of her bodice, along her collarbone, careful not to indulge her need to spend hours on Ruth's plump breasts lest she never emerge, but merely discovering.

All the while, the symphony of sounds and movements from Ruth underscoring her travels. Little gasps, sharp, high-pitched intakes of breaths. A squirm, a tightening of her grip. A shift in her hips, canting forward.

The rising of those beautiful, soft, and wonderful breasts until they threatened to spill over and make Artemis forget herself…

'Tell me to stop,' she breathed in between moments of laving the hollow of Ruth's left shoulder, whilst her hands—which she couldn't consciously remember moving from Ruth's face, yet which had done as much discovering as her mouth, for she could feel the imprint of Ruth's flesh on her palms even now—mindlessly kneaded Ruth's bottom. 'Tell me this isn't right, and to stop, or by God I'll have you on that desk.'

'Do you want to stop?' Ruth asked, gasping, her fingers threading through her hair, and scraping against her scalp as Artemis found a particularly sensitive spot.

'No, that's the problem.'

'Why is it a problem? Why wouldn't this be right?'

'You're emotional. Grieving. Our time is limited. You want more from life than I can give.'

In an astounding, and stunning display of self-control that filled Artemis with admiration, Ruth took her head between her hands, and forced her to meet her gaze.

She bemoaned the loss of flesh beneath her lips, but took comfort in all she could still feel, and grounded herself in the silver eyes that most certainly looked like stars now, burning in the twilight of the universe.

'I've wanted you from the first, Artemis Goode,' Ruth said with a serious steadiness that forced attention, her thumbs slowly caressing Artemis's cheeks. 'I may be grieving, but I know what I want. What you can give. And what you can't.'

Damn it all, Artemis thought grimly, any hope of denying, running from, or escaping…*this*, dissolved into the air, as though it had never existed.

Resolve, determination, and incandescent passion instead filling her heart, as she gave in to Ruth's beckoning gaze, and settled her lips once again onto hers.

Too damn good.

Too damn right.

Too much trouble.

Perhaps there were valid objections to allowing this to progress, but Ruth couldn't seem to think of any. What she'd said to Artemis was true. She'd wanted her from the first, and she knew…what Artemis could give, and what she couldn't. She knew what time they had, and what…she herself had to give, and didn't.

She also knew what she wanted in this moment, and that was to give in to this. To seize a chance she'd never imagined she'd have; to give in to her desire for Artemis.

To surrender to the potency of Artemis's desire for her.

It was both a continuation, and entirely separate from all they'd shared so far. Intimacy, only not emotional intimacy, but intimacy of a baser, more primal sort. And Ruth welcomed it. Relished it. The chance to feel, and only feel, and give herself over to pleasure, and not think, and not feel anything *but* the gloriousness of Artemis's touch.

The gloriousness of her taste—something akin to a warm, spiced wine.

The gloriousness of her scent—*meadows, and laundry drying in a crisp autumn breeze.*

The gloriousness of the feel of her, of being surrounded, and held. The comfort, and safety in it, even as it felt the most perilous, and reckless thing, to allow herself to feel such delights.

It all felt wild, untethered, and passionate, yet at the same time, the surest, rightest thing. So unlike anything she'd ever experienced before—but then perhaps that was merely loneliness. Not having been with anyone for…some time. Perhaps she'd merely forgotten what it was like to be touched, and desired, and *wanted* to this degree—though truthfully she didn't believe she ever had been.

Best not to think. Just feel.

Making good on her promise—a promise which had made Ruth's heart skip a beat, and the flames low in her belly rise to an inferno as though someone had thrown gunpowder onto embers—Artemis half guided, half nudged her back towards the desk, their mouths still entangled, Ruth still clutching to every bit of her she could get her hands on. Now that this… agreement had been made, it felt as if another version of desire had been unleashed.

One of clumsy messiness, and fervour, and—

'My papers,' she gasped, tearing her mouth from Artemis's, reason intruding in this most inopportune moment.

Artemis blinked, trying to clear some of the clouds of desire in her eyes—now the colours of a vibrant sunset over the Downs.

Their staggered breaths were harsh, and loud, their rhythm on opposing beats, sending the tiny hairs escaped from both of their basic *coiffures* toying to and fro, tickling Ruth's skin.

'I spent all day organising them,' she said weakly, and Artemis chuckled, her head dropping to Ruth's shoulder for a moment.

Then, Artemis lifted her head, shaking it slightly, an amused smile on her face, before gently kissing her forehead, and releasing her to clear the desk, carefully but perfunctorily.

Ruth would've helped, had she not been so stunned by that tiny gesture—that tender kiss to her forehead which somehow felt as though it crossed the boundaries of *animal passion intimacy.*

Turning to watch Artemis didn't help quell that feeling either, for that gesture too—the neat, graceful, and undebated clearing—held some measure of care she hadn't…expected?

Why shouldn't you? Artemis isn't a bad person.

Besides, lovers should have care for each other—even if their hearts are not involved.

And Ruth's heart certainly wasn't involved. All she'd said to Artemis was very true, and liking someone, desiring someone—even to this degree, this quickly—it didn't mean she was about to lose her head, or her heart.

Of course not.

Also, opting for the desk, rather than the bed they'd just cleared, demonstrated very well all this encounter was to be, and all it wasn't. It certainly wasn't because Artemis had *somehow* sensed Ruth might be reluctant to…do whatever they were about to in the room which felt less like, but still somewhat like, her father's.

Certainly not.

Ruth was torn from her silly musings when Artemis stood beside the cleared desk, and held out her hand, beckoning. For a moment, she wondered if the passion they'd felt had died because of her request, but as soon as her hand was in Artemis's again, she felt it rekindle with a searing brightness.

Pulling her close, and guiding her to sit on the edge of the desk, Artemis non-threateningly caged her in, wedging her thigh between Ruth's legs, one hand sliding up her thigh, and making room by sliding up her skirts in the same movement, the other, cradling her face again.

'What do you want, Ruth?' Artemis asked huskily, her eyes tracking across Ruth's features curiously, her lips hovering just above Ruth's own. 'What do you like? Or do you prefer not to talk?' A blush bloomed on Ruth's cheeks, the directness hitting its mark. 'Shall I take what I crave, and you tell me if you prefer I change…tactics?'

Pondering her options for a moment, Ruth lost herself, studying how the colour of Artemis's lips had changed, deepening, and blossoming.

What do I want?

What do I need tonight?

'The latter option,' Ruth breathed finally, acknowledging she wanted to hand over control.

To just feel.

A wicked smile, full of promise and intent grew on Artemis's lips and she nodded.

Lord, what have I just agreed to?

Something which made her heart beat almost intolerably in her chest. Which made her blood slow even as it did, turning to molten lava as it travelled through her veins, easing any tension but that of anticipation in every single inch of her body.

And she's not even begun...

Begin she did though, not hastily, but with a deliberate, teasing slowness that only fed the flames of desire and anticipation. Though already slick before, Ruth felt herself grow even readier, as Artemis stepped in closer, grabbing hold of her hips to draw her near to the edge—her thigh subtly, but steadily pressing against her core.

Then, she set to work, resuming her lavishing on the flesh available to her, before her fingers began undoing the buttons at Ruth's side. When the bodice was loose enough, she slid it off, and then undid her corset, and removed that, and what she could of Ruth's chemise, to gain access to what lay beneath.

Thus bared, Ruth waited, her breathing shallow, and her mouth dry, as Artemis...*looked.*

Gazes, admires...burns my flesh with her appreciation.

She even heard herself whimper as Artemis licked her lips then descended upon her as a hungry wolf might. But a hungry wolf would be less dangerous to her sanity. Because the way Artemis... *Touched* seemed too paltry a word. *Devoured* was closer, but still not quite apt.

She wasn't entirely sure why she was trying to define it, but she had a feeling it was because it felt like a safety. Keeping her from losing herself *entirely* to sensation. That may have been what she wanted, but she'd never imagined there would be...

This much of it.

Every nerve, every muscle, every bone, and every ounce of marrow within those bones, alight with...*life*, which had her squirming, and bucking against Artemis, who held her tight and fast with one hand, whilst the other cupped, and kneaded each of her breasts in turn, whilst her mouth kissed, licked, sucked, and nibbled at every inch of flesh. Her tongue, dancing over the bumps surrounding her nipples. Nails, slightly raking along the tender skin as she held it, and brought it further into her mouth. Lifting and pressing as she contorted gracefully to inhale deeply, then lick the beads of sweat gathering underside her breasts. Slowing, quickening, shifting, with every cue Ruth gave her.

All the while, all Ruth could do was hold on. Guide Artemis best she could, but also, fall into every caress as one tumbled into dreams. And had the warmth, the slickness, the gentle puff of Artemis's breath not been there, against her skin, she might've thought she'd tumbled into the best dream of her life.

And then Artemis was moving. With a hastiness that didn't belie, but was rather stark in contrast to the deliberateness of her attentions until now.

In a move—or rather, series of moves—which were graceful, efficient, and would've made anyone overseeing costume changes proud, Artemis had her skirts bunched up around her waist, underthings gone, so that Ruth sat open, exposed, and bare on the polished wood.

Dropping to her knees, again Artemis studied her innermost self as though she were gazing at the origin of the world. Awed, reverent, curious, and…

Still hungry.

Yet she also took care to glance back up at Ruth, who of course nodded, unable to do anything else. For a second, she considered lying back, giving in to this moment entirely, except she…couldn't. As much as she wanted to lose herself, she also wanted to be present. To memorise this moment—for future times of loneliness perhaps.

So rather than close herself off into her own world of ecstasy, Ruth merely steadied herself with one arm slightly behind her, leaning back, and opening herself that little bit more so as to allow Artemis better access.

Which Artemis took *full* advantage of. Her own excitement and need, tightly leashed, so that Ruth could feel the slight tremble in her fingers as she swept them across her thighs. Along the place where it met her most intimate lips. As they grasped the flesh of her thigh, and Artemis held her open to her mouth's ministrations.

It was as before. A thorough, decadent exploration, full of need, but with the drive of someone who needed most of all to find the perfect, most…triggering spots. A drive to learn Ruth's innermost self as another might wish to know their lover's soul.

Starting off slowly, little kisses, little licks, listening to how Ruth breathed, and seeing how she moved into or away from the caress. Working her way from outer lips to the inner folds, embracing, tugging, scraping, nibbling, licking, sucking, and breathing softly onto, every inch.

Sliding her fingers into Artemis's hair, she guided her gently, telling her silently—or not so silently, when she gasped, and pressed tighter against her mouth as Artemis's tongue ran just under the hood above her bud—what she liked most. *How* she liked it.

And one of the most exceptional things, was that… Unlike other encounters she'd had—Thomas being the exception, not that she was comparing—it didn't feel as though… There was any pressure of time, for her to reach her peak. The sounds Artemis was making… The way she left no spot—save for those Ruth didn't react well to—untouched…

She'd said she wanted to take, but it didn't feel like she was taking anything.

Or perhaps she is… Drawing my pleasure from my body…
With every swipe of her tongue, in and out, along, across,

and now her fingers… It was the most decadent, the most electric, the most sensual and complete rise to ecstasy she'd ever had. She was certain of it. Not a slow burning, but a wrenching of pleasure from every nerve, every muscle, every bone, until she was too close, too far gone, pressing against Artemis's mouth, holding tight to the silky hair bunched between her fingers, barely filling her lungs as Artemis held her tight, repeating ceaselessly the perfect combination of lips, tongue, and fingers, hitting those perfect spots in unison until everything within Ruth was clenching tight, and her head fell back as she sucked in gasps of air, and floated among the stars and felt as though she'd seen the origin of all things herself.

Artemis followed her lead until she came back down to earth, to the sticky desk, and the heat, and the smells of them both mingling in the air, and then she rose, and, burying her own fingers into Ruth's hair, pulled her in for a crushing, bruising, and spectacular kiss.

How long they remained thus, Ruth wasn't entirely sure, nor did she care.

Eventually, they slowly parted, Artemis's fingers toying across various parts of her—cheeks, nipples, the line of her hair, shoulders—as she looked at Ruth with the sort of self-satisfied smile one might've otherwise liked to wipe off her face.

But then… Her smile changed. It became complicit, tender, and full of something softer, and sweeter, and Ruth smiled back, taking a moment to bask in both the pleasure, but also the loveliness of that moment, and Artemis, all sweaty, and dishevelled, and glistening lips, and twinkling eyes.

Except a moment later, she changed again.

It stole Ruth's breath, and not in a good way.

Artemis shuttered away, not viciously, or meanly, but in a sad sort of way that made Ruth's heart tug, and want to—

'It's been a long day,' Artemis said, stepping back, shoving some strands of hair out of her face. 'You should get some rest.'

And with that, she left.

Left Ruth sitting there like a very exposed, very satisfied, but very cold ninny.

You knew what she had to give and what she didn't then, did you? Right.

Chapter Ten

Some sad and sorry young fool wanders about stormy moors, searching for refuge in some ominous ruin of a house, inhabited by the seemingly handsome, but secretly dark, haunted, and twisted lord...

It was a start.

All she had for now.

Looking back over those...*attempts* from yesterday—which had taken all morning—Artemis had come to the same conclusion she had come to upon writing them; hence the pile of balled-up papers near the wastebasket.

Triumphant return indeed. Ha!

Every attempt was more pitiable than the last, and she had no story. For either of these new works she was meant to be writing, though for now she focused on the main piece.

It was the whole reason she'd gone downstairs last night before...getting distracted.

Don't. Don't think on it.

You have to find a story. You have to get this done.

No thinking of Ruth.

No.

'Not for one second,' Artemis ordered herself.

In all fairness to...herself, she was doing a pretty good job of it too.

Mostly.

Occasionally, she would get these tiny snippets of memory, visions of Ruth in ecstasy.

Visions of Ruth's breasts—and yes, she was aware of the fact that she thought about those a lot, but it wasn't her fault she loved breasts as a general rule, and that Ruth's were magnificent.

And luscious, and delectable.

Just as the rest of her was.

A taste so sumptuous, so encompassing, and fulfilling, yet at the same time maddening in its ability to only make her crave it more, she—

Not. Thinking. About. Ruth.

Thinking on your...young, sad fool, wandering the moors.

Yes.

So...she had borrowed her gothic musings of the mind from that day Ruth had first visited her. It wasn't as if she had many other ideas.

Or any at all.

Besides, those gothic musings would do well for a melodrama, and a melodrama was always an audience favourite. Wasn't it?

Surely. Audiences flock to them.

It wasn't as if she had it in her to write a proper comedy, and she certainly didn't have what it would take to write... a drama. Not as she had in the past, full of soul, and heart, and...*everything*. She didn't have what it took to write *anything*, but she'd managed to convince herself she could write...things which took little effort. Little soul.

A sentimental melodrama, along with an idiotic little farce... Surely that she could do. Surely that would be enough to satisfy her debt.

Regardless. Sorry, sad young fool.

A lady obviously. Beautiful, all tragic, and forlorn and desperate, and of course she looks nothing like Ruth.

Her maid does, however.

Yes, a tragic, desperate lady, fled from...wherever with her maid.

Why?

Tapping the pen in her hand against her lips, Artemis stared out through the skylight, half praying for salvation from above. One of those poetic bolts of inspiration.

Of course, there wasn't one.

You know story. You can build one. You don't need inspiration, merely...

To find the natural next step.

'A lady running from wherever,' she muttered to herself. 'For some unknown reason.'

Yes.

So where from, and why?

Danger.

Always a classic tale.

Good. And...?

Throwing down the pen, and rising to stretch her restless limbs—which had *nothing*, patently *nothing indeed* to do with Ruth, and that...incredible time last night, nor Artemis's guilt on having left her as she had—Artemis paced about the room, hands balanced on her head as she tried to force something from it.

Fleeing from danger. Because she's...a spy.

Yes. The war with the French—any will do, plenty to choose from.

A lady spy, fleeing from...a spycatcher!

'Brilliant,' she congratulated herself, not truly feeling it.

She seeks refuge far from... London.

Everyone's always fleeing from London to the country. The country...

The moors. There's a storm. A house on the hill. Ghastly, and terrifying—another classic, mustn't do without—and inhabited by a handsome, but secretly dark and twisted lord.

You're welcome, Montague.

So... Taken by her beauty and desperation, the lord offers the lady a place in his household as a...housekeeper.

'That'll do.'

Finally, she was getting somewhere.

Who else did she have to cast then?

The old man, Thomas, the villain's aid, and...

Ah yes, the damned hero, Laurie.

For the old man...a vicar. Do have to bring in God and all those neat morals everyone loves.

'Your brilliance is astounding this morning, Artemis,' she sighed, rolling her eyes at her own...lack of originality.

But any story, any play will do.

You're not trying to be brilliant. Quite the contrary.

Right. So they'll leave me alone.

She ignored the stabbing guilt which arose with that reminder.

How Ruth might look at her when she found out that the play they were meant to be running for a *whole season*, the play meant to save them all from ruin was...*bad*. Ruth was *trusting her*, and Artemis was encouraging her to do so, purporting she could do this, and when Ruth discovered the truth... It would be so much worse than that look on her face last night when Artemis had left her...

Enough.

Never mind what Kit will think—

Oh, do cease!

The lady becomes friends with the vicar, who advises her spiritually.

We need our hero to appear soon, so... On her way back from one such meeting with the vicar, she is yet again caught in a storm, though she doesn't look anywhere near as appealing as Ruth did when she was—

Handsome stranger in the woods. Who is...masked. For

some inexplicable reason we don't need to explain because no one will care.

This handsome masked stranger rescues her, but warns her off the dark lord she's living with. However she cannot heed his advice for she has nowhere else to go. Even if...slowly— or quickly, this isn't a three-hour drama, Artemis—the lord begins making overtures. The lady is somewhat tempted by his handsomeness, but there is a darkness to him, an insistence that is too...much to be natural, and besides she's...

Married! Of course she is! Chaste, loyal, and good, despite her French spying ways. She's married to...

To the stranger in the woods!

'Who she didn't recognise?' Artemis asked herself, or the Heavens, she wasn't entirely sure at this point. 'Why run from him in the first place?'

Because he's the spycatcher, you ninny. Not that she knew that they were one and the same at the time.

Only that her life was in danger, and that she couldn't risk dishonour by telling her husband she was a nasty little French spy.

So...

Lecherous lord. Handsome stranger with a secret. The maid keeps trying to protect her, but things are becoming increasingly...dangerous.

Such danger. All the time.

Many storms. Much thunder and lightning.

One night, the lady flees the house to avoid the lord's advances, and meets the stranger again. They share an interlude, and he asks her to run away with him. Yet she cannot run, and is devoured by the fact she felt no guilt in being with a man who wasn't her husband.

'Who she still didn't recognise...'

No one said she had to have any sort of brains or instincts to be a proper spy...

And…so she confesses to the vicar.

'And St John? You bloody forgot St John!'

Another stranger.

Who arrives in the village. Purposely, pretending to be the spycatcher to scare the lady into agreeing to be…the lord's mistress. For the lord then offers her protection if she agrees to be his. She feels trapped, and lost, and so she agrees.

The night arrives and…the maid, and Thomas—another servant who has befriended the hero because why not—go fetch the stranger in the woods to save her. Our hero arrives at the manor just as the lord is about to ravish the lady, and kills our lecherous villain, saving his beloved wife.

However, devoured by grief—from having betrayed her country and her husband—she dies.

'Utterly tragic—well, not too much so, her death is also very beautiful and redeeming and all that—utterly boring, utterly unoriginal, and utterly moralistic,' she concluded with a most unsatisfied sigh. 'They'll… Love it, or hate it, I couldn't really care less. It's something. If needs be we'll add a dog.'

Throwing her hands up in the air, she resolved to return to her desk, and get that part down on paper at least, focusing hard on not wondering why she felt like the worst liar when she said: *'I couldn't care less.'*

As she began scrawling the sad and sorry tale onto the paper, with a fervour that most certainly was *not* due to anger or frustration, merely *haste*, she couldn't help but hear a nagging voice in the back of mind yelling at her that she did in fact, *care a whole lot.*

About making this play…good.

About Ruth.

About…everything she always denied she did.

Which was entirely problematic.

Because if she worried about making this play *good*, she would…inevitably fail. She had no doubts about that. It couldn't ever be good, when she'd lost her voice. Or more aptly, her friends. Those voices in her mind who guided her. Even if she *wanted* it to be good, she wouldn't manage it. All she had now, was her knowledge of writing as a whole. Of story, of character, of what audiences wanted.

It would bear her name, but nothing more.

As she'd told herself before, she'd agreed out of loyalty, and to pay her debt, and as…her final swansong. Which wouldn't be nearly as beautiful as one would hope such a thing might be, but yes, it was the final farewell, the final *leave me alone* before proper retirement.

Which you want.

Retirement.

Right. Of course she did.

It had been her choice then, and nothing had changed. She was done with this life of theatre, of writing, and, and… all that.

Precisely.

As for…caring about Ruth, and Ruth's future, and Ruth's theatre, and Ruth's opinion, well, she was done with that too. She didn't need Ruth's good opinion. Ruth's future and the-atre were her responsibility, and her choice, and had nothing to do with Artemis.

At all.

Never would.

What they'd shared…*good* as that was—*incredible as that was, use the right words, Artemis, though you doubt there are satisfactory ones to define the extraordinary quality of that encounter*—it didn't change anything.

They'd succumbed to pleasure and desire, and had a grand, jolly old time of it, and hopefully Ruth felt better for it—Artemis certainly did when she looked past the desire for *more*, or *all*—and that was that.

Besides. She is better off without…someone like me.

'Certainly,' she muttered, adding a little flourish at the bottom of the page as she finished writing out the story.

Now to write the rest...

In a week or hopefully less.

Nothing you haven't done before.

Though admittedly it had been a while.

Just as easy as...riding a horse.

Or giving another person pleasure, and—

With a half growl, half muffled scream of frustration, Artemis cast the pen back on the desk, and set about pacing again.

Visions of Ruth as she'd left her, glowing, dishevelled, and *hurt*, by her cold brusqueness, swam before her eyes. There should be no guilt sloshing around in her heart about that. Ruth herself had said she knew very well what Artemis could and couldn't give, so she shouldn't have been so surprised when Artemis just...left.

Or hurt. She shouldn't have been hurt by that.

Fine, so perhaps Artemis might've explained a bit better. Said *something*. Softened the blow. Reassured Ruth of her beauty, her gloriousness, the pleasure she'd given her by being so...wonderful. And *then* sent her off to bed.

Only I couldn't.

Yes, well, that was the crux wasn't it.

It wasn't about Artemis *taking* as promised, and leaving the woman satisfied, as agreed, and then resuming life.

It wasn't about Artemis giving only what she'd said—*pleasure*—and nothing more. Because the simple fact was that standing there, Ruth's taste still on her lips, seeing her smile, and all the shades of grey in her eyes, and how she sparkled, and glowed, and just how *perfect* it had been...

Artemis had been overwhelmed. With something she didn't care to name, but which terrified her nearly as much as the loss of her words.

Possibility.

There. She'd named it.

It would be so easy, to just…fall into Ruth. Fall into day-dreams, and wishes of…happiness, she supposed. It would be so easy to renege on all her unspoken vows—to be alone, to leave the theatre, to…fade away, all because Ruth was… tempting her like…like some…

Temptress.

What a brilliant writer you are indeed, Artemis.

Honestly, genius without bounds I say—

'What now?' Artemis growled, stomping over to the door.

Wrenching it open, no doubt a solid scowl on her face, she found herself confronted with the woman who'd been invading her thoughts—despite all she told herself not to allow it, and she looked…

Beautiful, but also nervous, and sad, and no.

You'll not…cave again.

'Yes?' she said, as politely, gently, and—*fine*, dismissively, as she could.

'How goes it in there?' Ruth asked brightly, Artemis's mood apparently giving her the impetus to be *even more cheery.*

'Fine. Was there something you needed?'

'Er…yes, well.' She smiled, the nervousness creeping back up, as she wrung her hands. 'Firstly, I thought we could set an appointment for tomorrow morning, or perhaps Sunday morning, unless you'd like to attend church, well, to discuss the new pieces, so I can begin to get everyone working on orders, and making, and so on…' Ruth said, trailing off. Artemis nodded, and after waiting a few moments, and realising she would get no further answer, Ruth continued. 'Fantastic. Also, we wanted to invite you to join us later. We have a few traditions when we open a new programme, and since you're part of our company now, we thought it would be nice. Before the dress rehearsal, and before the show, we—'

'I'm not part of your company, Ruth,' Artemis said, stopping her in her tracks. Again, hurt transformed Ruth's features, and not only did Artemis have to contend with guilt then, but also self-disgust. Still, she couldn't…help herself. *Or perhaps this is how I help myself.* 'I'm here for one purpose, and only one. I wish you all the best for this evening, but as for me, I've much work to do, as you're well aware. I'll see you in the morning.'

'Of course,' Ruth said weakly.

Unable to risk looking at her any longer, lest she let herself wander into mortal peril, Artemis shut the door again, and returned to her desk.

Get this done, and leave.

The sooner, the better.

For everyone.

Chapter Eleven

$\backsim\!\!\!\!\!\curvearrowright\!\!\!\!\!\curvearrowleft\!\!\!\!\!\sim$

Crouching behind the wall of one of the boxes Ruth sucked
in some deep breaths—as quietly as she could so as not to be
found. The Roman coin Father had found in the walls here when
he'd first bought the place, and which served as both a lucky
charm, and the object of this particular pre-opening ritual—
though technically it was a pre-*dress* rehearsal ritual—was
clutched tightly in her hand, and she had no desire to relinquish it today.

I need all the luck I can get...

Only, if St John—currently *it* in their game of hide-and-
seek—found her anything but last, she would be forced to
relinquish the coin, and the luck would be his for the day. It
wasn't that she was being selfish, only, she truly felt, today,
the coin, the luck it represented, well...it made her feel that
little bit better.

This game did too, if she was honest. She had no idea
where it had come from—Father had always refused to tell
anyone where he'd picked up the tradition—and no other
company she knew of did such a silly thing before a final
rehearsal, but she didn't care. It was lovely, energetic, and
put them all in a playful mood.

Well, for the most part. Even with the fun of the game,
Ruth was having some difficulty...shaking off Artemis's
mood. And yes, her rejection.

It wasn't only her rejection of...what had passed between
them last night, which wasn't actually a rejection of that,
merely a rejection of...

Me.

No.

A rejection of anything more than what it had been. A satisfying tryst.

Not some great love affair—which again Ruth didn't want anyway. She hadn't the time for it, at the very least.

As she'd said.

No, what bothered Ruth most of all was a rejection of civility—*again*—and a rejection of the entire company. Ruth had thought they were past this…*grumpiness*. This rudeness, really. She'd thought, well she hadn't expected Artemis to become an outwardly engaged and welcoming and chatty person—it didn't seem like her, and Ruth would never want her to be anything but herself—however, she did think that after the thawing they'd had, the slight opening, the complicity they'd shared…that she'd be more…

Nice.

At least less…

Horrid.

Yes, she'd been horrid again, and really there was no excuse for it.

Perhaps what bothered Ruth most was that she'd not said anything. Not stood up for herself, or her people, merely allowed Artemis to bloody well slam a door in her face again.

Spineless you are.

Surprised, was actually what she'd been. Bouncing, happy, excited—the show this evening was well booked already, and she'd spied some larger groups outside today, loitering, hoping to glimpse the elusive Artemis Goode, which boded well for future sales. And yes, she'd been eager, and nervous, to see Artemis again, hopeful perhaps, that they would be able to speak as adults would, discuss what had happened last night, and how *all* of it, including Artemis's abrupt departure, had made her feel, but of course not.

The woman shuts herself up tighter than an oyster.

Footsteps sounded below her, and Ruth held her breath.

'Come out, come out, my fellows,' St John crooned in such a typically old evil crone fashion she nearly burst out laughing, giving herself away. *Exactly what he wants—always doing silly voices when he's it*... 'I've already found most of you...'

Smiling to herself, Ruth shook her head as she heard him move away and go onstage.

Shuffling quietly further into the shadows—though there was no doubt he'd search the boxes eventually—Ruth took another breath, and forced herself to let all her frustration, disappointment, and yes, hurt, fade away.

You've a show to get on.

If Artemis wants to remain isolated in her tower...so be it.

Right. She wasn't about to force the woman to do anything she didn't want to, and she had better things to do than tiptoe around her foul moods and waste time trying to make any sense of it.

Even though making sense of Artemis was becoming a very dear, if not wish, then desire. Or goal. Or something not so strong as a wish.

For some inexplicable reason.

Regardless. She had work to do. A company to keep in check, and happy, and a theatre to save. So she would do as she'd resolved from the beginning. She would get a new play from Artemis, and get it on, and then say *fare thee well and bon voyage.* She had resolved that, hadn't she?

Well, I'm resolving it now in any case.

I've neither the time nor the will to become involved— least of all with someone who has no desire to be involved in anything.

My time and will must be used to aid and protect those who I care about.

And right this moment, she had a game to win. A lucky

coin to keep safe in her grasp. Running her thumb over the now nearly smooth surface, she prayed to her old gods silently.

Let this all turn out.

I cannot lose them.

Any of them.

With a kiss to the coin, she gathered up her skirts, and scampered away to another box before St John could discover her. In the end, she did win the coin for the day—though it was only a matter of sheer luck, as St John spotted her just as Fanny called time.

I suppose the coin works after all, she thought, smiling, as St John helped her up, and they descended to get on with the day.

Thoroughly exhausted and yet energised by their game, they made a complete muck of their group recitation of nonsensical nursery rhymes, then, of the final rehearsal itself.

More good luck.

Now, for it to hold...

Regurgitation. That was what Artemis was currently doing—what she'd been doing all day since she'd slammed the door in Ruth's face. *Regurgitating.* There were words on pages; scenes planned out, descriptions written, and lines which resembled dialogue right there, in black ink, but they weren't really hers. They neither looked, felt, nor sounded like hers, but rather facsimiles of a hundred other plays or books she'd seen or read.

It shouldn't bother her. She'd resolved this would not be some great work of genius, or even something remotely hers. She'd known that from the start—well, the start of putting words to page, and she should really be glad, proud, pleased, *happy*, that anything resembling *a play* was making it onto paper.

She was *technically* writing again.

But it felt…*wrong.*

Unsettling.

Bad. In every sense of the word.

Drudgery. That's what it felt like. Complete and utter drudgery.

An exercise in…recitation. There was no creativity. No… *life*. No passion.

No friends to guide the way.

Merely shadows, ghosts of *characters*. Little puppets, dancing about on strings made of ink, and—

There's nothing for it. It's all you have left.

Perhaps the worst part of it was the appearance of new doubts, or rather, a loss of the certainty she'd had before. Certainty, as to *why* she had nothing left of herself.

For so long, she'd been convinced, or perhaps *convinced herself*, that it was Killian and Winnie's final betrayal, their shattering of her heart—combined with her own weakness— which had extinguished her passion, soul, and taken her voice from her. Now…she wondered.

Things she'd said to Ruth, without thinking, without realising, kept niggling at the back of her mind. About how Killian had always been reluctant to tell the true story of her origins and rise. About how they'd disagreed on the nature and purpose of their work.

Things unsaid too, such as the umbrage he took with her success. How he'd purported she was selfish, for not knowing what *he* needed, and giving it to him, instinctively.

Despite herself, despite knowing the dangers, Artemis couldn't help but…look back. Only not as she had so many times before; with a different perspective now. A gaze, not of longing—of romanticising *the good old days*—but an inquisitive, and interrogatory gaze. And what she found…seemed to, if not contradict her initial diagnosis, then bring her to a new conclusion.

The loss of my soul and self was not a collapse; it was an erosion.

Over the years she'd spent with him, Killian had…chipped off pieces of her. *Smoothing* her out, shaping her into what he wanted and needed. He'd not done it alone, she'd helped him, felt his desires become her own because she just *loved him too damned much.* Bit by bit, pieces of her changed, transformed, or disappeared.

Gone was the truly revolutionary spirit of her youth—in favour of *not making trouble* or *angering those who could help us.* Gone was the drive for success, and excellence, lest Killian feel *left behind.* Gone was her loudness, her *joie de vivre*, her passion, her friends, so many of them, and in many ways, her freedom. She'd stuffed herself into another form, better to please Killian, and have him love her as she loved him.

Oh, and he'd not done it alone. He'd had help.

Theatre itself had wreaked havoc upon her, underlining, and enforcing his own points. Her love for theatre had, in its own way, betrayed her too.

The hypocrisy of it all. The necessity of favours. The reliance on cheap spectacle to supposedly appease audiences. The need to curry favour with those in power—in their world, and beyond. The disregard for her profession. The demand to write plays in less than a day, and keep writing them, onwards and ever. The exhausting pace, long days, and endless months. The business of it, the noise, the incessant churning of *new, new, new.* The taciturnity, the risk, the uncertainty— it had chipped away at her too. Making her silently, and perniciously question her very *raison d'être.*

It was an entirely unpleasant, disconcerting, and confusing

conclusion to come to, especially after all this time. It left her with so many more questions, doubts, regrets, and…sadness.

Yet regardless, the result remained the same, Artemis realised, and truly, there was really no use in this exercise.

You're still nothing but a shell, a dried-up husk of unoriginality.

'And a starving one at that,' she noted, as her stomach grumbled.

Tossing down her pen, she rubbed her eyes, glancing at the watch beneath the lamp on her desk.

Hm. Later than I thought.

The performance must've finished by now—*and no, I care not a jot whether or not it went well*—so food had surely been brought up. She'd not heard anything, but then, she'd been…

Engrossed in my work?

Artemis laughed loudly at that, shaking her head as she rose to check what had been left for her.

'More like too busy trying to pry somewhat coherent sentences from this useless mind of mine,' she muttered, opening the door.

Hm.

There was…nothing.

Frowning, Artemis was debating this oddity—and what to do about it, when a deep voice spoke from the shadows, making her jump.

'Hungry?' the voice asked, and she blushed slightly at having been so caught out, and transparent—though thankfully the dim light hid that show of weakness.

Glancing around, she found Montague emerging from the stairwell's gloom, and she straightened, raising an imperious brow.

He was unmoved by the gesture, and merely slunk forward, arms crossed, his expression halfway between a scowl and an open study of her. Artemis held his gaze, unwilling to blink, respond, or show any more weakness as he came to stand before her.

Part of her objected to his attitude, his approach, his audacity, wondering viciously *who he thought he was*; however, that part of her was silenced by the…strength of him. All subdued, leashed, and quietly obtained and held power that demanded not only respect, but attention.

Not so much a villain, but instead the silent hero no one expects.

'There will be no more trays for you, Mistress Goode,' he declared seriously, and despite herself, Artemis felt her eyes widen. 'Aye, I've been the one bringing them up to you. Thought you might need some time to…acclimate yourself, and Ruth had enough to worry about. But no more,' he declared. Artemis was too stunned to even think of a response, not that she felt Montague would give her a chance to argue anyway. 'We have few traditions in this house,' he continued. 'Toby Connell never expected us to live and breathe every second of our lives together, as some do. The kitchen is always full, and open to those who require or wish to eat here. However, *together*, we are the ones who make it so. We take turns, providing for each other, and when a new programme opens, we have a meal together. So either you come down, and eat with us tonight, or I can ensure that you do not eat at all. And if you think you can needle Ruth into feeding you regardless, let me assure you, you cannot,' he said, with the seriousness a judge might have condemning her to the gallows.

Artemis swallowed hard, her performative imperiousness melting under something which resembled…

Shame.

'If you're going to work with us, you work *with* us,' he continued, and in another life, Artemis might've had words to say, to send him away, crawling, and wounded, only in this one, she didn't. 'You've had your time to get settled, and you've had your time to wallow in your own misery. You'll not hurt Ruth Connell—who happens to be one of the kindest, sweetest, most hardworking people I know—any further because you're too mired in your own bitterness. She takes enough of others' burdens for her own as it is. We've all suffered in this life. Grow up, and for once, try and do something nice for someone else.'

With that, he left, slinking back into the shadows.

Listening to his receding footsteps, Artemis pondered for a moment her next move.

That part of her that had wished to tell him where he could shove his *traditions* and *sanctimonious preaching* begged her to be stubborn. Begged her to slam the door loudly enough so that they'd hear it—and her objection—all the way downstairs.

However, the other part of her, the part which had remained silent, and felt that wave of shamefulness… Well, it knew very well what she had to do.

And not solely because she was hungry.

That part of Artemis recognised that she'd behaved badly. Knew it very well, in fact. Up until now, she'd satisfied herself with the knowledge it was easier, and what *she* needed. To…protect herself. She was not so fool as to not see that it helped her protect herself from people. From everyone. From the world which had injured her so before—taken all it had from her.

'You'll not hurt Ruth Connell…'

Artemis felt like a child, who'd just been reprimanded for their behaviour. Though she wasn't about to change her ways overnight—if such a transformation was even possible, especially when one was very happy—*fine, content*—and safe and settled in their ways—well…

She was hungry.

A meal was just a meal.

And I can just sit in the corner and eat peacefully.

In the end, she did sit, not in the corner, but at the end of the bustling, full table, so busy it felt as if the mighty slab of oak would split in two. Despite herself, she found herself laughing—*chuckling discreetly*—on more than one occasion, as those gathered, filling the kitchen with exuberant and sickening joy told stories of this missed cue or that inopportune broken sword. Despite herself, she was swept away into a pleasant, warm haze she'd not felt in a very long time, as people gathered up instruments, and sang songs when the meal ended.

And despite herself, she found herself thinking once again, as she tucked into bed much later, that if sharing such a meal put such a glorious smile on Ruth's face, she'd sit through them for eternity.

Chapter Twelve

Though Ruth knew it was just a silly superstition, she liked to think that her luck did hold for having possession of that Roman coin. It had been four days since they'd opened the show, and *knock on wood*—which she did, tapping a piece of it loitering in the backstage corridor—all was going well.

The Revenge of Captain Marshall, though not ground-breaking, was doing well enough, and those who came to see it, and the other amusements on the programme, seemed to enjoy it. Sales weren't brilliant, despite the influx of travellers come to sample the waters, and other delights the area boasted, but they were solid, and the excitement about Artemis's new play was growing. London papers had even taken up the story, and already the hotels and other lodgings nearby had noted requests for rooms from people far and wide.

They'd received a letter from Mr Laughton, agreeing to their terms, and expressing, in rather effusive and numerous words, his excitement at Artemis's decision to abandon her retirement. Which had been a tremendous relief, obviously, even if the new pieces still needed to be written, sent off, and approved. By both Mr Laughton, and The Examiner.

Details. Minor details. All in good time.

In any case, now that they were one step closer, and word was spreading, they'd decided preliminarily to open sales for a good portion of the house in a fortnight—and invitations were being sent to her and her father's *friends* in the meantime, reassuring them that naturally, their preferred boxes would be held for them, in gratitude for their *support*. Ruth felt confident all they had to sell would do so quickly—if the growing crowds of admirers outside were anything to go by. Not that they'd managed to spy Artemis yet, though that seemed to merely add to their excitement.

'She's very busy, working away,' Ruth and others told them.

Which was true, as far as Ruth or anyone else knew— the company barely saw her any more than those gathered outside.

Since that whole *door-slamming incident*, other than at meal times—and even then, not regularly—no one had seen her. Well, Ruth had gone to see her the morning after *The Revenge* opened, as agreed, and got not only the news of Mr Laughton's letter, but also a preliminary list of characters, costumes, set, props, and effects requirements, but that had all been very quick, and though civil, nothing notable.

Perhaps the most notable encounter they'd had was when Artemis had joined them for their traditional first night dinner—which Ruth suspected *someone* of forcing her into, though how, considering the woman's stubbornness, remained a mystery. Even then, they hadn't spoken, though Artemis's presence had bolstered Ruth somewhat. Served as a sort of apology. A rekindling of trust, and…friendship.

Though friends is a rather strong word for what we are.

No wonder she was reluctant to call us thus.

Yes, well, that was fine with Ruth. This was about business, in the end. Her father's legacy. The survival of her true friends. So indeed, it was nice that Artemis had joined them, and that she'd been civil when they'd met the morning after, and even said *good morning* or *good evening* if someone met her in the kitchen. However, it was no disappointment whatsoever that there had been no more midnight conversations, or encounters, or whatnot.

None whatsoever.

I need to focus on the job at hand.

And the job in her hand.

The first pages of Artemis's main play, titled *The Widow of Windswept Moor*.

Ruth clutched them tightly—well, held the pile of copies newly handed to her by Fanny tightly to her chest—brimming with barely checked excitement as she made her way to the waiting company onstage. She was as eager as anyone else to see what Artemis had come up with thus far, how she'd made this seemingly traditional gothic piece her own. She hadn't had time to read any of it—Artemis had only given them to her at dawn this morning, and she'd needed to get the pages to Fanny immediately.

There were no pages yet for the accompanying farce, *The Thief & The Clown*, but from the few things Artemis had shared would be needed for it—a market setting, an old puppet theatre cart among others—it surely had promise.

So yes, everything was going according to plan. They were right on schedule, and...

It will all turn out just perfectly.

Even if...

Well, it was just that when Artemis had handed over the pages, muttering a *good morning*, she'd had this...look about her. She'd not met Ruth's eyes, and there was a sort of dejection, or defeat about her which had made Ruth's heart flip-flop—and truth be told, yes, also made her want to smooth the lines furrowed into Artemis's brow, and kiss her worries away, but that was neither here nor there. It had been a concerning look, or air, or whatever it had been, but before Ruth had even thought of questioning it, another door had closed in her face—though with less force than the last time.

Don't be daft.

She was only tired. She's been working...tirelessly to get this done.

Which Ruth appreciated, more than she could say.

Shaking off the twinge of unease, she let the excitement and fluttering take over as she made her way onstage, where everyone was gathered around *The Revenge*'s dining room table, brought out for precisely this purpose today.

'Good morning,' she greeted them, smiling broadly, the excitement in their own gazes bolstering her even more.

As did Thomas's inhumanely wide smile, and gentle chuck of her shoulder as she passed him.

They all echoed the greeting as she circled the table, handing them each a copy of the pages—though Fanny might've done it, Ruth felt the need to do it herself for some untold reason. To feel the pages between her own fingers, feel their power emanating into her being…

Focus. Work.

Or there'll be no play.

'So…shall we get started then?' She grinned, settling at her own place beside Thomas.

Everyone nodded, easing into serious concentration as Fanny began reading.

'The moors,' Fanny began in her gently authoritative tone. Breathing deeply, Ruth let it wash over her, letting it soothe her tittering nerves. *'A terrible storm assails the landscape, and the two bedraggled figures making their way through it, seeking refuge. A crack of lightning…'*

What a beginning to the play that will save us…

An hour later, having read through the pages together, Ruth was less than convinced by her own silent prophecy.

In fact, she was…

As everyone else onstage was.

Quiet. Confused. Dejected.

Terrified.

Slumped in her seat, folded over herself as much as she could without appearing entirely defeated, Ruth glanced around at the others.

They all bore the same expression: *doubt and disappointment*.

Laurie and Madeleine stared ahead, bland shock in their eyes.

Montague was quietly pensive—though darker than usual.

Thomas was fidgeting, sifting through the pages as if searching for something…*good*.

St John seemed to be doing the same thing—though merely recounting what they'd heard and said whilst his face alternated between *consideration* and *oh no*.

William, Fanny, and the others appeared to be caught in a silent daze, waiting for her to say something.

What the Hell can I say?

Her heart was sinking faster than gold in the ocean. She'd thought it had sunk all it could as they'd read on, but now she realised it was a never-ending drop into a fathomless abyss. She wanted to cry, to rage, and demand the gods come out and reveal what was so amusing in this jest of theirs, except all she could do was sit there, as bloody stunned as the rest of them.

We're doomed.

Montague opened his mouth to speak, and she raised her head excitedly—*I'm saved*—but then he closed it again and shook his head.

If you want to be their leader, act like it.

'I…' Heads raised, and eyes turned to her. Straightening in her seat, she sighed heavily. 'It's not good.'

Understatement of the entirety of human existence.

'Well, it…' Thomas began, waving his hand at one of the pages. 'It starts off strong. The stage directions are very… evocative.'

'It's shite, Thomas,' Laurie said bluntly, his cheeky smile and bluntness somewhat reassuring, but that it held a measure of *incontestable* to it. 'We'd be better off returning to not speaking at all than speak this utter drivel. I counted at least fifty instances of the widow simpering and screaming, and those were perhaps her best lines. The rest is all *"Oh, I have broken my shoe, I cannot go any further"*, or *"Why are you wearing a mask in the forest, sir?"* To which the brilliant reply, I will remind you was: *"It helps me remain unseen by the deer and other creatures I hide from."* We'll be laughed from the stage, and this isn't a comedy. I shudder to imagine what our promised farce will look like, though perhaps we should play this as one.'

'There's potential,' Montague argued with a shrug, before meeting her gaze. 'Unfortunately, Laurie's right. We'd be better off just continuing with *The Revenge* than putting this on.'

'They'll be throwing produce at us like in the old days,' Madeleine offered helpfully. 'And we can forget about *The Agora* helping us with this, let alone putting it on...'

Apparently Madeleine had no more words—she merely gestured disgustedly at the pages.

Though Ruth was loath to argue—she had no choice but to quietly do so.

Looking at the others who'd remained silent in turn—even the apprentices at the edges of the wings—she asked them: *are we all in accord?*

They all nodded, and Ruth rose.

Apprehensive, confused, and terrified, yes, but mostly, *resigned.*

There's nothing for it.

'I'll speak to her,' she announced grimly.

Though I have no idea what or how to say this, she mentally added, marching up to Artemis's room with the alacrity of someone going to tell the King his favourite coat was ugly.

Gods help me.

Artemis wasn't getting very far with her work again— that in itself wasn't anything really *new*—though it was for a very different reason this morning. It had nothing to do with a lack of inspiration, a lack of words, or notion of where to go next. Instead, it had everything to do with the guilt, shame, and nerves, bubbling up inside of her.

All that had been bubbling and brewing like that within the witches' cauldron in the Scottish play since…

This morning.

Yes. She would say *this morning* to avoid admitting it had in fact, been from the very beginning of this doomed endeavour.

Shame, guilt, and nerves born of the sad excuse of a play she'd written thus far, and would continue to write.

Because I've nothing else to give.

She'd not even had the damned courage to look Ruth in the eye when she'd handed over the pages. She tried to reassure herself that it was better than nothing, that she was still paying her debt—though this supposed debt didn't feel as though it had anything to do with anything now, if indeed it ever did.

She tried to tell herself her name alone would be enough to save Ruth from creditors and doom, at least for now— the crowds outside waiting for an appearance from Artemis Goode were proof of that—and then in time Ruth could… figure something else out.

I've only to pay my dues, and then I can return to my retirement.

Though perhaps I'll find somewhere else to live that out.

Yes… Remaining…here wasn't a good idea, and that was all she had to say about that.

Sighing, Artemis let her head fall over the back of the chair, crunching and slumping further in her seat, her eyes drifting up to the bare wooden ceiling. She'd given up even *pretending* to write a while ago now, and hadn't managed to think of anything else to while away the time, so she just sat at her desk, and waited. For what…she wasn't entirely sure.

For them to be finished. For this to be over.

A reckoning.

Typically, this was one of her favourite parts of the process. Handing her creation over to other artists. She'd sit in on every first reading, and as many rehearsals as she could—when there was actually *a process* and not just a quick mounting of some hastily scribbled piece, or she wasn't playing a role herself, obviously—watching her words come alive. Feeling them take on a new life. Listening for those moments which didn't quite work. Speaking with the actors to see what their suggestions might be.

True collaboration.

A coming together. A shift, from words on the page, to them being in the air. Tangible, and fragile as snowflakes. It had always been her favourite part. Now, however, she couldn't stand to be anywhere near where she might hear those words being made flesh. As though to hear them would seal them as a curse.

Oh, she'd thought about it. Thought about sneaking downstairs to spy on them as they read through what she'd written; thought perhaps it wouldn't be so bad as she imagined, and merely that she was seeking unattainable perfection. After three years of not writing, there were bound to be *some* issues with a piece written in a matter of days. Nothing… terrible about that.

Obviously, she'd not descended.

Not even been able to move from her bloody chair.

Surely they must be finished by now. This isn't Hamlet, *and I only gave them half of it…*

Ah. Speak of the Devil, she thought grimly as a knock sounded on her door. Her heart skipped a beat, her nerves firing up to a nearly unbearable degree. Rising with a groan, she schooled her features, and took a deep breath before opening the door.

Oh, Hell.

'May we speak?' Ruth asked, looking as though she'd just come to deliver the news that the Book of Revelations was coming to pass later today.

Not trusting herself to do anything but nod, Artemis did so, stepping aside to let her in.

As the first time they'd been in this room together—what oddly felt like months ago, not days, considering all that had happened since then—Ruth stood in the middle of it, as Artemis remained not *at* the door, but close enough to suggest a desire to flee.

Though she tried not to show it; not to demonstrate in any way that she knew what was likely coming, nor that she cared.

Even if I do, despite myself.

'I…' Ruth began, with the same measure of nerves and hesitancy as she'd had that day too, though after a glance at the skylight, deep breath, and shake of her head, she… *changed.* Her shoulders tipped back, along with her chin, as her spine seemingly filled with steel. It was impressive, to say the least—though Artemis focused hard on remaining… *prepared.* 'Well, there's no easy way to say this, Artemis, but what you gave us, *me*, it's not…good. I'm sorry, but it's the truth, and I see no point in trying to dull the blow.'

And there it is.

It hurt more than she expected, if she was being honest. Stung more, than she'd thought it might. In a sense, knowing that the work was terrible herself… Well, in some way yes, she thought perhaps an echo of genius would still be useful. Workable. Alive, within her.

Hearing Ruth's words however, feeling the sharp, piercing sting they caused, in turn brought up Artemis's hackles.

'Yes well, it's all you're going to get,' she bit back harshly, crossing her arms. 'It'll be good enough. Especially with my name attached to it.'

'When I came to you, I came for *you*,' Ruth said fiercely, unbothered by Artemis's outburst apparently. *Annoying.* 'I came for an Artemis Goode play. This…is derivative drivel. We could've picked a thousand pieces that lasted no more than a day on the stage, and done better than this. Hell, we'd be better off doing *anything* but this! There's no feeling, none of… *you* in it. Your plays… They were something special. I always dreamt of going to London to see one, rather than just reading them. Still, even just reading them… They spoke truths about the world, and people, and yet they were so personal, and passionate. They used form to interrogate…everything. They had soul,' she pleaded, her eyes so wide, and full of incomprehension, of passion, as she stepped forth… *I can't.* 'Your name will get bums in seats, but one word of how dreadful this piece is, and they won't keep coming. That's if your Mr Laughton will even stand by his agreement if he reads this.'

'Not my problem.'

They glared at each other for a long moment.

Normally, Artemis wouldn't be so bothered by it. She'd stared down many a demanding, egotistical actor, or tyrannical, idiotic manager in her day. Yet today, she felt like squirming, Ruth's gaze so piercing, so…*seeing*, it rankled. *I can't…*

'Why won't you tell me what this is really about?'

'You wouldn't understand,' she scoffed, shaking her head, pushing down the temptation to do just that. To tell this… *stranger* who felt like anything but what she'd never told, nor ever planned to tell, another soul. *Get rid of her.* 'You're just a silly little girl, to whom everything comes easily.'

'Explain it to me, then,' Ruth said flatly, again, unbothered by Artemis's attacks. 'Explain to me, as though I were a child, where the passion is. Where your soul is. Explain to me, why you are holding back now? Tell me this was all a jest, a giant mockery of me, and this theatre, even! Just tell me *something* true.'

'They're gone, Ruth!' Artemis yelled, surprising them both.

She'd meant to...keep on attacking until the nuisance went away, but the understanding, and pleading in those grey depths undid her.

If she was honest, so did her own desire to share her turmoil.

'I'm not holding back, Ruth. It's *gone*. The passion, my soul. The words, *me*...' Ruth frowned, and Artemis threw up her hands with a sigh. 'The vow I made... It was an easy one to make. It was easy to say I would never write another word again, because they abandoned me. The voices...'

Against any shred of will she had left, Artemis felt tears pricking her eyes and she shook her head, glancing over at the wall, which was slightly less threatening than Ruth's now gentle openness, and compassion.

'Ever since I was little,' she explained weakly. 'I had these...voices, in my head. People I'd never met, telling me their stories, inviting me to come along on their adventures. They were my friends. They were *me*. My soul, made bare in tiny pieces, and then, they left me. I've nothing left but regurgitations of past creations, or facsimiles of originality. I've nothing left, but deafening silence. A void, threatening to consume me. A blank page, taunting me, with its infinite despair.'

Sniffing, calling back the tears which would not fall, Artemis turned back to Ruth, challenging her to both understand, and forsake her for ever.

All I deserve.

All I'll ever have again.

'Write that, then,' Ruth said instead after a long moment.
'What?'

'I don't know what happened to the words.' She shrugged.
'Your friends, as you call them. I can venture a guess, and
think, you can too, as to why they've…left you, for now. But
I don't believe you've lost your soul, or that you've nothing
else to give, Arty. I think… Your heart is broken, in many
ways, and nothing makes sense any more. It's how I felt when
my father died. At least until I found out about the debts, and
then I was angry, but I realised… I have…this *thing*, this
incredible, beautiful, impossible thing we are all part of to
help me heal, and give me joy, and light.' She smiled, tears
brimming in her eyes, and Artemis's own eyes refused her
edict, and shed theirs too.

*Only they aren't tears of sadness. I feel they are almost
tears of…hope.*

If Ruth believed she hadn't lost her soul—not for ever—
then perhaps she was right.

If even the ghost of Toby Connell which had refused to
let her leave, promised she might find it again…

Dare I even believe?

'Maybe you're trying too hard,' Ruth offered. 'To find
what you lost, instead of…inviting new friends to tell you
their story. Or simply admitting that it's your story you're
telling. That it always has been. So many may not be able to
relate to your hurt exactly, but they will relate to your loss.
Write the despair. Write the turmoil. Write the blank page.
Write who you've become.'

'Writing all that I am now…and writing something which
would keep people coming… I fear those would be two very
separate things. As for the lighter piece… I dare not even
think how dark that would turn out to be.'

'You're underestimating audiences, I think.' Ruth grinned,
raising a brow, and Artemis let out a wet chuckle. Edging

forward a step, as if approaching a wild beast, Ruth continued. 'There was turmoil, despair, loss, in all you ever wrote, even from the first. There was in *Laney Grace*, that ridiculous trifle or whatever you called it. There has been in nearly every piece we've ever performed, be it tragedy, comedy, melodrama—even some of our burlettas and harlequinades. Some might argue theatre might never again reach the great genius of the Greeks, or Shakespeare, or whomever else they idolise from past centuries, but despite what they believe... it isn't all just vapid entertainment. So the great majority of what we perform here, or even what they do in London now, may be *popular*, romantic, and at times, simple, but I fail to see the wrong in that. Making things which people of all walks of life enjoy, and can relate to. You're not limited to writing *one thing*. Just...write the truth, of you, of how you see the world, and people will love it, no matter what shape it takes. And if it takes some new form which doesn't exist yet, well...create it. Let yourself make something new.'

'I don't think I would know how to do that even if we had all the time in the world,' Artemis said quietly.

No longer...so terrified of the empty void which had taunted her for too long now.

No longer convinced finding herself again was an insurmountable feat, never to be achieved in her lifetime, and it felt strange—both of great magnitude and an incredibly simple change of mind.

Or heart.

Still, it didn't mean she saw the road ahead any clearer, or knew how to...fix herself.

'Well, I'm not a writer,' Ruth pointed out. 'But I do... I do have an idea.' She grinned, her eyes lighting with it. 'Something that helps me when I feel stifled.'

'I don't—'

'You've been cooped up here for days, and if I were to ven-

ture another guess, I'd say you didn't get out much before.'
Her brow raised higher, and Artemis grimaced, shrugging
in assent. 'Thought not. So, get your things,' Ruth ordered,
charging towards the door. Artemis stepped aside to let her
and her now—*yet again*—enthusiastic self, full of annoying
verve, pass and open the door. 'We're going for a walk. I'll
meet you at stage door.'

'You're not giving me a choice, are you?'

'I can always send Laurie, Thomas, and Montague up to
fetch you if you prefer.'

'I'll be down in a few minutes.'

Ruth smiled broadly, nodding, before whisking herself
away.

Leaving Artemis feeling at once dazed, relieved, lighter,
and…

Hopeful.

*Certainly that is hope, flickering in what I'd believed
long-extinguished embers of life.*

Who'd have thought?

*And who'd have thought I'd ever let someone call me
Arty?*

Perhaps the latter was the greatest mystery.

Chapter Thirteen

'When you said we were going for a walk, I wasn't expecting such an…expedition,' Artemis said, half a laugh in her voice, and a heartening smile on her face. Small, yet present, and therefore, promising, and encouraging. Ruth smiled, glancing around at their assembled party atop the common's hill—from which one could see, if not for ever, than at least much of this corner of the world.

From the beginning of their acquaintance, Ruth had sensed there was something more. Not only to Artemis—there was always more to people than met the eye—but more to her retirement. She'd pondered that vow Artemis had mentioned, though refused to give it *too much* thought, if only for self-preservation. Now… It all made sense. Artemis's reluctance to write the play. Artemis's withdrawal from the world, and general demeanour. The doubt, the hesitation both she and Thomas—and likely others—had sensed in her.

It hurt Ruth's own heart, to hear all Artemis had been struggling with. Silently, without aid. Believing her passion, her purpose, had been taken from her. Believing she'd lost her soul. She'd wanted to reach out, and hold her, hug her again, touch her, make her feel…

Something other than pain.

Instinctually however, she'd known Artemis wasn't ready, nor able to accept any such care, not then, so she'd done all she could. Used her own words, to try and show her there was a way out of despair. A way back from darkness.

As you showed me, however reluctantly.

Ruth thought the message had got through—no doors had been slammed in her face, and Artemis was here, with them—though she knew it was a long road which still lay ahead.

Which I fear we must somehow travel quickly...

'Well, they were all gathered already.' She shrugged, shaking the thoughts of trickling time from her mind, and glancing over her shoulder at the gathered company. Some were sprawled as she and Artemis were, on the grass—though the food Rose and St John had gathered in haste was on the blanket here—others tossing balls or performing acrobatics to amuse the passers-by, and themselves. 'And if not for them you'd not have made it out of the theatre unspotted,' she pointed out, referencing the gaggle which had surrounded her, keeping her from view of any gathered admirers as they navigated the side streets up to the common.

Smiling, she turned her attention back to Artemis, who patently did *not* look more beautiful than ever in the warm summer sun, the weight she had carried so long *somewhat* alleviated from her now relaxed shoulders. She wasn't, for she couldn't be, because Ruth couldn't...

Artemis doesn't need that sort of gawking right now. Her heart is hurting, and she's lost.

'True. And I suppose one must eat.' Artemis grinned, playfully picking up, then nibbling on a shortbread.

So far, she hadn't eaten much, not that Ruth didn't understand the likely lack of appetite.

'We do love a good picnic. And when one has views like this so close... It would be a shame not to enjoy them.'

'I admit I've not been down here since the coach brought me from London,' Artemis said solemnly, her eyes drifting over the orderly, growing collection of neat new builds, and pointed spires littering the rolling hills. 'It's certainly something, and has changed quite a lot from what little I recall of it.'

'It has, and will continue to do so, if Mr Burton and others such as Dempsey have their way. I suppose it's good for trade, and to attract visitors and new industry, and I like the order of it…'

'But…?'

'I don't know,' she said, shaking her head, and picking at a chunk of spiced bread. 'I suppose I wonder how we fit into this ever-changing, growing world. If we'll survive whatever this next great change is. If there will be a place for us in the new, modern world.'

'We've survived since the Greeks.' Artemis smiled, bumping shoulders with her gently, and Ruth tried very hard not to make anything of the small touch. Not to be reminded of… *all that passed between us.* 'And this might be contentious, but I always had the sense we existed in some fashion even long before that. Whatever this world becomes, I think… there will be a place for theatre in it.'

'What's this I hear about the Greeks?' Thomas asked, playfully ruffling Ruth's hair before settling below her on the slope. Grabbing up an apple, he crunched into it loudly, and Ruth made a face. Thomas grinned. 'Love the Greeks, don't I, Ruthie?'

'*Obsessed* would be a more apt word for what you are. Please, I beg you, and warn you,' she added fervently, turning to Artemis. 'Do not, under any circumstances, let him get you started on the Greeks.'

Artemis glanced between the two of them warily, and finally seemed to understand this was no jest—not going by Thomas's crazed eyes—and she nodded.

'You're neither of you any fun. Aristophanes would be ashamed of you both.'

Popping a cherry in her mouth, Ruth made quick work of it, and spat the pit at Thomas's head.

He swatted it away, and was about to initiate a skirmish, when St John and Laurie joined them, so he settled for a glare which said: *I'll have my vengeance later.*

'So,' Laurie said, plopping down beside Artemis, while St John settled beneath him on the slope. 'Has whatever was causing your...terrible words been sorted now? Has this expedition cleared whatever cobwebs had gathered in that great mind of yours?'

Everyone stopped and froze—even those gathered a little away, and even, Ruth felt, the birds and the bees.

Laurie was unbothered, simply waiting for a response as he made himself a piece of bread with cheese and chutney.

The rest of them held their breath as Artemis stared down at him, aghast at his bluntness, and Ruth's mind scrambled to find something to say, *anything*, to tell him this was neither the time, nor the place, and that Artemis was struggling with *very serious* things—

'It will take a great deal more than what this morning has offered me,' Artemis said meaningfully, glancing over at Ruth with such gratitude, and *knowing*, she felt... *Don't.* 'However, I believe I am of a different mind now,' she continued, returning her gaze to Laurie, thankfully. 'One more able to...do what I must.'

'Oh good,' he said simply, popping his food into his mouth. *Oh, Laurie.*

'We could play around a bit later,' St John offered, as more of them congregated in a circle on the blanket, helping themselves to food. 'Perhaps that could help. Alleviate you of some of the burden. We're very good at thinking on our feet.'

'Aye, you're good at thinking on your feet until the time comes to mind your costumes, and clean up after yourselves in the dressing rooms,' Rose scoffed, making everyone laugh.

'Or when comes time to remember what doors are doors,' Guy added. 'And which are but paintings of them.'

Everyone laughed again, remembering the numerous times one of them had tried to unsuccessfully open a non-openable door.

Laurie being the guiltiest.

'All that notwithstanding,' Montague said quietly, fixing Artemis with his always piercing gaze, and for a moment, it seemed to Ruth that something more significant passed between them then. 'We are very good at conjuring nonsense. And we've the time, as we've no pages to learn. Perhaps we could be of assistance.'

'Yes.' Artemis nodded after a moment. 'I think, perhaps you could. I would appreciate any and all help you have to give.'

Montague nodded, and there was a chorus of voices which rose, either deciding plans for later, discussing ideas, or simply speaking of the weather, or this news or that.

Ruth merely sat there, watching Artemis for a long time, as she slowly began engaging with them, eating small bites here and there. Trying not to think too hard on how her heart seemed fit to burst at the sincere change in the woman. The vulnerability of her. The courage, and strength she demonstrated in that moment.

Oh dear, Ruth.

You really are in trouble now, aren't you?

ACT III

Chapter Fourteen

❧

Miss Connell,
    As requested, for inclusion in the playbill.
    Do advise if it is too simple, or does not say enough.
    I was unsure as to whether I should attempt to make it
    more interesting than my typical newspaper notices.
    G Dempsey

Be it for BUILDING, RENOVATION,
or PROPERTY MANAGEMENT,
Mr G DEMPSEY,
whose offices may be found in Culverden, opposite the inn,
offers LOCAL EXPERTISE & EXCELLENCE.
'There is no task too daunting.'

It wasn't a sudden shift. A magical overnight transformation. A spark lighting the first beacon along the coastline. It wasn't water suddenly gushing forth from a well after years of digging into dry earth. It was…slow. Unsteady. A relearning. A foal stumbling to find its footing moments after gulping in its first breaths. It was painful, and aggravating, and felt like trying to force gravel through a tiny sieve. It was harrowing, confronting, and liberating.

Artemis savoured every single minute of it.

After their expedition to the common, the players kept true to their offer, and spent the day and most of the evening, simply *playing* with her, true to their name. It wasn't a process she'd ever really experienced—not at the beginning of the writing process—but perhaps that is why, and how it worked to further fan that new fire lit again within her.

The fire of hope.

Hope that I may find and reclaim my soul again.

Scene by scene they would, as the Italians would say, *improvise* the action, and conversations, then start again. Each time, Artemis found something new to take for herself. An idea, a sentence, an action or a gesture. Their own creativity, sparking hers in turn.

Just like the old days.

Collaboration.

She'd barely slept that first night, and eaten only because Montague had given her a look which suggested she couldn't retire to her room until she did. She stayed up all night, fixing what she'd written so far, and when she handed them the new pages the following day, remaining as they read through them, she knew…she was on her way to beginning again.

So it had been for three days.

The company would alternate between reading whatever new pages she gave them, playing with her through new scenes, then rehearsing as she rewrote old ones, and moved on to what still needed to be written. In the evenings—apart from Thursday—they performed, and though she made a point of descending for supper, from midday to well past midnight every day, she was in her room, writing. And not solely because she had a deadline looming—she'd written to Kit asking for a few extra days, but they could afford no more delays—but because for the first time in a very long time, she could do nothing else *but* write.

See, Killian. I am writing again.

Other preparations went on around them, but Artemis saw none of it. Beyond her time with the company, neither did she see Ruth, nor engage with her. Not for lack of desire, but because she was terrified to lose the thread she'd struggled to find thus far. A gleaming, magical gold thread—much like Ariadne's—which in time would lead her back to her soul. She could see it almost, some ethereal, shining, colourless orb, pulsing in the darkness of the labyrinth's maze. So no matter how she wished to…be with Ruth, she couldn't allow herself the distraction.

And a distraction she was.

Would've been, if only by all Artemis had unwillingly allowed herself to confess, and by how she'd handled such revelations. How she'd looked atop that common, all free, and lovely, and as though she were the sun herself. But to boot, when Ruth came onstage, when *she* played about with the others…she shone even brighter. There was something about her which reminded Artemis of that which had been said when she'd first conquered the London stage.

Magnetic. Compelling.

Something still held Ruth back from entirely…fulfilling her potential, but in time, hopefully she would be able to release it.

In the words Artemis wrote, she did. For there was no denying that was one of the things which had shifted since she'd restarted this endeavour. The roles each actor were meant to play shifted in her mind as she saw things in each of them which didn't allow her to cast them in her imagination as she should. She said nothing to any of them of these changes—perhaps in time, she might—but for now, all she needed was to choose her own inspirations as she saw fit.

So Ruth shifted from *helpful maid* to *heroine*, while Madeleine went from *heroine* to *conniving and deceitful maid*.

Montague shifted from *villain* to *unexpected hero*.

Laurie… Laurie went from *hero* to *villain* and became— as Madeleine did—a representation of someone else. A representation of Killian.

That was something else which changed. Something which compounded the struggle she faced when writing not only the main piece, but the other too; something she'd never done so *consciously* before. Something she'd never allowed herself before.

She wrote parts of her own story; let her own journey, influence those she set to paper.

Those imaginary friends who had guided the way had always been *her*, part of her own soul; she'd always known that. But this was different. These voices in her head now, they were echoes of her past selves. Echoes of those she'd known in her past—be it Killian, or others. The characters dancing about in her mind's eye, telling her their story, were no longer metaphors of her own heart, or inspired by things she'd witnessed. They were undoubtedly…all she had to say, and never had.

They spoke the words she had or hadn't been able to. They felt all she had, not only these past three years, but even before that. They were all the poison, all the heartbreak, all the doubts.

Hours she spent at her desk, watching the light change in her room, and then, by flickering candlelight, giving everything which she'd kept steadily locked away in chests, behind great iron gates in her heart, free rein to come out. It was…cathartic.

And aggravating, and a struggle, and all she'd said before. Not a great gushing, an unleashing, but a slow trickle, which only grew as she allowed herself to…do what she had to. What she'd never thought possible, or that she would be capable of even if it were.

An unlearning of all she'd believed up until that point; the learning of a new way to…be. To fulfil the purpose she'd always believed to be her own.

Until she had finished her farce, and only the ending of the main play remained.

An ending which was still giving her trouble.

The *happy* ending, to be specific.

Yes, at first, as she'd told Ruth…she felt that her life, her struggles, all of it, were more suited to some grim tragedy no one would come to watch. Yet as she'd begun writing it, shaping it…she'd known, it was to have a happy ending, lest it not be…as it must to be true to itself. It must be, for she *wanted* it to. The only problem being, she didn't know…

It had been a long time since she'd been happy. Truly happy. Fulfilled. Settled. Hopeful. Triumphant. Able to heal. This process was helping, but there was something missing. So far, there were snippets of joy, the flashes of triumph—

A knock at the door.

Sighing, Artemis set down her pen, and rubbed her eyes before glancing at the watch, barely lit as the candle was near its end. It was late—just gone midnight again—but tonight she didn't mind the interruption. It was going slowly— evermore so as she approached that bloody ending, and struggled to find the meaning, the lessons, and how to tie up all the bows.

I welcome any break just now.

Even if I don't know that I'm ready to see who I suspect this is…

Opening the door, she indeed found Ruth—precisely the only person she would've expected at this hour—looking rather grim, exhausted, and temptingly simple in a loose, flowing shirt and skirt.

'What's happened?'

'I need you to write in a new character,' Ruth sighed heavily. 'Nothing grand, something small will do, a random footman or whatnot—it's just a gesture, for Mr Dempsey.' Artemis raised an enquiring brow and Ruth shook her head, a tired chuckle escaping her. 'It's a long story.'

'You'd better come in then.'

Ruth hesitated, and Artemis might've too, if she'd been at all clever.

Only tonight, she didn't feel clever, or anything beyond a need to see Ruth a little less grim.

So much for no distractions...

Chapter Fifteen

'It all started when one of the apprentices said the name of the Scottish play,' Ruth began, flopping onto the end of Artemis's bed without preamble, care, nor concern. It had been…a day. To say the least. She was tired, on edge, grumpy, defeated, wrung out like a soggy lump of over-extended tea. Which meant she likely should be in bed. Sleeping. Not here.

Except she didn't want to sleep.

She may be tired, but mostly in body. It had been a long, trying day, full of unexpected and unwelcome surprises, and all Ruth wanted right now, was a friend. Well, not just any friend—*fine*—she wanted Artemis. Artemis, who was her friend, of sorts—insomuch as she wasn't exactly *an acquaintance*. She might've gone to Thomas or Montague or Rose instead—anyone else she'd known for more than a fortnight, especially considering they'd offered to help her drown her worries at the inn—but no. She wanted Artemis's company.

In some way, perhaps she wanted to check on her too. To see how she was faring with the work—work which had become undeniably personal, and which couldn't be easy to wrestle with. Ruth had actually been pondering checking on her before…everything happened.

So, two birds, one stone.

And if she was being *completely* honest, well, ridiculous, nonsensical, and utterly unimaginable as it was, she missed Artemis. Her presence while they worked was *something*; something which made Ruth at times feel like an insect being studied, so intense was Artemis's gaze, but which was also…

faraway. There was a connection, yet there also wasn't. They were all there to work, and there was a sharing, but also not.

Though Ruth was glad to see the change in Artemis, in her work—painful, and trying though it must be, considering the lines they now spoke, and the story they now told— and understood solitude was necessary, selfishly, she also wished…to spend time with her.

Personally, not just professionally.

No matter how often she tried to convince herself it would be an ill-advised, and unnecessary distraction.

No matter how many times she told herself she would likely be imposing, forcing a furthering of their relationship in ways Artemis could never desire it to be furthered.

She is here to work, to pay a debt, and perhaps in the process, help herself conquer what might've vanquished her.

A tryst is a tryst, and someone such as her has no need of your…interest.

Not that I have any beyond…spending more time with her.

So, yes. Many reasons why she was here—no matter *how* inadvisable and selfish—sprawled on the end of Artemis's bed like some dejected child, and not in her own bed, sleeping, content that the day's disasters had been fixed. Besides, she hadn't lied—she did need Artemis to write in a new character for today's saviour, Mr Dempsey.

The bed shifted as Artemis came to settle beside her, lying down to stare up at the ceiling too, hands behind her head, and Ruth tried very hard not to notice how much better she felt then, just for having her so near.

What did we just say? She neither wants nor needs your… girlish infatuation, so do desist.

'I imagine the apprentice was made to undo the curse,' Artemis said after a moment.

'Immediately,' she agreed, recalling how they'd quickly explained the ritual, waiting with bated breath as he ran round the theatre thrice, before returning with a curse. 'Still, I cannot but think it was too late to counteract it. A delivery of materials came, and it was all wrong, only they wouldn't take it back despite Guy and I arguing with them for nearly an hour,' she sighed, massaging her brow. 'In the end we had no choice but to accept it, and they put it in the wrong place, and…then there was the whistling.'

'Oh no.'

'Oh, yes. That time it was Laurie. He didn't mean to, he and St John and Thomas were working on some music, and Laurie whistled a tune for them. Guy and the others were changing over some set pieces, and trying to make room to move the delivery, and one of the lads working the lines heard the whistling, thought it was Guy, and started lifting the wrong thing. Guy tried to stop him, but the pulleys stuck, and then the whole painted scene came crashing down on him.'

'Is he all right?'

'He has a broken leg, and fingers,' Ruth admitted miserably, turning to look at Artemis.

'I'm sorry.'

'He'll live.' She shrugged pitifully. Artemis gave her a small, reassuring smile, and took her hand, running her thumb over the bump of Ruth's. *Do not make a mountain of this. Not how warm, and lovely it feels, nor how it makes your heart soar and feel better.* 'Rose has agreed to have him at hers just down the road, and tend to him, but he cannot but give directions now.'

'So how does Dempsey figure into this?' Artemis frowned.

'I met him on the way back from fetching things from Guy's to bring to Rose's. I was more than *slightly* harried, and he asked if all was well, and I couldn't help myself. I blurted it all out. I honestly cannot say why, but he sorted the delivery for us—taking what we didn't need in exchange for what he had and we needed—and promised to come and work in Guy's stead.'

Artemis's expression was as surprised as Ruth's had been when Dempsey had offered.

She'd not been able to understand it—the man who wanted her home helping her to see she didn't lose it by sheer bad luck—and said as much.

'He said he'd always wanted to see one of your plays,' Ruth said, grinning at Artemis, whose surprise didn't quite fade, rather transitioned into bleak apprehension. 'He's quite an admirer of you, and theatre, and always fancied himself a patron. Or something else, *"in another life, Miss Connell."* So I agreed, and told him that if he wished, he could be something else, even if only for a night. Hence, the new part.'

'Well now,' Artemis sighed, nodding thoughtfully as her gaze returned to the ceiling. 'That is quite a tale. Quite a day. I'm sure we can find him something. Random footman or whatnot.'

'Thank you.'

'You're welcome, Ruth,' she said, turning back to her, something warmer, and softer than Ruth had ever seen before in her eyes. 'I may not… I thought I'd made it clear now, that I don't wish to work against you. Whatever I can do to help, and ease your way, I'll do it.'

It sounded…like so much more of a promise than Artemis intended it to be.

But it isn't, Ruth reminded herself as she nodded, unable to do anything else.

'How goes it up here?' she asked after a moment. 'I'm not asking because I'm worried about…time or anything,' she added quickly. Well, she was—they needed to get everything to London *very soon*—but that wasn't why she was asking. 'We've not spoken since you…began again.'

'It isn't easy,' Artemis sighed, looking away, and Ruth

tightened her hold on her hand. 'But then, I don't suppose it is meant to be. It feels as though I am raking myself over white-hot coals most of the time, yet when I am done, I feel better for it. Though I'm struggling with this ending… Doing as you prescribed, using myself, my own experiences as explicitly as I have, it has helped, but now I come to the time when I must write all the good… I fear I've lost my inspiration.'

'So we're to have a happy ending then?' Ruth mused, surprised, yet also, not, and wondering… *If we're to have a happy ending.* 'You'll find it again,' she whispered reassuringly before she could lose herself in that thought. 'What you've given us thus far… Arty, I don't think you quite realise how magnificent it is. How brave and inspiring it is. You'll find your way to the good. I'm certain of that. As before, if you need help, you've only to ask for it.'

'I know. Though I am unused to doing such a thing, I do know. And I am grateful. To the company, but most of all to you, Ruth.' Artemis breathed, her hold tightening this time, though her gaze remained affixed on the beams above them, while Ruth lay there, transfixed by all she saw in her in that moment. 'I… I am not one for sentimentality. Everything I ever had, I gave it away. Onstage, to those who came to watch me, or hear what I'd written. In my own life, I never seemed able to speak…the truth of what, and all I felt. But I need you to know, that there are no words for the gratitude in my heart. You…woke me from what might've otherwise been a nightmare to last a lifetime. You challenged me to seek out all I'd lost, to reclaim my own soul, and that is something… *thank you* could never be enough for.'

The emotions which coursed through Ruth then were too much to separate, or delineate or define.

It was one great, heart-wrenching, and heart-warming rush of…something she certainly didn't wish to even think of naming.

Neither would she ever attempt to cheapen Artemis's declaration—which had taken everything she had to express, Ruth knew—with words of reassurance, gratitude, or pride of her own. Instead, she sucked in a quick breath, and let her body do what it had longed to...*for ever.*

Rolling slightly, shifting their still-linked hands so that neither would be hurt, Ruth tucked herself against Artemis's side, waiting, in case Artemis wished to refuse her.

Only Artemis did not. When their gazes met, once again Ruth saw the very same combination of relinquishment and desire that lived in her heart, and there was nothing for either of them but to give in.

So Ruth closed the distance, and kissed Artemis with all that had flooded her heart.

Definitely something worth the lifetime of unextraordinary things which is sure to follow this time.

For nothing else could ever compare to this rare and phenomenal exquisiteness.

All the possibility, the simple rightness of their connection, the blinding wonder of it, all which had terrified and sent Artemis running was still there, in Ruth's touch. Except tonight, she could neither run, refuse, nor fight her need of it.

Perhaps she was too tired; that would be the easiest explanation, or excuse.

Only Artemis knew it would just be that. An *excuse.* She knew that the truth was, there was something of fate, as well as of possibility in the connection she shared with Ruth; an element of inevitability. It still terrified her in theory, but in practice, tonight... It somehow felt less overwhelming.

Everything seemed to feel less overwhelming with Ruth. Admitting her darkest secrets. Opening herself up. Confronting her past. Being honest. Ruth seemed to—without even barely trying—prise things from Artemis she'd otherwise have kept close to her chest. Including…all she'd just said. About Ruth awakening her from a nightmare she'd convinced herself would last a lifetime.

Where once there was only gloom, now, there was a light in the distance.

Because of Ruth.

Perhaps it was all that which made the kiss they shared then feel so different. Still—*very much*—as passionate and exciting, driving Artemis nearly mad with desire, yet also settling her more than any other kiss had. It wasn't all butterflies swooping around her belly, and nerves fluttering. Quite the contrary. There was a languidness that invaded along with the desire in her veins, an indescribable sensation of having arrived. It was as addictive as all else Ruth gave her.

They remained thus for a time—Ruth tucked into her side as they kissed progressively slower, and with more intention, remembering the other's preferences—and as ever with Ruth, she couldn't have said whether it was minutes or hours. Any tiredness or frustration she'd felt melting, as she herself was, into the mattress, while they explored, boldness, and depth growing with every passing moment, their hands still entwined, as Artemis's other hand went to Ruth's silky strands.

Eventually, their breathing became *too* shallow, the quick snatches of breath and scent whilst tongues and lips entwined sadly not enough to sustain them any longer. Reluctantly, they broke the kiss, Artemis snatching every last taste she could. Ruth hovered just above her, every detail of her yet again in the sharpest relief despite the slowly dwindling light.

I could stay here for eternity just…looking at her, and still I wouldn't know every infinitesimal detail.

The manner in which Ruth studied her suggested she might be having similar thoughts, and once, that might've made Artemis squirm, but not tonight. Even if the mutual…*appreciation* which went far beyond *appreciation* felt a lot like…

Something I am no longer capable of.

Something I fear more than anything, for I know its dangers now.

'Are you tired?' Ruth asked quietly.

'I don't feel as though I could ever feel thus with you in my bed. Finally.'

'Finally?' Ruth scoffed. 'I'll remind you that you left *me* that first night.'

'I won't make that mistake again,' she said seriously, meaning it…for so much more.

It scared them both—Artemis caught the flicker of fright in Ruth's eyes, right before she closed the distance between them once again, this time not hesitating to straddle Artemis's hips.

Much better, Artemis thought, groaning at the shift in heat, and passion. Releasing her hand, Ruth began exploring, first running her fingers down her cheek, then neck, down to her breasts, and waist, and Artemis had just begun to lean into the touches, to revel in them as she hadn't in a long time, when Ruth yet again broke the kiss, and contact.

But…

'I need that dress gone,' Ruth said, rising, avoiding Artemis's attempts to reconnect. 'And the rest too.'

Raising a brow, whilst also letting Ruth see just how much Artemis was enjoying the reversal of roles, she grinned, slowly raising her hands above her head.

I'll not make it easy.

Smiling crookedly, Ruth shook her head, then slid up slightly, to better access the dress's buttons. Tortuously, making sure to only touch her fleetingly, Ruth undid them. Once she had, she slid her hands up Artemis's arms, leaning over so their chests nearly touched—but not quite.

So their lips were barely apart.

Close enough that Artemis could taste all Ruth was in the

air, but not have it for her own quite yet. Twining their fingers, Ruth guided her arms down, then, much as Artemis had done to her, she slowly released Artemis's torso from the fabric's hold.

Still, she continued the torture, refusing Artemis any contact, but for slight brushes of fingers against fabric, and the tantalising caress of breath against increasingly sensitive skin. Artemis's eyes fluttered closed as she let herself fall into sensation, and into Ruth—no matter that she knew how dangerous it was to do so.

Even once Artemis's top half was free, Ruth did not relent, working her way down, pulling every stitch of clothing off as torturously as she could whilst still straddling Artemis—one way or the other—which might've been comical to watch in all its acrobatic fumblings, however which was anything but in terms of sensation.

With every disappearing layer of clothing Artemis felt Ruth's heat a little bit more. Evermore encompassing, and drugging, and she wondered at how she was already a puddle of molten desire when the woman had barely touched her yet.

Because she touches more than your mere mortal coil...

Except that now she *was* touching her mortal coil, and Artemis grabbed hold of the blanket above her head as she felt Ruth's skin come into contact with hers. As she felt Ruth's slickness just below her belly. Bucking slightly, her eyes flew open, and were met with the sight of a fully naked Ruth atop her, and...

The thing of angels singing and poets marching into Hell.

If Artemis had thought her beautiful before, it was nothing compared to this vision of...erotic loveliness that yet again, held an edge of immortal settledness. She didn't have much time to think of anything else to define it, before Ruth finally lay down and met her lips again, her delightful, gorgeous breasts meeting her own, and their hands twining once again.

This kiss was feral, and messy, and desperate. Artemis was not the only one affected by either the slow torture, or final meeting of their warm slick skin. She wanted…to touch every bit of Ruth, to slide her hands down every inch of creamy skin and make her see the stars again, but Ruth wouldn't have it, keeping her hands in place while she drank from Artemis, and she from her, as two lost in the desert for centuries might. Her heart soared and tumbled all at once at the symphony of sounds, scents, and sensation.

Then, it skipped and scrabbled as Ruth released her, a satisfied look in her eyes, before laving every bit of Artemis from temple to nipple in hungry caresses. Artemis bucked and squirmed as Ruth found her way to the most sensitive spots, taking extra time and care at those, and at her taut and demanding nipples. Ruth suckled, scraped, and licked with every fibre of her being, and Artemis hadn't ever felt herself… not this responsive, but rather, as willing to give herself fully over to another.

Ruth's clever fingers, palms, breath, tongue, lips, made sure no inch on her body was left untouched or unattended, and Artemis envied her. She'd missed out her own first chance at discovering *all* of Ruth, left some corners untouched and unexplored—though eventually she promised herself she would make up for it.

Perhaps when she could think a little clearer. When it didn't feel as though her heart might beat clear out of her chest, or her muscles give out for all the clenching they were doing, life flowing through them as never before.

Ruth slowly made her way up from her toes to her thighs, and Artemis let out a stilted gasp as the temptress spread open her slick and demanding lips, and succinctly but ever-so-thoroughly, kissed her from core to bud, her tongue dancing and teasing, but not lingering. With a mournful, but determined moan, Ruth then slid back up her body, straddling only one of Artemis's thighs now, her own wetness tantalising.

Skin to skin again, Ruth took her mouth fiercely, as her fingers delved into Artemis's slick folds, now exploring and learning with determined slowness. The moan they both released, vibrating in their kiss, was Artemis's undoing. The silent pact they'd made was broken—not that Ruth seemed to mind—and Artemis enjoyed the luxury of having the use of both her hands to caress, knead, and tease as much of Ruth's body as she could find.

The dips of her waist, the softness of her thighs. The delicate roundness of her bottom, and yes, naturally, those breasts she was not afraid to admit she adored.

She returned to the dripping folds she longed to taste again—*later*—sliding her hands between them and her own flesh, and Ruth leaned into her ministrations, though she never lost her focus on Artemis.

Their pace became wild, and frenzied as they both sought their peaks, both finding and aiding the other to find the rhythms, motion, and angles they needed to reach completion. Yet it never felt hurried, rushed, or frantic; though it felt to Artemis as if she was relearning knowledge acquired long ago, perhaps in another life. Relearning what it was to be with someone who—

Ruth's fingers slid into her hair, scraping and gently grabbing, beckoning Artemis to open her eyes as she broke their kiss. Artemis hesitated, knowing that if she did…if she looked Ruth in the eye then, she wouldn't be able to deny what she must, any more.

Nonetheless she did.

And as she met that determined, grey gaze, full of fire, and something else, she knew, with a blinding, but reassuring certainty, that there was purpose in creation, for she'd been made for Ruth, and Ruth for her. Worse still, in that moment, as Ruth drove her to the edge, and beyond it, chasing stars, but refusing to break their gaze, that there was so much more in Ruth's touch.

There is love, and care, and a tenderness and generosity of heart I've never known nor ever shall again.

As Artemis focused on dragging Ruth over the edge of bliss with her, struggling to both enjoy the waves of pleasure, let them seep through and revive her, and not fail to satisfy Ruth, she realised something else.

My heart isn't so shrivelled and worn out any more.

It was on that thought, that she watched yet again in rapture, as Ruth tumbled with her into ecstasy.

Who'd have thought?

Chapter Sixteen

When Ruth woke to the first streams of light piercing into the room, snuggled tightly in Artemis's arms—Artemis having coaxed her to stay, or rather, distracted her from leaving by initiating a second round of most exceptional sexual congress—she woke with an odd clarity. Odd, in that it was so profound, *so* clear, so utterly undeniable, it was as piercing, and blinding as the sunlight streaming in.

For the first time in her life, she was *in love*.

As she'd told Artemis, she had loved before, but this...

No wonder that before she hadn't been able to find any words befitting the sky-high wave of emotion. No wonder she'd tried to call it *like*, or *besotted*, or *really nice*. She was a stranger to it—and no, she hadn't lied, had thought perhaps she was not formed enough in heart, or spirit, to experience it. Yet when she woke, clear-eyed and bright, she had no choice but to admit the truth.

I'm in love with Artemis Goode.

It stole her breath, that thought, and had Artemis's arms not held her tightly, she might've leapt from the bed. Her heart beat so fast once the realisation washed over her, filling every corner of her being with that blinding light, but not *because* of the wonder, because of the terror which quickly followed the *good*, *happy* feeling.

The terror of potential loss, yes, but also the terror of not knowing...what came next.

Not as in *how to behave or make this last*, but instead, as in *how do I love someone?*

Having never been in love before, she didn't know… anything really. It felt like a fault of the world's, to not have a set rulebook on that. There were books, and poetry, and plays, and stories, but they all seemed to…skip over the mechanics of it. Leap from *falling in love* to *being happy*, or adversely not. People spoke of *the work it took*, but never said precisely what it was, and yes, she'd seen…people in love, and how they were together, except it didn't seem enough. Any, or all of it.

And yes, Ruth had had relationships—well, one lasting one, with Thomas. Other, shorter-lived affairs, and of course, she had her friendships. But was it the same? What did one do *specifically* when one was in love? How did it change things? Or not?

How did one function?

Worst of all was probably the fact that Artemis…well, that she didn't know how Artemis felt. What Artemis wanted. Would she be open to a relationship? Last time they'd been intimate, Artemis had just run away, but last night she'd *sort of* apologised for that, and asked—implicitly and explicitly— for Ruth to stay… Still, did that mean she would be open to even more? To remaining here? Or would she return to retirement, as she'd decreed? Hadn't things changed?

And what was Ruth meant to do? Just…*say it*? Just *speak* of her feelings?

Then there was of course the fear that Artemis would reject any such declarations as the silly notions of a girl falling in love for the first time. Or that Artemis would merely reject her, for being…*a silly little girl*. Not the sort someone such as Artemis could be in love with, find lasting happiness with.

Perhaps Ruth was being carried away, wondering about the future when really she had no information available to make a reasonable approximation of it. Perhaps she was being a silly girl, experiencing love for the first time, yet also…

It felt…

Not like that.

It felt, on the contrary, that this love, for all its doubts, came with a certainty she couldn't deny. An inevitability she couldn't disagree with. That this was not just *first* love, but *real* love, which could be lasting, if only she gave it a chance.

If only she was given a chance.

Except I've no clue how to do that, or ask for it, and let's not forget all the rest I need to take care of just now—

'G'morning,' Artemis murmured in her ear, holding her even tighter. Ruth's heart calmed, as she sucked in a breath, and allowed herself to nestle into the embrace even further, not that she'd have thought it possible before. 'How did you sleep?'

'Like the dead.' She grinned, as Artemis nibbled on her earlobe. *Most distracting.* 'You?'

'As I haven't in some time.'

'I'm glad to hear it.'

That sounded trite and silly.

Honestly, Ruth, have you no idea how to behave at all any more?

Perhaps I should just tell her.

'Are you hungry?' she asked instead.

'A very open and leading question you've posed, Miss Connell.'

Oh, Ruth thought, realising the double entendre.

Wide awake and bright-eyed indeed.

'I meant for breakfast,' she corrected quickly, but already Artemis's hands were wandering.

Onto her breasts, gently squeezing, and flicking, and down her waist to her hips, and…

'Are you in such a rush to leave this bed? To leave me?' Artemis asked, and perhaps Ruth was imagining it—her mind did seem to be running away with her this morning—

but there was a note of vulnerability in the second half which made her wonder...

'No, I'm not,' she answered seriously, with as much truth, and implication in her own voice as she could muster.

I would never leave you again were it my choice.

'Oh good,' Artemis sighed, relief dancing between them in the air.

For a split second at least, before she leaned over, and kissed Ruth for all she was worth, her hands busy both caressing her breasts, and dipping into Ruth's already soaking core.

Ruth poured all her newfound love into that kiss, and the many which followed, as Artemis held her tightly, driving her to lazy, but supreme rapture. Then, when she had returned to this realm, to this bed, feeling a woman possessed by the need only to consume, ignoring all her morning responsibilities, Ruth turned in Artemis's embrace, slid down her body, and poured that love in her heart into a most intimate kiss.

Only then, when she'd drunk, not her fill of Artemis, but enough to sate her for a time, did she force them to get out of bed, and find some breakfast.

I suppose I'll just figure out the rest later.

As I go along.

Sometime.

Gods, help me.

Chapter Seventeen

If Artemis had had more time to ponder her whole situation, to ponder the fact that her heart now seemed to beat in time with Ruth's, every second reviving it from its shrivelled, paralysed state of inertia, she might've found herself baulking, terrified at the prospects.

Prospects. Such a strange word for me to make my own again.

Prospects.

All the possibilities which were born of what she now felt for Ruth.

Love. Again. In a more complete, and settled form than I have ever known.

If she'd had the time, she might've wondered more—*too much*—and doubted more.

About what came next. About whether or not she was ready to love, and accept love again, when for so long she'd thought she wasn't. When the depth of the wound suffered at the hand of her last love had nearly killed her soul. She might've wondered, if a wound born of Ruth's hand, of Ruth's love, so much…more than Killian's had been—purer, and more genuine, undemanding, and unrelenting—how such a wound might injure her.

As luck, or perhaps Venus herself would have it, she didn't have much time to do any of that, though some of her questioning, fears, doubts, and joy, found their way into her writing.

Two days.

She had two days after that delicious night, and morning, with Ruth, to complete her work, and get it to Kit. A feat which should've been daunting, yet which she found herself relishing.

Almost there, objectively, though.

Apart from the bloody ending.

Yet again, it wasn't easy. It wasn't magical. It was…a feat of Herculean proportions—at least to Artemis—yet one which she threw herself into with a fervour, a verve, she'd not known since she was just starting out, scratching thoughts on scraps of discarded paper.

Perhaps it was pathetic to admit it, but the truth was, she knew what she'd found with Ruth—and Ruth herself—inspired her. She didn't like *owing* inspiration to *love*—how could she when she knew what a fickle mistress Love could be in the end—only she wasn't about to spit on it. Not when it allowed her to finish her work, and pour all which needed to be into it.

Joy. Profound lessons.

A happy ending.

It felt…*good.*

As much as she'd relished the catharsis of expounding the poison in her heart, she also enjoyed…living vicariously through her characters, as she allowed them to see the light, and happiness too. Not that she didn't have *some* light and happiness in her own life—hence how she even had the words to *somewhat* express it on the page.

For any moment she could spare, she spent with Ruth. There weren't many—snatches of time, little touches, kisses in the wings, or hurried tumbles in the twilight—yet they were like air, or food. They kept Artemis moving forward with vigour and hope as she'd never known, up until the final pages.

Fin.

Curtain Falls.

* * *

Were the gods of this place trying to tell her something? Was this just another giant sign that she was refusing to see as such with all her will? Another sign that she should just… give up? Pack it all up, sell Father's theatre to Dempsey, relinquish Tunbridge Wells to Warlington and his company, and move on elsewhere? Or was she cursed?

There are always last-minute problems, Ruth thought weakly.

Things which go spectacularly wrong and make you believe you'll never have a show in the end. Still, somehow, you inevitably do.

Quite. This was just another…*thing*.

If losing one of your principal actors could qualify as merely *a thing*.

It has to.

Otherwise I might take it as a sign, and give up.

And things were going so well…

Perhaps that was how Ruth had cursed herself, actually. She'd spent too much time thinking on *how well things were going.* Too much time…being happy.

If she'd learned one thing from life—be it onstage, or not—it was that happiness never lasted; likely what made it so enduringly alluring. In the end, however, it never did last. To begin to think it might because one was so…*enchanted* by a glimmer of it, was to court disappointment. It was like chasing a will-o'-the-wisp, and thinking that if only you caught it, you could keep it alive for ever.

And oh how Ruth had let herself be enchanted by these last…was it truly only two days? Time seemed to… Slow, and pass in an instant, all at once, when you had love, and hope in your heart.

Even though Ruth hadn't managed to snatch much time with Artemis, what little they had was wonderful. So natural, and urgent—because yes, they were both incredibly busy. Artemis, finishing *The Widow*—which Ruth hadn't even had time to read the last act of as Artemis had only finished in the early hours, and it needed to be copied so it could be sent off to London.

It had bothered her, but also…not. She had faith in Artemis, and not solely because of what she had seen so far of the work, including the accompanying farce—a satire with some very pointed thoughts on the rather fraught relationship between the legitimate, and illegitimate houses—which was…exceptional. No, Ruth had faith because there was something driving Artemis now… Ruth couldn't name it, but she could see it. The invisible force, the air, feeding the flames in Artemis's gaze.

So yes, she was giving in to faith. In every aspect of her life.

Or perhaps, it was simply that she'd not really had time for doubts or fears.

Between staging everything, learning lines, learning music and movement, keeping on top of the business side of things, performing the other show, integrating Mr Dempsey—Guy was not doing well being, in essence, immobile—well, no, Ruth hadn't had much time to work herself into a frenzy over her feelings.

Probably for the best—though I can't blame Artemis for distracting me this time.

Perhaps I can blame everything else.

How could I not see that Madeleine was preparing to leave us?

Though apparently Ruth wasn't alone in having noticed nothing.

Slightly reassuring.

Only slightly.

In fact, on any other day, the rest of her company and

crew's spirited revolt might've lifted her spirits, and made her want to conquer the world. As Thomas's impromptu inn speech at the beginning of this whole endeavour had. Except that she was slightly too exhausted, too preoccupied, too devastated and desperate to be anything more than *slightly* heartened.

Ruth stood there, like a dazed ninny, in the midst of the whole *brouhaha*, just tired. She'd managed to say three words when Madeleine had strode into the auditorium, travelling bags in her hands, and announced she was leaving.

Three words.

'What?'

To which the response had been: *'You heard me'.*

'How?'

'An offer from Warlington I'd have been daft to refuse. As you were daft to refuse Dempsey's—and don't think we all didn't know about that.'

Luckily at least, the man himself hadn't been there for that one—Ruth wasn't sure she could've borne that.

'Why?'

'I'll not stay and go down with the ship. You couldn't manage a cast of puppets, and we can all see it. I'll make something of myself as I never could in this pathetic theatre.'

That's when the others—equally as aghast—had revolted. The words *traitor, shrew, swine,* and other assorted colourful insults ranging from dockside euphemisms to Shakespearian delights poured from everyone's mouths. Then, somewhat satisfied they'd made their point, they'd moved on to words like *contract, legal suit,* and so on.

Even if Ruth had the means to do such a thing—force Madeleine to stay, or even think twice about leaving—she couldn't. She'd never be able to work with someone who didn't want to be here, and had made their feelings on the whole enterprise well known.

Not that I've any idea what to do or who to bring on instead...

'Just go, Madeleine,' Ruth said quietly, utterly done with all of it. It may have been said quietly, but everyone froze, turning slowly to stare at her. 'The contract between you and my father was verbal. I'll not pursue any legal avenues, it's only your own conscience you've to justify this choice to. I wish you what you seek.'

Madeleine nodded, turned on her heel, and disappeared from the theatre.

And our lives.

You'd think I'd be used to such departures by now.

Perhaps she's right.

Perhaps I've not got what it takes to be...a manager, just as I didn't—

'Ruth...' Thomas began.

'I know,' she said, stopping him, knowing very well what they were all thinking. 'And to answer your question, I've absolutely no clue what we're going to do now.'

Everyone fell into a grim silence at that.

Eventually, Ruth hoped at least they'd start offering suggestions of people who might be available to fill Madeleine's role, or any other ideas they might come up with to get them out of this new pickle they found themselves in.

Because of me...

Don't.

Not the time.

Right now, they needed her to be strong, and in truth, they all needed to take some time to...feel the hurt, the betrayal, and the loss, for no matter their thoughts on her leaving thus, Madeleine had been part of their company for years, and a valued, if sometimes aloof member of their strange family.

'The way I see it,' Thomas sighed finally, and everyone turned to look at him. 'It's either replace Madeleine, since we've no one already here who could take over,' he said meaningfully to Ruth, and she gave him a *don't even think about it* glare, to which he nodded, disappointment in his eyes. 'Or we close the show until we open *The Widow* and *The Thief.*'

'We'd have to do the latter in order to do the former,' Laurie pointed out with a shrug. '*The Revenge* is new, and anyone I can think of who might've worked on the others is engaged elsewhere for the summer.'

'Helen might be free,' Montague offered with a frown. Helen, being a young woman with whom they'd worked last season on some larger shows, and who was delightful. 'She's a quick learner…but Laurie's right. Even if she is free, there's no way we could confirm it, get her here, and integrated by tonight. Not to mention, she's not used to taking the lead.'

'And that doesn't solve the problem for *The Widow*, though I suppose it's a small mercy Madeleine had no part in *The Thief,*' William noted grimly.

'We could…' Ruth began hesitantly, knowing it would be *a lot* to ask. Of everyone. And even then, she wasn't certain it could be done. *We've done more in less time, haven't we?* 'Change the programme. I'm sure we have pieces we know well enough which don't have…a heroine. Any of the smaller pieces Madeleine always refused to do, and as for the songs she had…we can bring back some of the bawdier favourites. We could cobble together sets for tonight, couldn't we? It would be a lot, but our audience isn't particularly attached to *The Revenge* and, well, they like *The Black Beast* but Madeleine wasn't in that one!'

'Because she was never in the filler pieces,' Laurie said wryly.

'Exactly!' Ruth exclaimed, looking at them all hopefully. 'Everyone is looking forward to *The Widow*, and we'll still have the problem of that, but we have just about three weeks before we open. In the meantime, if we close the theatre, even for one night…'

'We risk our reputation,' William agreed. 'It can be done, I think.' He nodded after a moment, and Ruth beamed at him. 'It will likely be a mess tonight, and I'd suggest adding in more musical intervals and singing, but I think we can pull something together. If they don't like it, refunds might be in order, but I wager we can offer them their money's worth.'

'If you say so,' Montague agreed. 'We'll go through what pieces would be best, surely there will be some you'll have done before elsewhere.'

'If not, I'll manage. Even if it means having Fanny in the wings to whisper to me in her mellifluous tones.'

Fanny snickered and rolled her eyes at that one, and everyone chuckled, relaxing slightly.

'Let's do it,' Thomas declared, and those assembled nodded in assent.

'Thank you, everyone,' Ruth said, relieved, though of course, also hugely aware of all they now had to accomplish today. 'I know—'

'Is that Madeleine I just saw leaving?' Artemis asked, startling them, coming to stand right where Madeleine had been not moments ago. 'Bags in hand, heading for the coach? Which she'll have missed on that note, considering I watched it leave. Dare I even ask what's happened?'

'It's rather self-explanatory,' Laurie said wryly, flopping onto the edge of the stage, though his tone also suggested he was—as others surely were—amused by the fact Madeleine had missed the morning coach. *Perhaps she'll catch the mail*. 'She's gone off to greener pastures, so now we're changing the programme for this evening, and we've got to find ourselves a new widow.'

Artemis glanced at them all, presumably trying to determine whether this was some great jest—a trick played on new members of the troupe as a ritual or something such.

Their expressions very clearly told her it wasn't anything of the sort.

'Oh dear. I'm sorry,' she said seriously, her eyes fixed on Ruth's, which Ruth had to admit, made her feel *slightly* better. At least, until she continued. 'Why can't you play the lead in tonight's pieces, and then the widow, Ruth? You likely already know the lines, you've just as good a voice as Madeleine, we can just make adjustments as you're a *contralto*, and I'm sure Rose could alter the costumes. It would be easier to find a replacement for—'

'No,' Ruth said, harshly. Only she couldn't... She wouldn't let them—*any* of them—get fanciful ideas in their heads. *Not that they would. They know very well why this is my answer. Why it must be.* 'There's a reason I play the roles I do, Artemis.'

The look Artemis gave her then clearly said: *we'll speak on this later.*

Which Ruth was...*fine* with. They could speak of it eventually if Artemis was truly that bothered or interested. If she—who surely knew *why* already—needed to be explained in plain English that Ruth had not the life experience, the depth, the allure, nor the maturity, to play the lead role of *any* play, let alone the heroine Artemis had written for *The Widow.*

'We must all play the roles our talents make us suited to,' Father ceaselessly reminded her.

So I shall.

'We'll sort it—we have a few days to do so,' Ruth reassured her, or all of them, or herself, she wasn't quite certain just then. 'In the meantime, we've tonight's performance to worry about, and much work to do to ensure we have one.'

'Consider the new programme sorted now,' Artemis said challengingly. 'I'll do it. I'll be your widow.'

A whole chorus—nay, a legion—of ghosts might've appeared before them then, strutting about the stage, and no one would've been more surprised than they were by Artemis's pronouncement.

Gods, I cannot make sense of your signs if this is yet another one.

Chapter Eighteen

Well today had certainly been an interesting one. *Whirlwind. Confusing. Troubling. Exciting. Impulsive. Surprising.* All words which came to mind when Artemis sought to sum up the day. When, if anyone had asked her upon waking, all she'd thought today would bring was a sense of relief, and perhaps accomplishment. Which it had, though in ways, and to degrees she hadn't expected.

Finishing *The Widow*, handing the copies of it, and *The Thief*, to Oscar, the young apprentice who would take them up to Kit in London personally—well, handing them to him, then walking him to the coach and watching him leave—Artemis had felt…proud of herself. Hopeful, *yes*, grateful, *yes*—to a dizzying degree—but especially proud. To have beaten back the void, perhaps for ever.

It had also felt…strange. Oddly final, yet somehow, as though she'd left a candle burning somewhere which she couldn't even recall lighting. It was linked, surely, to the feeling of bittersweet completion.

Yes, there was still work to be done—particularly if any issues arose with Kit or the Examiner—but beyond being here in case she was needed, potentially watching some rehearsals, and being there opening night to take a bow… Well, her work was done. She could move on. Move along. Return to her cottage, and her retirement.

Though perhaps, she'd thought—and this of course being before she committed herself to replacing Madeleine—*not the latter.*

It all felt in flux. Uncertain. So many plans—well, her one big plan—changed now that she was writing again.

Now that her heart wasn't so dead.

Yes. Ruth had changed things for her in more ways than one.

Which explained why she was standing here, in front of Ruth's office door.

Hesitating. Knowing two options were before her.

The first: to let things end between them. To do the work—including the additional work she'd committed herself to today—and then leave, gratitude in her heart.

The second: to walk into Ruth's office, and talk to her. Not necessarily about the future, but about today.

Only speaking of today, going in there with the purpose to not only express some of the reasons *why* she'd decided to stay on, but especially to get Ruth to open up, talk, share… It would be abandoning any chance Artemis had of *just leaving.* Of walking away in the end, pretending this hadn't been but a lovely little restorative interlude.

It would be admitting that perhaps, she wanted to speak of the future. Of all those possibilities she saw whenever she looked at Ruth.

It would be admitting my heart is well past involved.

So it is, she thought, not bothering to knock—mindful Ruth might try to avoid her, not for mere dereliction of manners or show of force.

If Ruth did notice the intrusion, it didn't show. Buried in paperwork, by the soft glow of the lamps, she looked both tired, and obstinately determined to be…*well.*

Determined to pretend she's fine, and that she can shoulder it all alone.

It's what she'd done since she'd known her—Montague had been right about Ruth taking on others' burdens and putting herself second—and it was what she'd done all day since Artemis had volunteered to take over the widow. Now, as to *why* Artemis had done that…

Madness.

A need to not see this enterprise—her chance at redemption—crumble before it even began. A desire to help the company that had helped her. A need to relieve Ruth, to take some of that weight she carried off her shoulders. A need to seize the chance to…not have to leave, or decide other aspects of her future quite yet.

To stay that feeling of leaving things unfinished.

She wasn't particularly keen to return onstage, but neither was she entirely averse to it. It had never been her truest love, and it would be *a lot* on top of the rest after three years of retirement, however it also didn't terrify her as writing again had. And truthfully, she hoped she could eventually convince Ruth to take over the role, having written it for her after all. Ruth had been her muse, so in a very real sense, Artemis had volunteered as a stopgap. Until she could get to the bottom of Ruth's reluctance.

Which she hadn't had a chance to, since all day, it had been *work, work, work*—which granted, there was a lot of for them to do. And yes, Artemis had pitched in where she could, helping to change over sets, props, costumes… Unearthing old things from trunks and moving bits, as the company relearned the pieces they would be putting into the show.

It *had* been a lot, but in the end, they'd managed to cobble something together which had their audience, if not *ecstatic*, then satisfied. Then, after it had finished, Ruth had taken her belated dinner to her office, requesting she not be disturbed.

That had been a while ago now, and sooner or later, she'd have to…

Open up? Oh, how the tables have turned.

'How long are you planning on hiding in here?' Artemis asked, crossing her arms, and leaning against the door frame when Ruth continued to insist on pretending she could neither see nor hear her.

'I'm not hiding,' Ruth said finally, her eyes remaining affixed on her work. 'I'm busy. Every day, there's more to do, and there's only me to see it done.'

'That may be so, but I have a strong suspicion you've been avoiding me. Or anyone else who might confront you on your adamant, and vehement refusal to replace Madeleine.'

'You're the only one who would question my refusal, or offer up such a ludicrous idea. The others know very well why I'd never do such a thing.'

'So it is just me you're avoiding then,' Artemis remarked, straightening, and closing the door, before stepping closer to the desk, though not *too* close yet. 'Good to know.'

'Look, Artemis—'

'No more Arty?'

'Artemis,' Ruth repeated, more tartly than someone else might've thought her capable. *But as with all else about you, I believe I see more than others do, and even you yourself at times, I think.* 'Do us both a favour, and let this go. It merits neither the time nor energy we've already spent on it. Things are as they are for a good deal many reasons, and it's not like you actually care. So go to bed, we've quite a few long days ahead of us, and we'll all be needing our rest.'

'I do care,' she said, with a deadly seriousness, and vulnerability which at last caught Ruth's attention fully. That Ruth believed she didn't care… It injured her, but more so because she knew the fault lay with her. In not…*making it clear this wasn't merely a lovely little restorative interlude.* 'If I believed, *truly* believed, that you refused to take over for Madeleine because of a host of *good* reasons, I would let

this lie. My insistence on understanding comes from a genuine place of incomprehension. Because I cannot see any of
these good reasons.' Ruth shook her head, rolling her eyes as
though Artemis was the daftest person on Earth. 'If I didn't
truly think you capable of it, I wouldn't have suggested it in
the first place,' she continued insistently. 'You must know,
at least from what tales you've heard tell of me, that I do not
suffer bad casting, even in such cases as ours. Unlike others, I would never put someone in a role they weren't suited
for, no matter if I was in love with them.'

Damn.

Ruth stared at her in shock, however Artemis could only
pause, freeze, whilst a million thoughts passed through her
mind at once.

Did I truly say that?

Do I mean it?

How did I manage to fall in love?

What the Hell was my heart thinking?

Why am I not so terrified now that I've said it?

Why am I not feeling as Ruth looks?

Shit.

Damn.

'However,' she continued after a rather long, and telling
pause, ignoring the feeling of quiet, and settledness invading her veins now the truth was out, to both of them. 'There's
obviously more to this than merely believing you're ill-suited
to the role. There's something more bothering you.'

'Did you…?'

Artemis shrugged and grimaced.

'Can we ignore that for the time being?' Ruth nodded
slowly, looking somewhat relieved by that suggestion. *Well
if I get her to open up by offering up the greater of two evils
in its stead, why not?* 'So… What is this really about?'

'You missed, in my father's box of programmes, the one for *Mary Abbott, or Benevolence in Bedenbury*, which we staged seven years ago,' Ruth sighed, shaking her head again.

Her eyes flitted to the shuttered windows, and Artemis dared this time to approach, sitting on the edge of the desk beside Ruth.

It was as if another wall had been torn down between them; all resistance to what was between them, gone.

If only because we're both too tired fighting other battles to fight our own hearts any longer.

'Father agreed to let me take on the lead role. The others had been pushing, saying it was time things changed. That I'd become a woman, that I could handle something more challenging, more substantial. Father agreed. In fact, I think he'd always planned for it to be thus. As others have, I believe he hoped this theatre would be…mine in every sense. A stage where I could shine, and so much more… He worked with me for weeks. Day and night. As did the others. They put so much time, and effort into it. Into me.'

Ruth fell silent, the pain in her eyes hardening her entire being, gutting Artemis.

So she did all she could.

She took Ruth's hand in hers, and held tight.

'It was all a waste.' Ruth shrugged despondently. 'An unmitigated disaster. That's when Madeleine came to us; Father brought her on because he had to. *"We must all play the roles our talents make us suited to,"* he said. *"And you are not, nor do I believe you ever will be, suited to lead a play. One needs experience, and maturity, and you've neither."* Say what you will about him, for I have in my time, but Toby Connell was a man of theatre, and knew what was good and what wasn't. Others may settle for less, but he never would.'

'I'm sorry. I can't say I understand how precisely that feels, how it must've felt…but I imagine such harsh words would be enough to keep you from ever attempting the experiment again. I won't push you to do something you aren't comfortable with, and which could add to the weight of what you already carry. However, I will say this: we both know Toby Connell wasn't always right.'

Artemis lifted a brow, and Ruth chuckled despondently.

Somewhat better.

'It's easy to forget, but throughout all my years working, I had some harsh critics too. Yes, I gained favour, and notoriety, but it wasn't *all* of London who loved me, and thought me brilliant. Criticism can be useful—we cannot grow without it. However, had I listened to those who thought me *vapid*, and *excruciatingly dull*, and given up, I'd not be here with you now. So you tried, and failed. Try again. And trust me, I beg you, when I say that your talents, your experience, your maturity, all you are, make you uniquely suited to take on this role. I should know, considering I wrote it,' Artemis said gently, and with all the love, and truth she held in her heart.

Ruth swallowed hard, her big grey eyes pleading, and uncomprehending.

In time, you might believe me.

Until then, I'll…be here for you.

Artemis decided to give that thought body, form, and proof, by leaning down, and kissing Ruth. That *something* she hadn't been able or ready to name earlier—*love*—pouring from her, and transforming their kiss into something even more intimate and precious than any which had come before.

Infinitely exquisite in its perfect simplicity.

'Can we talk about the other thing now?' Ruth whispered when Artemis finally broke that kiss she might've indulged in for millennia.

In another lifetime, or days ago, that question would've terrified her, and sent her running.

No more. However...

'In a while.' She smiled. 'For now, can we just…rest, and be here?'

Ruth nodded.

'Yes.'

Chapter Nineteen

So they did, merely rest, and exist together, for quite a while, though there was nothing *mere* about any of it. It was a surprisingly arduous task in fact, Ruth quickly discovered. She'd never considered herself to be someone patently incapable of stillness, of existing without doing, yet the concerted effort it took her to just sit there with Artemis, sometimes touching, mostly just sitting and breathing together, told her that perhaps she'd been wrong in that prior conviction.

But then, many of my prior convictions are of late, being put into question...

Eventually, they moved to Ruth's bed, not even bothering to change into nightclothes, merely lying atop it, holding each other's hand as they stared up at the ceiling full of shadows. Both were exhausted by the day's—indeed, the *days'* and weeks'—events, yet somehow wide awake.

Perhaps it is our full hearts, beating stronger, keeping us awake.

When Artemis had said *those* words, or rather, the implication of those words had slipped out apparently against her will... Well, it had been another shock to add to the day.

Ruth was having enough trouble wrapping her mind around her feelings—not that again, she'd had much time to do so, opting instead to just enjoy what time she had with Artemis—but there had been, deep down in the bottom of her heart, this conviction that though Artemis might feel something in return, as her touch, her manner, the way they were together, suggested... That it wouldn't be enough.

For her to choose… Ruth. To stay. To build something. Even as Ruth wondered at the possibilities, there was a feeling in her gut which told her that those possibilities were nothing more than her own impossible fantasies. They *still* felt like impossible fantasies, *and yet*.

Artemis's confession of sorts gave them…new life. Like a foal learning to walk, her newborn fantasies were growing stronger. They held a sense of *real* possibility now. And Ruth no longer felt alone, adrift in emotion she couldn't quite make sense of.

Between that, and Artemis's…knowledge of her in a sense, her refusal to let things lie about why Ruth wouldn't play the widow… It broke something within Ruth. Her willingness to hold on to her prior convictions, which she'd held tight to, like crutches. Now, she felt as though she'd broken those in half, and cast them aside, which was terrifying, yet liberating.

Terrified and liberated. How I always seem to feel when I'm with her…

As for Artemis's belief that Ruth *could* take on the lead role… Well, that was one conviction Ruth wasn't quite ready to make her own, not entirely, though it did make her think. It made her feel…*good*, for Artemis believing all she did about her. It made her feel less of…someone lesser, and unworthy of someone like Artemis. But at the same time, it also made her…sad. For it made her rethink yet again… *Father*.

All he was. All he taught me to believe. All he taught me I am and am not.

So yes, Ruth was feeling quite joyful, yet still very much confused despite the growing clarity this new love of hers seemed to be giving her.

And that clarity was telling her now that in order to move forward in any way, something needed to be said before anything else was.

'I love you, Arty,' she breathed, before she lost her courage. Neither moved, except for Artemis's hold tightening slightly. 'At least… I think it is love. I know it is,' she corrected. 'Even though I've never felt it before—not like this—despite that seeming somewhat impossible. Knowing it is love, without having experienced it before. Still, there's this undeniable certainty inside me, and I also know… This isn't just the first love of youth either, though it may be, you may be, my first love. I'll admit… I've no real idea of what to do with it. How to be, how to…love like this. What it means, what it changes, if anything. Still, it's there, alive in my heart somehow.'

'I've no idea what to do with mine, Ruth,' Artemis admitted quietly after a moment. 'I don't know whether that makes you feel reassured, or scared…'

'Reassured, I think.'

'Good,' Artemis said, a smile in her voice. 'The truth is… I thought my heart irreparably broken, and wasted for good. Like the words, I never thought love could be mine again. That I would even want it to be if it could, and I still don't know. I'm terrified, of losing it all again. Of courting the void of nothingness again. I don't think I'm ready to make plans for the future yet, you should know that. But perhaps, for now, we could…see where this leads us. At least until this show is over, and then…we can see where we are.'

'That sounds like a sensible plan.' Ruth smiled, even more relieved. It wasn't that she didn't want to speak of the future, but right now, putting less…stress on herself, on both of them, with all else that was going on, it was for the best. So that any decisions were made with a clear heart, and mind. 'Why… Why did you volunteer to take on the widow today?'

'Many reasons,' Artemis sighed gently, her thumb stroking over the back of Ruth's hand mindlessly. It had become in the short time they'd shared so far, one of those small things…

many lovers surely did, but which felt somehow specifically *theirs*. 'I wanted to help. The company, and *you*. I won't lie, I hope you'll decide to take over in time, but I didn't want… If I could help relieve you of this one thing, I wanted to do it.' Ruth nodded, hoping Artemis would feel the gesture, unable to say anything about how touched she was, or that she *would* consider taking over in time. *Perhaps. When I am on more solid ground.* 'I certainly don't think I could be counted as an expert,' Artemis said after a time. 'But from all I know, all I've seen, and learned… There is no one *way* to love. There's…no dictate on what to do with it, what it means, how it changes things. Everyone must decide that themselves, with the person or persons they love.'

'Is that…how it was for you before?'

'No. Those thoughts are…reflections of my retirement, and some of them rather recent in fact. I think, I've realised… that's one of the reasons it went wrong,' Artemis told her, shifting slightly to put an arm beneath her head. 'I…was devoted to Killian. Consumed by my love for him. He exploited that, and my talents. I think he loved me, but I also think he loved…possessing me, and my love for him. For all the power and control it gave him. I couldn't see it of course. All the great books, and poems, and works of art, all these stories we tell each other of love…they're full of his version of love. Subsummation, forgetting yourself for the whole. In some way… I think I also accepted, revelled in it, because it felt good. To have Killian…tell me what to do. Control my decisions, take charge of my life. I'd fought, alone, for years, to… become something, playing taverns, and markets, earning a pittance, and risking liberty performing some pieces. Even after your father found me, and brought me to his theatre… He was something of a radical himself, you know,' Artemis told her raising a brow.

Ruth grinned, and nodded, having heard as much.

Though her father's subversive spirit had diminished when he'd left London, choosing safety and stability instead.

For my sake.

'So when Killian came along,' Artemis continued. 'Though I was young, and eager to change the world as any artist is, I was also tired. He promised to guide me, and keep me, and… I was eager for that. I gave him control, and trusted him, and lost myself in him. Likely why I lost my words. I forgot who I was for a…long time. Until you came along, and reminded me, much against my will.'

'I thought I knew who I was,' she said softly, agreeing with all Artemis said, terrified of…losing herself to this in the same way. 'Until you came along.'

'I suppose we've lots of learning to do, the two of us. I'm glad we'll be together for it, though.'

'Me too.'

They fell into silence, and with every breath Ruth expelled, she felt a weight she'd not realised she held on her heart, lifting.

We don't have to have the answers now.

We can just breathe, and be, and learn.

Seems like love can be simple sometimes.

ACT IV

Chapter Twenty

'Sleep, sweet child not of my flesh, yet for ever mine,
Dream of love lost, and love found; none should
be forgot.
When you wake, keep your dreams close, they'll
help you divine,
The path ahead, through thorns and claws, to all
you sought.'

The Widow of Windswept Moor, A. Goode, 1832

'How much have we lost?' Ruth asked, entirely numb to disaster at this point. Not that there had been many—and again, not that she ever expected smooth sailing when mounting a show—still, it felt like this was someone, or something, somewhere, trying to tell her something. *Or perhaps merely testing me.* If they were...she wondered how she was doing.

Yet again, everything had been going *so well* this past fortnight. Despite Madeleine's abrupt departure, they managed to carry on smoothly. Artemis integrated the company and rehearsals for *The Widow*, not only because she knew her own words rather well already, but mainly because of her enthusiasm to truly *integrate the company*. To play with them, explore, and work with them. To laugh, and share with them.

There was still a caution, from both of them, a need to protect their hearts, yet there was also an undeniable openness. A relinquishment of all which had preserved them up until now. Even going so far as…allowing themselves to demonstrate their affection in front of the others.

It was no longer stolen kisses and touches in the backstage corridors, or once everyone had left. It was holding each other's hands, or wishing each other luck for a scene with a quick kiss. It all felt so natural to Ruth, so…wonderful, she woke every morning with a smile on her face, and excitement in her heart to greet the day—and not solely because she woke beside Artemis.

Mr Dempsey had also transitioned into their group rather well—as much as he could considering he was a busy man elsewhere. He and Guy found a rhythm of working together, and a common appreciation for *hard work well done*, and so their sets were nearly ready, needing only to be properly put in. In just less than a week, so would rise the manor, woods, and eponymous moors of *The Widow*, along with the marketplace, players' carts, and puppets of *The Thief*. Dempsey had fun it seemed, walking in and delivering his two lines as a random footman towards the end of *The Widow*, and still refused to take any more thanks than Ruth had already given him.

Everyone else was working with all their hearts, bodies, and minds, Artemis's presence if anything spurring them on not only to live up to her words, but her reputation, and talent as an actress. Ruth too was *spurred on*, though admittedly the one grey point of the week had been her…rediscovery— if it could be called thus considering she'd never seen the woman perform before—of Artemis's onstage brilliance, and magnetism. Ruth, like the others, wished to…live up to her, and what she brought to the stage, in every way, though at the same time, she felt perpetually inadequate. Unable to ever do such a thing—*give all I have and all I am away as she does*—though every day Artemis dropped hints like breadcrumbs about Ruth taking on the widow, and told her how good she was.

Perhaps it is merely that I cannot believe it myself...

So yes, preparations, rehearsals…all was going well. Visitors hoping to get tickets or spy Artemis Goode were more numerous every day, which was reassuring, and bolstering—especially considering they'd not announced Artemis would be performing, it was to be an opening surprise—and four days out of seven Ruth actually felt as if she had a proper handle on the business side of things. They'd not heard back from Kit Laughton yet about any notes or decisions from the Examiner—only a strangely brief note to say he'd loved the new pieces, and had sent them along to be approved—but surely they would hear something soon.

Everything was going so well.

Until now. Again.

There'd been a storm last night—one of quite a few this season, and apparently, the one too many.

A stream ran under their stage, just beneath their trap room. Typically, it wasn't a problem. Typically, even with seasons of heavy rain, they had no issues. It was a fun little quirk. A cute part of the building's history.

Not this time.

This time, water had managed to, if not flood, then *seep heavily*, up into a corner where they'd put the trunks of ready props and costumes when they were done with them in rehearsal—so nothing would be confused with what was needed for the current show, or take up valuable space else-where.

A brilliant, brilliant plan.

'We've not lost *that* much, not truly.' Rose shrugged, her head bouncing as she surveyed the damaged and soaked costumes hanging and laid out before her. 'I suspect it's much like the props,' she continued, fingering a ruined piece of lace which Ruth knew for a fact she'd made herself some years ago. 'The more fragile things we'll need to replace—there are a few of the gamekeeper's leather pieces for instance I have doubts about, and bits like this lace which have taken in gods know what with the water—but all isn't lost, Ruthie.'

Turning back to her, Rose smiled gently, and came over to rub Ruth's shoulders.

A gesture which had always made her feel…warm and loved, and reassured, and which she sorely needed just now. She'd not had the heart to tell any of the others about this, not even Artemis—luckily Fanny had discovered it before anyone else, and she and Ruth had made sure everything was taken care of before anyone arrived, Ruth distracting Artemis by asking her to wait for Montague and work on their scenes together.

They'd find out soon enough, but for now, Ruth just needed a few moments of quiet, and calm, so she could measure up her losses, and make a new plan. She wasn't entirely sure why she didn't fancy sharing this particular burden with Artemis, but then she didn't really want to think about that right now.

I've quite enough as it is, and it means nothing.

Together or not, we have our own battles to fight.

'It's really not so bad, Ruthie.' Rose smiled, still rubbing her arms, and Ruth smiled weakly in return. 'Anything which needs replacing, we'll find somewhere. You don't need to worry about the cost. We'll manage. I'm used to working with a very small budget.' She winked.

'You knew about the debts, didn't you?' Ruth asked, frowning slightly as Rose wandered away to begin her work of sorting through this mess. 'I won't… I won't be angry if you did, Rose, I'm just curious.'

'I knew,' Rose said quietly, settling down at her table to begin unpicking that ruined lace from the dress. Ruth went to stand before her, waiting for the rest. 'I told him to tell you, especially once he got ill. I was sorry to discover he didn't. But you mustn't be too angry. He loved you very much, and I think… He wanted to remain a hero in your eyes in his final days.'

Ruth's heart squeezed painfully, and she nodded.

She *was* still angry, but when Rose put it that way…like that which she'd experienced, spoken about with Artemis, she began to see things in a different light.

'He loved you too, Rose,' she said after a moment. Rose nodded, a smile which said *I know* on her lips. 'As do I. I've not said it nearly enough over the years, but you were always good to me. A second mother, and… So I need to know. Do you think I'm daft? Wasting my time, energy, and money, trying to keep Father's theatre? Trying to make it into something? Even before Madeleine said so… I know you all knew about Dempsey's offer. I don't need reassurance, Rose,' she added warningly. 'I need truth, as only you've been able to give me all these years.'

'No. I don't think you're daft, or wasting your time. No one here does. We are proud of you, for fighting to keep us together, and keeping our livelihood here alive.' Ruth expelled a very, very long-held breath of relief. *Perhaps that's why I never asked any of them before. I wasn't sure I wanted to know the answer.* 'However,' Rose added, raising a brow, and with the tone Ruth knew too well, and which told her she was about to hear something she didn't wish to. 'You'll not manage to make much of it, if you keep thinking of it as your father's. He made it into what it is today, but his legacy will be wasted if you seek to continue it only for him. In his name, or in his image. I thought you had the right of it, bringing on Artemis Goode. It showed courage, and imagination, and if it fails, it fails. Sell the theatre, start again. We'll follow you, all of us I think, if we can. Just…be mindful not to step in your own way.'

Sighing, Ruth leaned further onto Rose's worktable—laid across it more like—and Rose patted her head gently.

There was…so much in what Rose said to think on.

So much more than merely potentially ruined costumes.

In a sense, Ruth understood, and knew Rose was right.

Hell, despite trying, she'd not even truly been able to think of her quarters as her own. It was *Father's office*, or *Father's bedroom*. Thinking of it in any other way…perhaps in a sense she feared erasing him from her own memory. She had so few of him to begin with; only a little more than a decade's worth, all added up together.

But you cannot live for ever in his shadow. You know this.

I am his daughter, but I am my own person too, even if I'm not sure who that may be.

'Thank you, Rose,' Ruth mumbled against the cool wood.

'Don't thank me, Ruthie. We're family. Giving each other advice we need but don't want, and sometimes want, but don't need, is what we do.' Ruth sniggered at that one. *Oh, I am lucky in my family, though sometimes I forget it.* 'And whilst we're on the subject of advice, what I said about not stepping into your own way, I meant it for more than merely building your own legacy. That goes for taking on lead roles, too.'

'Roooose,' Ruth groaned mutinously.

'Ah-ah-ah,' she tutted. 'You'll hear me out to the end. Your father was a smart man, with a keen eye. But you were his daughter. No man wants to see their children as different from the children they once were. And one last thing:

don't think so hard on whatever it is between you and Mistress Goode. You've a tendency to think too hard, on too much. Love requires thought, and care, but you'll only find more doubts and fears if you forget to let it…sweep you away sometimes.'

'You're too wise for your own good, Rose, you know that?'

'It's why I stay up here. Better for everyone.'

They both laughed, and Ruth dragged herself back up to standing.

With one last glance at the not-so-ruined costumes, Ruth nodded to herself, and, feeling better about the day, and whatever it might bring, she resolved to go down and meet it. She kissed Rose on the cheek, and left her to her work, feeling inordinately better for that talk. Feeling as though all these things going wrong were neither tests, nor signs.

Rather, just life. Only I've been too much in my own head to realise. And to…live.

Smiling to herself, she stepped out, only to be greeted with a harried-looking St John.

'The man from London is here,' he told her breathlessly. 'Kit Laughton.'

Of course he is.

Life, you are having your fun with me today.

Gods…help me.

Chapter Twenty-One

'Kit, it's been such a long time,' Artemis greeted, hiding her surprise with a wide smile as she made her way down the stage's steps to meet him, currently striding through the pit towards them, Thomas on his heels. When St John had told her she had a visitor… In truth she hadn't quite known whom to expect. Now…she still didn't.

Her heart stilted somewhat at seeing Kit again, *here*, no matter how nice it was to see him again. Here.

It wasn't that she *hadn't* thought they'd meet again at some point, but corresponding with him had been much easier than seeing a remnant of her past striding towards her, through her new life.

Forcing herself to take deep breaths, and calm her heart, she let the pleasure of meeting an old friend anew take over the discomfort as they met just at the bottom of the stage, and she held out her hand. Kit took it, and shook heartily, smiling back at her.

She'd always liked Kit, and not solely because…he'd been one of the few to remain at her side, loyal, and kind, to the end. They'd met some…well, she couldn't recall exactly, but many years ago. Friend of a friend of a friend, with whom she'd shared many a conversation after a show in the dark-ened corners of an inn. Only slightly older than her—not that he appeared it, his boyish looks still in full force, though there were a few more lines around his deep brown eyes—he'd been raised a fisherman, then turned acrobat, then actor travelling the country, before coming to London to make his own name, becoming a theatrical entrepreneur when he took over *The Agora*, and built its reputation and position as a licensed house unafraid of boldness, and provocation. Kit, beyond engaging her as an actress, had also helped her with her first works, by being a keenly critical eye, then, by putting them on.

Eventually, between Killian's influence, and Kit's focus on his new wife and family, they'd drifted apart somewhat, to her deepest regret.

But he was there in the end, and so he is here now, still a friend.

Though I cannot help but wonder why he is here now...

'We weren't expecting a visit,' she said as they released each other's hands. 'You should've said you were coming.'

'I wanted to surprise you.' He winked, telling her there was something more to his visit than mere spontaneity, making her heart skip a beat again. 'I knew you'd make a fuss if I told you, but I just had to see this new haunt of yours. See what it is about this place which has coaxed you from retirement.'

'I would blame it on the waters, but I've not had the chance to sample them. Perhaps we could later, and you can call yourself a proper tourist.'

'Perhaps,' he laughed.

There was a quiet disturbance onstage, and Artemis turned to find Ruth coming towards them, a breathless St John recuperating *somewhat* discreetly beside Montague, who, like the rest, was waiting, staring at them avidly.

Artemis threw Ruth a smile, and gave her a look which said: *all is well, come meet the man, he's a friend.*

'I should introduce you to everyone.' She smiled, turning back to Kit, before shifting to stand beside him. 'Starting with of course, Miss Ruth Connell,' she said, as Ruth joined them, holding out her hand. 'Proprietor, manager, our lovely maid in *The Widow*, and the talented puppeteer in *The Thief*. Ruth, Kit Laughton, manager of *The Agora*.'

'A pleasure, Mr Laughton,' Ruth said, somewhat anxious, Artemis knew, but hiding it well. 'Thank you for taking the time to come and visit us. We're honoured.'

'Overdoing it a bit, Miss Connell, but I'll take it nonetheless.'

They shared a smile, Ruth inclining her head, before taking up a position at his other side.

Artemis began the introductions once Thomas had slipped onstage with the others, then once everyone had been introduced, she led him onstage.

'It's fine, Ruth,' she whispered in her ear discreetly as Kit wandered about the set a bit, sharing some words with the others. 'Offer him a tour. He wouldn't have come down, and be thus, if he had bad news.'

Ruth offered her a gentle, relieved smile of thanks, brushing her fingers against Artemis's and nodded before doing as Artemis instructed.

'Would you care for a tour, Mr Laughton?'

'Well yes, I think I would, Miss Connell. Do lead on.'

Which Ruth did, Artemis following in their wake.

She offered reassuring glances and smiles to the others, who would quickly *pretend* to start working again, though all the while, she couldn't shake the feeling that perhaps, not everything was *fine*.

There was more to Kit's visit than met the eye, and until she knew what it was, she wouldn't be able to fully relax and breathe again.

As it happened, Artemis didn't have to wait overly long to find out what it was. After their thorough, but rather quick tour of the theatre—which Kit declared to be a *most worthy*, and *exceptionally tasteful house*—and after putting them out of their misery and announcing loudly that the new pieces had been approved with no changes or deletions—at which point Ruth looked ready to kiss him, and Artemis actually did—Kit asked if Artemis would be so kind as to show him around the Parade he'd heard so much about.

Knowing it was the moment she'd been waiting for, the moment Kit would finally out with his true reason for being here, she accepted; not that she could realistically give him any manner of proper tour considering that even after all this time, she knew London better than she knew Tunbridge Wells.

Ruth shot her an inquiring look of concern as they made their way out, but Artemis threw her another reassuring smile—an occasion for acting if she'd ever known one—and led Kit out to the Parade through the back so as to avoid any of the admirers sometimes waiting about.

Gently, they ambled about with the granted, already plentiful crowds, between the shaded line of trees, and colonnaded shops and buildings, quiet for a few moments, Artemis leaving him space to finally tell her his business.

'As surprised as you were by my visit,' he said after a while, glancing about pensively at the myriad of sights and sounds, so different, yet so alike to those of London. 'It was nothing, surely, compared to the surprise I had when I received your letter, telling me you were writing again.'

'It was a surprise for me too,' she chuckled gently. 'I'd thought myself long done with such things.'

'I'm glad you weren't, Artemis. I know many have extolled your talents over the years, and so have I, but it must be said. Losing a voice such as yours…it would've been criminal. For what it's worth, I'm not sure how much you know,' he continued carefully. 'But although Killian has seen success, no one really forgave him for what he did to you. If only because he chased you from London, and what he produces now is nowhere near as good as it was when you were together—popular shows though they may be.'

Artemis's heart twisted gently in her chest for the show of…loyalty, belief, friendship; the true, honest opinion of a peer.

And for once, not at the mention of Killian. She realised then, that his success, or lack of it, didn't matter to her any more. Her heart was no longer full of anger, and bitterness—of spite, and revenge. It was only full of love, gratitude, and pride.

Here I thought I'd never be able to forgive and move on.

As for the rest of what Kit said…

All that time in isolation…she'd never once, or perhaps, often, but often dismissed, the impact she'd had on others. Her leaving, was her decision—of sorts—and she'd never thought… Others might see it as a loss, not when there were so many very talented people to, if not take her place, then take up the mantle.

I never thought myself good enough to be missed thus—only ever as merely another writer, who eventually retired to normalcy, and was all but forgotten…

'Thank you, Kit. That means more than you can know.' They exchanged small smiles, and Kit nodded. 'In truth… you were right, all those years ago, when you told me time and space away might be *"just the ticket."* I couldn't see it then, never thought I would…rise from the ashes of the destruction I let him wreak in my life, but it was the truth. There was so much more…eating away at me than merely Killian. You should know that. Just as you should know, I never forgot your kindness, and your endurance when others moved on. Never forgot your support in those final days, when I believed myself utterly alone.' Kit nodded again, and Artemis tried to shake away some of the emotion clogging her voice. 'As for Killian, and Winnie, I can now say, in all honesty, that I wish them well.'

'These new pieces, particularly *The Widow*… I think it might be some of your best work,' he said seriously after a moment. 'I devoured it. It reminds me…of my youth. Of ferocity, and ingenuity, and cleverness, and of all those tricks we, and those who came before us, employed so that they could continue making theatre, despite the law. It's a piece of both our time, and all which has come before. I loved the return of scrolls, and rhyming couplets, and how deeply the movement and gesture is written into it. You've taken bits from every form, and made it into a beautiful whole; fragmented, yet coherent. There's subversion of expectation, and a nuance and truthfulness to the emotion… You've somehow combined spectacle and poetic morality. It's so personal, so profound an exploration of the psyche, and sentiment itself. Twisting our expectations of every character, and making the lessons…*not* the traditional moralistic findings… It all truly sets it apart. It's a tragicomedy, a melodrama, and so much more, blended into one. It's gorgeous, Artemis, and I don't just mean *The Widow. The Thief* is a clever, satirical and challenging little piece that admittedly I had to…work very hard to get approved as is. But then we have to work hard for approval on most things nowadays. You did walk the line very tightly on that one, but then I suppose you did remember some of George's preferences.' He grinned slyly, referencing the Examiner.

Artemis smiled and nodded, unable to say anything, for fear of crying, or hearing her own voice shake, beyond *moved*—absolutely overwhelmed with Kit's effusiveness, and also…

Still wondering, what else is coming?

'Artemis…having seen what I have this morning, hearing you just now speak of the past… I understand. I'm happy for you. I came down here, as I said, to see what had got you out of retirement, and so I have. Which is why… I hesitate to say what I've come to.'

'You're scaring me, Kit,' Artemis admitted, her heart beating faster as her palms dampened. 'Just out with it, whatever it is.'

'I didn't mean to scare you.' He smiled, shaking his head, and patting her arm gently. 'It's a good thing, I promise. Well, I hope it is. I want you to come back to London,' he said plainly, stopping them, his eyes flitting about, checking no one they knew was about. Artemis couldn't but stand there, in absolute shock. *London.* 'Things are changing, quickly. There's reform in the air, and I need the best people working for me, making the kind of shows which mean we cannot be ignored any longer. My position may afford me security in many ways, but I have not forgotten where I come from, and I can see as plainly as others that the way things are… is untenable.'

'I… I don't…understand?' she sputtered out. 'I… I've only just…got back to myself, returning to London…'

'Would be a lot, I understand. Only, I promise, it wouldn't be the same as it once was. I've bought a new theatre, *The Adelaide.* I intend for it to be…all *The Widow* is. A place of entertainment, and catharsis, and excitement. And it would be yours. Once the first show has opened the theatre, I would give you free rein for the rest of the season, and the next two. You would have lodgings, a *very* comfortable wage, a secure contract as my principal in-house dramatist, and I will fund publication of your works. Your return would be triumphant, and launch you…as far as you wish to go. You could resume your path, find your success again. Return to your life.'

'What's the catch, Kit?'

'I need you up by this coming week's end,' he sighed, starting to walk again, as Artemis struggled to process…

everything. 'The first person I had engaged…wasn't quite up to snuff, and I need a replacement now. The theatre is to officially open at the end of the month, with an adaptation of *The Canterbury Tales*. I know,' he added, spotting Artemis's wide eyes. 'It's ambitious. It needs to be a true exploration, to play with genre and style, and push so many different boundaries of what we can make, and how, and that's why I need you. I believe it's Fate's hand that brought us together again. And if you're worried about it taking attention and custom from this place, it won't, I assure you, just as I promised bringing *The Widow* and *The Thief* to London wouldn't. You'd be starting off with an adaptation, so your *original* return would still be limited to *Connell's Castle* and *The Agora* until the end of the summer.'

'The show opens at the end of this coming week, Kit. If I leave, it isn't just a playwright they lose. They'll be losing their widow again, and they've already lost one.'

'I know.'

'I'd be…'

'I know, Artemis.' He nodded. 'But I wouldn't have brought this to you if I thought it wasn't worth your consideration. I can see…all this place, those people, have done for you. In the end, however, you have to consider yourself. You were positioned to be one of the greats before you left London. Perhaps this generation's Aphra Behn. If you remain here… Making your name in the country is not the same as making it in the capital, you and I both know that. It's wrong, but it is as it is.'

'So it is,' Artemis agreed, her mind whirling a thousand miles a minute. *I…* 'Thank you for bringing this to me, Kit. I do appreciate it, it's an incredible chance, and I will consider it. I… When are you leaving?'

'On the evening coach,' he told her.

'I'll have an answer for you by then.'

'Good. Now, come on,' Kit said, sensing she needed time to get herself in order. 'Let's go sample these vaunted waters, and then we'll get you back.'

Artemis nodded distractedly and on they went towards the chalybeate springs.

It should've been an easy enough decision to make—one way or the other.

Her old self would've leapt at the chance to make a name for herself again, to live in London, to be part of that vibrant, and ever-changing world again; and yes, potentially find a place for herself in the pantheon of great playwrights.

Her new self would've never entertained the notion of abandoning those who had brought her back to life, even this new life of quietude, play, and simplicity; of abandoning Ruth, and this new, unexpected love she'd found.

The only problem was, it seemed both of her selves were warring with each other. Neither was she fully her old self, nor confident in this newer version either. And chances such as these…they did not come around every day. If she refused now… In ten years, where would she be, and how would she feel if she let this opportunity pass her by?

Surely, there must be…some middle ground.

Except, as she and Kit sampled the waters, then slowly made their way back to the theatre, Artemis couldn't quite seem to find it.

So which love will win out?

That of your profession, or that of flesh and blood?

Chapter Twenty-Two

Something was…if not amiss, then happening, that Ruth had no awareness of beyond the fact that she could *sense* it happening. It was like when the company had organised a surprise birthday celebration for her, and for months, she'd sensed they were…*up to something*. All that susurrating in corridors, and hurried exits from rooms when she entered— not that there had been any of that today. And not that many were involved—only Artemis and Mr Laughton in this case.

It bothered her because she couldn't quite put her finger on it, since there was no susurrating in dark corners or hasty exits from rooms. It bothered her because there was some sort of…unspoken conversation going on between the two of them that affected… Artemis's energy? Her newly gained enthusiasm, zest for life, and sense of fun. It affected her smiles, and the sparkle in her eye. It affected the way Artemis touched her whenever they were near—which before, had been *often*, and today, had been *never*.

Perhaps it was merely Mr Laughton's surprise presence which…discombobulated Artemis somewhat, this return of a sliver of her past, but Ruth didn't think so. She'd been different after their walk, at once more removed from the general revelry—which had been rather intoxicating once Mr Laughton told them they could in fact, legally perform the new pieces with no changes—and also more watchful. In a studious, almost calculating way.

Of course, Ruth tried to ask what had gone on, thinking perhaps Mr Laughton had brought unpleasant news down from London, but Artemis had smiled dismissively and told her *all was well*. Which *seemed* to be, yet didn't feel as though it truly was.

Perhaps what bothered Ruth most was that she'd spent the day thinking, pondering, watching, running through the various possibilities in her mind, half distracted from what she *should* be thinking about. Namely, ensuring this new show was ready to be performed. Which it generally was. Barring any more misfortunes.

Gods, save us from any more of those. I don't think I have it in me to face further ones.

I feel as though I am slowly losing my strength to fight again, and I doubt a speech from Thomas will have me back from the brink this time...

They were in the final week now. Inevitably, there would be small things which would go wrong, but otherwise, if it could just be smooth sailing...

I would be most grateful.

Distractedly, she rubbed her fingers along the Roman coin in her pocket—she'd taken to carrying it about always now, and didn't look forward to potentially relinquishing it when they played their game again next Friday.

Perhaps I won't.

And I admittedly am looking forward to our game, if only because Artemis will be playing with us this time.

That brought the hint of a smile to her lips, as her eyes passed over the shadowy, ominous-looking cottage onstage, the strange flickering glow of the dim gaslight making it appear utterly otherworldly. She'd come here...to wait. Wait for Artemis's return—which should've been hours ago, considering the woman had told them she was only leaving to see Mr Laughton off—though in a sense she hated herself for *waiting*. There was so much to be done...even if only celebrating.

The others had gone to the inn after tonight's performance to celebrate *all being well*, and Ruth too, should've been glad. Ecstatic, really. It was all happening, all coming together, yet all she could do was sit alone, and wait, this odd feeling in her bones that something was...off.

With Artemis, but not solely with Artemis.

With herself.

It seemed like all she'd dreamt, and even that she'd not dared to dream of—namely, love, in her life—had come true, *was* coming true, and yet... She wasn't happy.

Well, she was. She was of a generally happy disposition, no matter what trials and tribulations she faced, and perhaps it was lingering grief over Father's death tainting her... appreciation of all she—*they*—had achieved so far. Maybe it was something else.

Disappointment at my own self for...not risking enough. Not taking the widow on.

Not...

She wasn't quite sure what else she wasn't doing that was making her feel slightly unfulfilled, but there was *something*. It felt as if everything in her life, and herself, was being put into question since her father died, and the answers were...slow to come. Hidden, just beyond her view. Even sitting here, much as she had at the beginning of this whole endeavour...

Who am I now?

For I do not feel I was the girl, sitting there, wishing for her father's ghost to haunt and comfort her.

Instead I feel like a woman. Surveying her castle, built atop the ruins of another, gazing out onto grey, mist-filled skies which hold no answers as to what lies on the horizon.

A castle of illusion, and not...truth nor certainty.

'Though I do still wish you would haunt me, Father,' she whispered softly. 'I could use some of your certainty just now.'

Sighing, she pushed up from her seat, and wandered into the pit, then onstage, through the cottage's front garden, her thoughts flitting in every direction, from her father, naturally, to Artemis, to herself, to *The Widow*, to theatre, to its future, her own, and even how they'd need to remake some flowers for tomorrow's show as St John had got a little too excited tonight as he bashed Thomas over the head with this posy.

A noise caught her attention, and she glanced over her shoulder to find Artemis marching up the steps towards her—she'd not even heard her come in nor traverse the room—looking…

A woman possessed.

Ruth opened her mouth to say something, but before she could, Artemis was upon her, taking her face in her hands, and kissing her as though…this was their last day, their last moment on Earth. All Ruth could do, was grasp onto Artemis's waist, hold fast, and let herself be swept away by it. By the fierceness, the edge of roughness laced with deep, passionate desire. The demanding need, and desperate…take.

It wasn't that Artemis wasn't *giving*, or that she was attempting to do what both agreed was unhealthy—*possess*—but it was as if Artemis had been underwater for centuries, and Ruth was…her air.

The suddenness of the gesture—not unwelcome, but confusing, and disconcerting—surprised Ruth in both good, and bad ways.

It was certainly exciting, and passionate, the way Artemis drank from her, and sought out every recess with her tongue, and lips, and teeth, absolutely setting fire to her veins, giving no quarter.

Yet it was also worrying. A shift of…emotion and pace, so far from what they'd experienced together as of yet. There was something…behind the love—for it was there, in the tenderness of every rough-edged kiss, every sigh, and whimper, and stroke of Artemis's thumb against her cheek.

A part of her…considered stopping this, confronting Artemis, asking her *what the Hell was going on*, but then she realised…

I don't want to know right now. I just want to feel.

Everything was a mess inside of her, and she couldn't add to it right now. And whatever it was lingering behind Artemis's desperation…she knew it would only add to the mess, in a terrifyingly spectacular fashion.

So she took the cowardly way out.

She moved her hands to the buttons of Artemis's dress, and began undoing them. A pitiful sigh of relief escaped Artemis as she did, and then she was taking care of Ruth's dress. Her mouth moved on, to those tender spots she seemed to have mapped out perfectly now, and Ruth struggled to focus on her task, namely: *get Artemis naked.*

She managed it, somehow, her own desperation mounting with every nibble of her collarbone, every swipe of the tongue against her already painfully erect nipples. Artemis had less issues it seemed in the pursuit of nudity, though Ruth did wonder at a few points whether her clothes would survive the encounter. By the time they were both unclothed, and Artemis had a handful of her hair, and was delving further and further into her mouth once again, she found she didn't quite care.

And then Artemis was moving her mouth again, that sinful, pleasure-inducing mouth of hers, devouring every inch, kneading her breasts, and her thighs, and every bit of flesh she could get her hands on as she pulled her down to join her kneeling on the cool boards of the stage. Pausing for the briefest moment, which felt a lifetime, Artemis met her gaze. There was so much in those vibrant eyes of hers, a new, strange shade of vibrant blue in the gaslight. So much…it seemed she was trying to say, but that Ruth couldn't quite comprehend.

So much that I am not ready to know, I think.

Perhaps Artemis sensed that, for her jaw tightened, flicking in time with the lights, and she nodded, before lying back, her head on a pile of someone's clothes, and guiding Ruth to kneel above her mouth, her legs tucked along Artemis's body.

In another life, at another time, Ruth would've felt exposed, uncomfortable in such a position, but tonight, in this moment, she felt…a prize fighter. Holding nothing back, for neither she nor Artemis could withstand holding anything back from each other now.

Beyond what's in her heart, and in her eyes.

All thoughts flitted away into the ether as Artemis encircled and grabbed her thighs, and set her mouth to Ruth's intimate lips. There was no teasing, no coaxing, no slow discovery this time. It was only…

Consumption.

Artemis delved into her folds, into her core, relentlessly, and without mercy, determined, it seemed, to drive Ruth wilder than ever before. Determined to reach deeper depths than she ever had before; to soak up every last drop of Ruth's essence. Ruth let herself fall into the profound, and encompassing sensations, letting her body move, sway, and buck as it would, Artemis's touch, her grip, her breath, and her sounds, vibrating against her inner self, guiding her.

All the way, to a peak unknown in both power and feeling. Crying out, to the ghosts, to her gods, as she strained to not collapse, her legs shaky and tired, her knees smarting, but the rest of her being soaring and flying in blissful release. Until finally, with one final suck of her nub, she did collapse, Artemis guiding, and falling with her to the boards.

They lay there a long time, tangled together, heaving breaths in, gazing at each other in the semi-darkness, before their need to fall into pleasure and ignore all left unsaid between them, creating a mighty gulf, became too great, and so they began anew.

I pray the lark never sings again, for I dread what the morning will bring.

Chapter Twenty-Three

Ethereal, pale blue and rose-pink light seeped into the room from the skylight. Artemis had been stood here beneath it, watching it shift and change since…the final cold breeze of twilight pushed the stars back into darkness. She felt it—the light, and its changes—on her skin, as though she were the moon herself, reflecting the sun's eternal rays.

For a time, she'd watched Ruth sleeping, her bountiful brown locks splayed across the pillow and her back, her flesh blending into the rumpled sheets, but finally she'd had to turn away, unable to bear the breathtaking, heartrending sight of her. Or rather, not so much her, but the memories of what they'd done together, etched on her surely as ink stains on blank paper. It was almost as torturous as the smell of her, which seemed to have infused every pore, becoming one with her own flesh.

Artemis knew she shouldn't have…done what she had last night. Avoided the conversation they must have, taken Ruth as she had, all whilst carrying her decision in her heart. She knew it was unfair, and unkind, and cowardly, and despicable, and the sort of thing… The sort of thing Killian might've done. The sort of thing one didn't do when one loved another, not truly, and selflessly.

Only she'd learned that about herself last night, or perhaps, only remembered it.

She was not…selfless in love. At least, not this time.

Her selfishness was something she'd had to come to terms with even before the incredible night she'd shared with Ruth, first onstage, then here, in this room which had seen Artemis change from *lost soul* to *playwright*. She'd had to come to terms with it all day yesterday, as she'd examined every angle of herself, her desires, her needs, and her plans. As she'd examined every aspect of the offer Kit had brought her.

It hadn't been easy. She was rather certain, that somewhere, some demon was dancing in glee in fact, at having found a special kind of torture, just for her—and yes, in some ways, this offer felt like…a Devil's bargain. But as not many could refuse the Prince of Hell, so Artemis, in the end, found she couldn't refuse Kit Laughton.

All day yesterday, she'd watched them. Watched herself with them, as though a member of the audience herself. She'd…spent hours examining how she felt about them all, and what it would mean, to leave, and to stay.

To stay… It would mean so many extraordinary things would come into her life. She could see it, clear as day, as though someone had painted a series of pictures telling the story of her life here, like a strange version of the *via crucis*.

There would be love. With Ruth, and with this company that had accepted her…without second thought. Without compromise, and without stopping themselves from telling her when she was being…a grumpy old witch.

There would be fun. A new family.

There would be adventure. She could write a thousand plays, Ruth as her muse. In the evenings, there would be laughter, and passionate, beautiful love.

But there would also be…wondering. Regret. A sense of having given away too much of herself, and not in the same manner as she always had before.

There was fear too, marrow deep. That Ruth, being as she was, so selfless, and determined to believe herself…second, in all things, would do as Artemis had once upon a time. That Artemis herself would become Killian, subsuming another into herself. If she stayed, she could see Ruth never quite taking the leap, fulfilling her potential. Refusing to take over the widow, because Artemis would be there, and she didn't think herself as worthy.

There was a very real fear, that she would, in time, destroy Ruth.

A small consolation to know that enmeshed with her selfishness, there was *some* selflessness too.

As for the future if she left…

Leaving meant breaking her own heart. It meant shattering the thing she'd just repaired. It meant risking happiness for another kind of happiness and fulfilment. It meant abandoning a new dream, to pursue an older one, which felt more vital to her very being, because like it or not, Kit was right; success in the country was not success in London.

It meant returning to the city, to the noise, and the dramatics—offstage and on—and the politics, and the…*business*. The constant motion, the vibrancy. It meant returning to a game she'd not enjoyed playing when she had, and breaking Ruth's heart. Breaking the whole company's heart. It meant being selfish. It meant…becoming who the child she'd been once, dreamt she could be, so long ago.

It had been whilst they rehearsed in the afternoon that she'd finally found her answer. She'd been watching from the wings as Ruth and Laurie played out a scene of scheming and betrayal. Ruth was…utterly magnetic, and hypnotising, and it was surprising actually, that her mind had found its way away from the moment.

But it had. Something about the scene…it forced her mind back to the first time she'd ever seen Shakespeare performed. Not in a theatre, but in the streets of Shadwell, by a band of travelling performers. She'd been young then, it was before Papa died, though she'd been alone that day for some reason.

Othello.

The other morsels and speeches had been good, but when one of them had begun the *'it is the cause'* speech, she, and a hundred other people, had stood still, transfixed. People who had busy lives, or were in the midst of working. Many of whom had never seen Shakespeare before, nor could've rightly told you precisely what was being said in the soliloquy, or why it mattered. However, Artemis was certain that if she could find any of them now...

They could tell you how it had made them *feel*. How it had made them stop, and feel Othello's pain, and the danger of that moment. How it had transported them far away from that busy street, to another world entirely. And she remembered thinking...

One day, I too shall write words to transfix a crowded street.

Words to, if not change the world, then change one person's soul.

For hers had been changed that day.

And though she didn't believe herself to be the next Aeschylus, Shakespeare, Goethe, or Aphra Behn, or Sheridan, or Molière... She remembered being part of the audience that day, and knowing, deep inside, that this was *the something more* there was to life.

The ineffable thing she'd found with her father at those puppet shows, and every time she heard a young woman sing a haunting song in a tavern. She had no idea how to... create it, but she knew she had to find a way. The voices, her friends, *this* is what they'd been telling her stories for.

To enchant, transport, teach, and commune with.

This is the more. The human, the connection, the beauty beyond life.

Immortality.

And so as Artemis had stood in the wings today, watching, and remembering, all at once, she'd known, deep in her heart, that there was only ever one choice she could make.

To feed the love in my soul. To feed my soul, which I've only just regained.

Now to tell my love, she thought grimly, her eyes shuttering closed as she felt her heart beginning to crack, preparing herself for what came next, when Ruth shifted and groaned behind her.

And hear, she wakes.

'Good morning,' Ruth murmured.

I will miss that sound, and that sight, Artemis added, when she turned to find her smiling, and stretching delectably in the tangled bed.

Though Ruth's smile didn't last long—there was only so much acting Artemis could do just now, and her being fully dressed didn't help either.

'What's wrong? No, wait,' she added hastily, tearing from bed. 'I have a feeling that for this, I'll want to be dressed too.'

Artemis waited, as one might for their executioner, whilst Ruth tore from bed, not angrily, but shaking, fear, and foreboding flashing in her eyes.

She waited, as Ruth threw on her clothes, hastily, and she knew better than to ask whether she wanted help.

Then, when Ruth stood across from her, the bed between them like a shield, braced for the worst, then, finally, Artemis said the words she knew would break both their hearts with one fell strike.

'I'm leaving.'

'You're…leaving,' Ruth repeated, dazed, and uncomprehending.

'Kit made me an offer yesterday,' she told her, nodding. 'To return to London, as the in-house dramatist for his new theatre.'

'That's…that's why you were…so strange.'

'Yes,' she admitted, the betrayal in Ruth's voice slicing through her. *But you knew this wouldn't be easy.* 'There was much for me to consider.'

'I see it didn't take you very long in the end.'

'There was a time constraint, I didn't have a choice.'

'And I imagine there's a time constraint on you leaving as well,' Ruth retorted bitterly. 'If not I don't imagine you'd be telling me thus, or that you'd have…come to me as you did last night. That was one final farewell tumble, wasn't it?'

The cracking in Ruth's voice had Artemis moving towards her in an instant, but she froze at the glare of pure steel and warning.

'Yes,' she admitted.

'Did you even consider…other options? Compromise? Asking me to come with you? Or we could've spoken of dividing our time between both places, or… I don't know, *something*! Did you consider any of it? Did you even consider *talking this through* with me?'

'Of course I did,' she retorted angrily, her own hurt manifesting in frustration. 'I considered it all. Asking you to abandon your father's theatre, and following me. Asking you to live the life your mother did. But I couldn't. London would eat you alive, Ruth. I don't even know if I have it in me to survive it again. And I… One of us would abandon something of ourselves to please the other, and I can't ask or do that. The likelihood is, you would become as I was with Killian. You'd never rise, and become all you can be, because of me, and I can't do that to you!' Swiping away angry tears from her lashes, Artemis heaved in a breath. 'As for talking this through… It was my decision, though it affects us both, and so I am sorry for that. I should've told you.'

'Why?' Ruth breathed after a moment, and there was something worse than heartbreak in her now. Something which was…a shuttering. A closure, that hardness that even from the first had made Artemis baulk. 'It's not like you owe me anything. That you owe…*us* anything. You said you didn't wish to make plans for the future. We promised each other nothing.'

'Ruth…'

'What do you want me to say, Artemis?' Ruth shouted, throwing up her hands, making Artemis flinch. *This wasn't… how any of this was supposed to go.* 'Go. Please, waste no time in marching off, and seizing this grand opportunity. Be happy. We had a deal. You kept your end of it, so there's nothing keeping you here.'

'This wasn't an easy decision, Ruth,' she said fiercely, daring to take another step closer. 'Everything I said, before, I meant it. I love you! If there was a way I could…have both, I would do it.'

'But there isn't, according to you, and so you had to choose. Between your career, your success, and me.' Ruth shrugged, and Artemis's silence was assent enough to that accusation. 'Believe me, I understand.'

'I…'

'I suppose you'll be on the morning coach,' Ruth said, moving towards the door, and Artemis might've…followed, considered telling her, that no, she hadn't planned on leaving just yet, but on staying a few days, but actually…

This is best.

No use staying now the decision is made, it will only make it harder.

She might've tried too, to make Ruth understand, but she couldn't move.

This feels…wrong.

Or perhaps it merely hurt too much.

Yes. It must be that.

'I'll leave you to pack. I've much to take care of, it seems I need to find a replacement for the widow after all.'

'It should be you,' Artemis managed to say, her eyes prick-ing ceaselessly, though she yet again refused to…submit to tears.

I am making the right decision.

Ruth stopped, and Artemis pressed on, knowing…there was so much she needed to say, that Ruth needed to know, before she could leave…*in some manner of peace.*

And if I'm taking the morning coach, it must be now.

'For what it's worth, I wrote it for you.' Ruth shrugged and shook her head, but Artemis pressed on. 'If you only ever be-lieve one thing I've said to you, believe this, right now. Even before I knew… Even before I knew I was doing it, I wrote that part for you. There is so much of myself in this play, I think you know that. But there is so much of you in there too, surely, you have to know… The first day I saw you onstage… There was *something*. I couldn't figure out what was wrong, and then I realised, you were miscast. You were never any-thing but the heroine. I could never properly imagine you play-ing a secondary role. Not in life, and not onstage. It's only you stopping yourself from being the woman I wrote.'

'Maybe I don't want to be the woman you wrote,' Ruth said quietly, turning, a smile so sad, and regretful on her lips it twisted Artemis's heart even more. 'The only reason I would want to be that now, is so that you might not leave me.'

'I would leave anyone for this chance,' she bit back. She'd thought Ruth knew, knew *her*, and had she not warned her that she couldn't lose herself again? And to refuse this opportunity…it would be sacrificing a piece of herself which had been lost for too long already. 'You should believe that too. You are not *second choice*, or *second best*, and I'm not leaving you because you're not good enough, or I don't love you enough. I'm leaving you, this place, for myself. Because I couldn't rightly stay, and not resent you for it in time.'

Ruth nodded, though Artemis could tell her words bounced off her armour like dull arrows.

In time, she will understand, and forgive me.

In time, she too, will be fulfilled.

At least, so I pray. To my God, and to hers.

'Goodbye, Artemis Goode,' Ruth said flatly, with so much…grief it almost made Artemis rethink her choice. 'May you find the success and life you crave so.'

'Goodbye, Ruth.'

Almost.

Chapter Twenty-Four

By the grace of the gods she prayed to, Ruth made it to her room without encountering anyone—not that she expected to, considering the very early hour—and without crying. It really was worth congratulating herself on, the not crying part. She nearly had up there. Started…sobbing, started begging Artemis to stay, started begging her to…choose her.

To let her go with her to London; that she would follow her anywhere.

To find *some* way so they could be together, and pursue their dreams, and have everything…

But she'd managed to restrain herself from saying any, or all of that.

Well done, Ruthie.

Though, she really shouldn't be congratulating herself. It hadn't been so much *actual* restraint, as…the depth of the wound inflicted. It was one of those wounds which reached so deep inside of you, tearing out…everything, every feeling, all at once, so you couldn't feel any more. It was a wound which reopened very old ones, always fresh on the soul if not on the heart. It was a wound which at the same time… came as no true surprise.

Yesterday… Ruth had sensed Artemis's distance, and now, her calculating, evaluating stare, made sense.

She was measuring us up, and in the end, she found us wanting.

That didn't truly surprise Ruth either. From the beginning, she'd not believed…someone like Artemis could be for her, and she'd been right. She'd thanked her lucky stars for a chance to know the woman, and so she'd had it.

A chance. But nothing more than that.

Sitting on the edge of her bed, Ruth enjoyed the dazing numbness encompassing her for a moment. The tears, the pain, the crying, it would all come soon enough; she could feel it, *right there*, under her skin, itching its way to the forefront from her shredded little heart. She'd felt thus when Father had died. Grief, biding its time while shock dissipated, though this time, the shock was…less. For the lack of surprise.

At Artemis choosing to leave.

At Artemis choosing another love over that we shared.

At being second choice, second best, always, no matter what she says.

Ruth wished…she wished she could hate Artemis, as Artemis herself had hated the man who'd nearly destroyed her. She wished she could have some anger, some hatred, *anything*… But she didn't. Oh, she was angry at Artemis's abrupt departure, only it was because of all the work she'd have to do now to even attempt to save the show they'd worked so hard on. The show which was to save them.

But she didn't hate Artemis for her choice. She didn't, couldn't find any anger for the woman choosing her dream, her purpose, over Ruth.

I'd not choose me either.

I'd not choose a life here, when the world could be at my feet.

I'd not choose second best, exile, when success and an immortal legacy could be mine.

Ah, here are the tears, Ruth thought simply, as they began to well up and drop heavily. They weren't delicate tears, oh, no, they were big, fat, blobs of salty horribleness, falling down her cheeks, onto her hands, irritating her, though not enough to force her to move.

And they just kept coming.

Her heart and chest wrenched, her throat tightened, and she wanted to sob, to scream, to release the pain inside, but all she could do was just *sit there*, and suck in breath after breath, pathetic noises escaping every so often as they just kept pouring from her.

Perhaps, a lifetime's worth.

Oh, she'd cried before. But this…it felt like the culmination of *all* the sad things. A culmination of every hope and dream being crushed, not because of anything she'd done or not done, but merely because she was…herself, and nothing more.

A million memories and voices circled each other in her mind. Echoes of so many past hurts, and past hopes. Memories of seeing her father off on coaches to London. Memories of she and Thomas playing in fields of summer sunshine. Memories of her dull, meaningless time working at a shop, trying to have the life everyone did before Father returned and showed her another path. Memories of that first day she'd met Artemis. Memories of Artemis as she'd taken her last night. Memories of her first time performing before an audience. Memories of…everything.

The sum total of my life and myself which don't seem to amount to much.

Mother's funeral.

Father's.

Father telling me I wasn't good enough to be a heroine.

Artemis telling me I am.

Hopes of falling in love. Finding my place with someone else in this world.

Wishes of never loving ever again for it isn't…enough.

Wishes of security, and comfort, and certainty.

Fears of what will happen now.

Of us all scattering to the wind because I couldn't fix it.

Hours Ruth sat there, and still the tears kept coming. In waves, in droves, sometimes pausing until another memory, another fear or broken wish would appear, and then they'd begin again. She was exhausted, but remained unable to move, even as every minute stole more of her breath, and her throat became rawer, and her heart pulsed in pain.

Fanny found her eventually, though Ruth had little memory of it. She thought she tried to say *go away*, only nothing but tears and a scratchy sound came out.

Then they all came.

Thomas, Fanny, Rose, William, Montague, St John, Laurie, even Guy. No one asked anything, no one said anything.

They merely surrounded her, held her, and stayed with her until her body refused to stay awake any longer, and still they stayed, as she fell into a blessedly empty slumber.

Chapter Twenty-Five

'Helen is the only one available,' Montague declared late that afternoon, as they sat in a circle onstage. Ruth was feeling…better. Of a fashion. Still desolate, lost, and terrified beyond belief, heartbroken, of course, except…she wasn't crying any more. Which should be counted in one's favour.

As should the love they'd shown her today. It didn't heal, but it did help soothe the hurt.

After she'd slept for…some time—it was difficult to say considering she had no clue as to when they'd appeared and she'd fallen asleep—and woken in the warm embraces of too many people to count, Rose had helped her wash, and change. Laurie and Montague had brought in some food, and they'd had a delicious picnic, snuggled up tightly in her room. Though she'd had no appetite, Ruth had been strangely ravenous, and ate heartily, sipping on buckets of tea, which everyone had apparently been pleased to see.

Once somewhat revived, they'd insisted on taking her for a walk to the common—though they'd been gracious enough to thoroughly avoid the spot where they'd taken Artemis what seemed a lifetime ago now.

Perhaps it is.

And this is yet another new life of mine beginning.

All Ruth wished to do, was fall into a dark hole somewhere, and sleep, and never emerge, but the others likely knew that quite well, and prevented her from doing so. Every so often, someone would murmur words of reassurance between random conversations about the weather, and local news.

'We can still do this.'
'Nothing is lost yet, not until the final curtain falls.'
'We'll find a way.'

Heartbroken Ruth didn't wish to admit every reassurance felt like a warm stroke against her heart; still, it did.

Though it didn't…change anything. Sitting here, as they had been for a while now—no show tonight as it was Sunday, a small consolation considering Ruth wasn't entirely sure she'd be able to do…anything, let alone perform—it didn't change anything either.

In fact, in some way, it seemed to make things worse, their reassurances slowly chafing against…so many feelings. Feelings which had been brewing since the beginning of this endeavour in truth, unnamed, and unspoken. Those same feelings which had brewed as she sat here last night, only now, they were beginning to form themselves into words.

Into something she could express.

'What's the point, Montague?' she asked, and everyone turned to look at her, frowning, or narrowing their eyes in confusion. 'So we find someone to take over the widow's role. We open this new show, and if we're lucky, the crowds keep coming long enough to keep us open for a few more months. Then what? We can't perform these pieces until the end of time. Eventually, we'll have to go back to performing the same…useless, pathetic pieces we always have been. Scrimping by every day, to what end?' She shrugged, throwing up her arms as their confusion grew—along with flickers of concern. 'My father spent his whole life working in theatre, and what did it get him? Barely more than a score of people at his funeral, and a mountain of debt. When everyone who knew him is gone, what will remain of him? He'd be lucky to be a footnote in a tourist's guide.'

'Ruth…' Thomas began beside her, and she whirled on him.

'What, Thomas? We spend our lives strutting about these

damned boards, pretending. Living in imaginary worlds made of plaster and paper flowers, and fake sunrises. What's the point?' she cried. 'I used to be so certain it was vital to who I am. I used to think…so many things, but in the end, what is the point of us?'

'She really destroyed you, didn't she?' Laurie remarked in a serious tone, most unusual for him.

'This isn't about Artemis,' Ruth bit back. 'I've felt this… for a long time, yet never could acknowledge it. Voice it. But here, now, with everything telling us this is futile, I finally can. Wonder, at the futility of it. The world is changing, perhaps we should change along with it.'

'We do this…to make people laugh,' St John offered. 'To delight them, make them cry, and feel, and bring beauty into the world.'

'We do it because we cannot do anything else, and be true to ourselves,' William added, to a chorus of nods.

'We live outside of the realm of normality so that we can remind ourselves, and everyone else, that there is more to life, and being human, than what we can sometimes believe,' Laurie said.

'Or do we just tell ourselves such things so we won't face the truth?' Ruth asked bitterly. 'Do we convince ourselves we have great, ineffable aims, and purposes, so that we don't stop, and look, and see that we spend our time playing at life rather than living it? So that we don't regret sacrificing comfort, and safety, for…*this*?'

'Then sell the theatre,' Montague said flatly, garnering all their attentions. 'Do it,' he challenged. 'Sell it. We'll find our places elsewhere, and you can return to living your life, or what you believe it seems, living is.'

Ruth clenched her jaw and fought back the tears threatening to fall again.

And I thought I had no more.

'None of our pretty words will convince you if that's how you truly feel. Only... I don't think it is. You, like many of us, believe in the old gods of this place. And you, as many others of every creed on Earth, are having a crisis of faith, because life has wounded you, deeply. I think I can fairly say everyone in this room has been where you are.' Montague glanced around the circle, as did Ruth, and her heart pinched when she saw the sombre nods. 'I do what I do, I strut upon these boards, and live in imaginary worlds day after day, because I *do* believe as the others do. That in our brightest, and darkest hours, we...need to be reminded of our humanity. Our communality. I believe theatre, art, can change the world, because it can make one person believe, or think, or feel. You cannot touch, nor measure our purpose, our impact. You may never be able to see it. That isn't the point. Immortality isn't the point.'

'What is?' Ruth breathed.

'We humans have been creating since we were put on this Earth. Art *is* our humanity, fulfilled, to its highest order.'

Silence invaded the space, as Ruth...pondered everything again.

She...felt Montague's and the others' words. She had always held such beliefs. Why doubt now? Why such a crisis of faith as he called it, now?

Life has thrown a fair few unbearable punches of late.

Perhaps you're merely seeking to leave the fight before you lose everything.

Perhaps you're trying to make it easier on yourself, this game of life.

Would it be easier? Ruth supposed that was the question, wasn't it.

Would leaving it all behind, be easier?

Unfortunately, the answer came swiftly, as though every

ghost in this theatre—including that of her father, whom she could finally feel—whispered in her ear at once.

You would regret it until the end times, and beyond.

Looking up at Montague, her heart flooded with certainty, gratitude, love, and grief, she nodded.

'So as I was saying.' He smiled, inclining his head, as Thomas took her hand. 'Helen is free. I rode down to see her this morning, and she had an engagement fall through in Brighton. It isn't ideal, but as before, I don't know of anyone else who could fill in in a pinch.'

They all fell silent again.

What he said was true, yet again. Anyone they knew was already engaged elsewhere, and seeking out new performers was possible—but not in the time given to them. Helen was lovely, a genuinely talented actor, but Montague was right in that it wasn't ideal, since again, Helen typically played…

The roles I do.

'I wrote it for you.'

'I wrote it for you...'

'Let's bring Helen on,' Ruth said, her voice, firmer, her heart surer than she'd ever have expected either to be, considering she was also…*panicking.* 'As the maid. I'll take over the widow's part.'

If the others had any objections, or doubts, it didn't show as she looked around the circle.

In fact, it rather seemed like they were…excited. Proud, happy, and relieved.

Perhaps so shall I be, in time.

Oh gods, what am I doing?

Chapter Twenty-Six

It was harder than Artemis had imagined to readjust to London. To her old life. She kept telling herself that was entirely normal, considering she'd only been in town barely two days now, and that it had been…a very precipitous arrival, and departure. Hell, she'd left Kent without even sorting the cottage properly. She'd just packed her bags at the theatre, and jumped on the first coach to London, forgetting that she even had another…home.

Of sorts.

The cottage had always been a refuge. In many ways, she'd made it her own, and not solely by *buying* it. Thinking back, however, on those years spent there… Artemis realised she'd never felt as if she'd found her home. Her place. It had felt…

Well, she'd felt as she imagined Medusa perhaps had. The version of Medusa which said the maiden had been transformed to beast for her treachery against Minerva, that is.

There was much to be said about drawing such parallels, but Artemis focused on the idea that they'd both…removed themselves, or been removed, from the world. They'd both found a refuge, which had been a place to live, but never a home. Only to have that refuge breached by…

Now, Artemis wouldn't place Ruth on the same scale as Perseus; still, the idea of an intrusion of the outside world remained.

And here I am, back to the place I once called home freely. London.

Where she was indeed having some trouble readjusting,

which again, was entirely to be expected when her arrival had been so precipitous and *unexpected*. Once she'd found a room, in a coaching inn near the docks—not everyone's preference, but then all those thoughts of home made her think perhaps revisiting her roots would be welcome, and being removed to the east would keep her from encountering old acquaintances before she was ready—she'd sent a note to Kit telling him she'd arrived in town.

He'd been surprised—or so he said when he came to visit Monday morning—though he'd not questioned her on the precipitous arrival, likely seeing enough in her face to dissuade him from doing so. Lucky, not because Artemis wouldn't have had an answer, but rather because she would've had one. A most unconvincing one to her own mind now, and voicing it…felt as though she'd be lying, though she wouldn't have been.

That's positively clear as crystal, and not confounding nor confusing in the least.

So yes, she and Kit had merely had tea, spoken of his family, and then made plans for the week ahead, including setting a time for her to visit *The Adelaide*—today in fact, which was where she was headed just now.

Overall, Artemis had tried to keep herself busy, yes, in large part to avoid *thinking*. What point was there really, when her decision had been made? In full consciousness, and in possession of all the facts? So, she was…distressed. Sad. Heartbroken. It was normal. To be expected. She'd *knowingly* left something good, and precious behind. Made a sacrifice. It was bound to hurt. At least, she'd ended it before…ending it meant her destruction like the last time.

It wouldn't. It was nothing like last time.

Tssh, she told herself, attempting to focus on the task ahead. Namely, meet Kit so she could begin this new old life of hers.

It's done and over with. In the end, it was merely a lovely little interlude.

You can cherish the time and memories, and still move on with your life.

Love does not always mean happy endings—if theatre has taught you anything, it has certainly taught you that.

So it had.

In the end, this was the best decision for everyone involved.

It didn't matter that Ruth's theatre had begun to feel like home, or that, much like the widow in her own damned play, she'd begun to feel as though she'd found a family again. That was nothing but…the magic of the theatre. Of working on a show together, with good, talented, and kind people. One grew attached. And then, more often than not, one moved on.

It may not be the way of *the* world, but it was the way of *their* world.

They'll all be just fine.

Perhaps Ruth will listen, and take on the widow's role. Find…everything she's searching for.

Find herself.

As I did. Again.

Artemis sent that prayer up to the Heavens, and whichever God or gods may be listening. Then, squaring her shoulders, she continued her way westward along Fleet Street towards *The Adelaide.*

Reassuring herself that the fact she was so anxious at stepping into Kit's new theatre, and generally so reluctant to actually *rejoin* her old life, meant nothing.

Nothing at all.

Chapter Twenty-Seven

For the next few days, Artemis found that using that reassurance—*it means nothing at all*—helped her stop thinking on, and avoid, a great deal of things. A great many doubts, and questions. Things like *why did I refuse Kit's offer to move into the promised lodgings*, or *why haven't I accepted any invitations to join him for dinner, an ale, or a show.*

Things like *why do I feel more lost than I did before without my words*, or *why can't I revel in London's sights and sounds any more?*

Why does it feel as though I've made the worst mistake of my life?

To all those things, those questions, those niggling doubts and fears, she'd learned to reply: *heartache.* Discombobulation resulting from said heartache.

None of it means anything at all.

Not even her…lack of excitement at the meeting with Kit, and their visit of the admittedly, spectacular theatre he'd bought.

Oh, she'd *outwardly* been excited; it wouldn't do to appear as she felt inside, which was…glum.

Unconvinced. Drudging.

It was merely, a lot.

They'd discussed terms. Her wage would not only be good, it would be *more than comfortable.* Artemis would start the following week with work on *The Canterbury Tales*, thus beginning her long season at *The Adelaide.* Next week the announcement of her new role would officially be made—

a stipulation of hers, that Ruth's show open before it became official that Artemis had returned to London, though of course the city was already abuzz with rumours. Papers had been drawn up this week, and contracts would be signed later today.

Friday.

The day *The Widow of Windswept Moor* and *The Thief & The Clown* would open.

If…they'd managed it. Artemis hadn't heard otherwise, not that she'd really bothered to inquire either. Surely though, even with her isolation in the docks, she'd have heard if it had been cancelled.

Postponed.

Or something.

Especially since rumour had it a great many people were travelling down from London to see the show, despite the fact it would open at *The Agora* in a month.

At the very least Kit would've heard, and sent a note.

Yes, she would've heard.

Surely.

It doesn't…matter.

That one was harder to swallow, for it did; though it didn't matter in that there wasn't anything for her to do about it either way.

It had been a strange few days. At first, after the meeting with Kit, Artemis had tried to convince herself she'd start working on some ideas for not only the *Canterbury* adaptation, but further plays she was to write for him, and how they could be integrated with *The Canterbury Tales*.

They'd discussed some initial ideas, so she could absolutely go ahead, and get some work done. In fact, she'd returned to her room at the inn with that intention, only to find…she wasn't particularly inspired.

So she'd gone downstairs—dockside inns, taverns, and

other such places of human congregation, were ideal locales
to find inspiration and stories—and she'd had a jolly enough
time of it, not that she'd got any work done in the end. Merely
a fair bit of talking, and ale-drinking.

And eating, that too.

She'd heard about a Greek sailor's favourite ports across
the globe, and a lady of pleasure's upbringing in Aberdeen.
She'd thought about sharing too, her woes, her heartbreak—
they, and others had asked—only she'd found herself not
quite able to. Reverting too easily into her old ways, merely
asking others questions, distracting them from…digging too
deep, or at all really, she supposed.

In any case, beyond pacing about her own room, and
spending inordinate amounts of time at the inn, she'd not…
done much. Which was both strange, and not, considering
for the past three years—the past few weeks being the exception—she'd not done much. She'd busied herself with chores,
and preserves, and mending, and cleaning, and gardening,
and reading, but otherwise she'd been stuck just…existing.
And even though she knew a new life would be properly beginning for her in just a few days, and that perhaps, some
rest and recuperation to…heal, was best, she also couldn't
help thinking that perhaps…

I need to go for a walk.

Right. She'd done a lot of walking in Kent.

Fine, so perhaps not *a lot*, but a fair amount. She'd been,
as Ruth had put it, cooped up in this room for too long now.
Fresh air—well, the London version of *fresh* air—would be
just the thing to get her back to…fighting form.

Which she would need to be. To sign the contract today.

To just get through today.

Right.

Without further ado, Artemis strode out of her room,
straight out onto the already busy streets. As she'd told Ruth

what seemed so long ago now, people who knew nothing about these areas, always thought they knew what the docks were. What places like Shadwell, Rotherhithe, or Wapping were about.

They didn't. They never could, not without living, and breathing, as she had for so long, in such places.

Like most of London, it was crowded, and noisy. Like much of London, there was poverty, suffering, and crime. Life, beauty, community, and industry. It was full of sights, sounds, and yes, smells. The cawing gulls, the shouts of workers. The industry—so many industries—and so many people from different horizons, all gathered here, to live from the beating heart of the city, as people had for millennia.

The river.

The putrid, disgusting, soup of a river. The beautiful, glorious Thames, which Artemis had sorely missed. It felt as though the river flowed through her as surely as blood did, pulsing through her as it did the city.

Weaving her way through dockhands, lightermen, kiln workers, weavers, chandlers, ropemakers, merchants, children, and visitors from halfway across the world, Artemis felt her step quicken as she made her way further east. The sights, and sounds, so familiar, yet so foreign and forgotten, it was both hypnotising and painful.

On she walked, inhaling every note of spice, food, sea, and refuse, as the sun rose above her, changing the skies from a dusky orange rose, to a bright, blue summer's day, as if by magic.

On she went, as if possessed, seeking…something she couldn't name.

Until she found it. Until she stood before it.

A plain wooden door, which opened onto a plain room, in a plain bricked alley, just a little ways from Shadwell's High Street.

It was quiet in there, no one at home, surely out to wherever they worked already, and there were people living here—the sweet, dainty curtains which others would think out of place here a giveaway to that fact.

It didn't matter; Artemis remembered.

The life, the laughter, the tears, the trials, the love, and the warmth which had been aplenty in that room. That room which had been her family home.

It hadn't changed much.

Have I? she asked herself silently, tears gathering, and tumbling quietly as she stood there, lost, confused, and so very sad. *For I suppose that is the question...*

Home. That is what this place had been.

Why does that word haunt me now?

I...had no use of such concerns as home for so long. Whilst I wrote, that was...home.

And then she'd thought it was...her life with Killian.

Only, standing here now, she realised, she'd not found a true home again since she'd left Shadwell.

Until Ruth.

But one person cannot be another's home. Can they?

One cannot rely on another to...bring them fulfilment, joy, happiness, purpose.

No. They couldn't. That was dangerous. Madness. The road to rack and ruin.

In the end, our desolate, and woeful widow, in the haunting house on the moors, with the dark, brooding lord and his young son, finds family, forgiveness, and rebirth. Learning that fortune, true good fortune, is found, and made, but has nothing to do with money. Learning to hope, and love again. Learning that appearances can be deceiving, and that love appears in ways we cannot always expect. Learning that destiny, fate, even free will, often lead to an unex-

pected destination. Dreams can change, and be made anew, as one changes with the seasons.

The sounds echoing off the air washed over Artemis like a wave, them, and her imaginary voyage as the widow, bringing forth a realisation she'd held in her heart for some time, yet been unable to see—though she'd felt it.

Written it even, without ever truly seeing.

It had been there, behind every doubt, every question, every moment this choice felt *wrong*. Behind every moment she'd wished she could tell Ruth something, point something out to her—even a gentleman's silly waistcoat—just *share* with her.

My love for her is soul-deep.

Not consuming, not all-encompassing, yet part of the fabric of me now.

I want no success, no notoriety, no immortality, if she isn't there to share it with me.

To live without this love, that would be losing my soul.

'Damn it,' she sighed, shaking her head at her own foolishness.

Marching back off from whence she'd come, she only hoped she could fix perhaps the gravest mistake she'd ever made before it was too late.

ACT V

Chapter Twenty-Eight

⁓⧁⧂⧁⁓

'Collect your playbill for a penny when the curtain falls!'

So we come to it now; the end, the beginning...all we've worked for and which I did truly doubt would ever come to pass, Ruth thought, as she took a moment in the shadow of the wings again, to look at them all, waiting onstage for her to complete the final ritual.

Even through the thick curtain, and over the gentle music played to entertain them before the show, the buzz of the audience was loud, electric, and pulsing through each of them, as it always did, but even more so tonight.

To say this week had been a whirlwind, or merely *difficult*, would be the understatement of her life.

It had been gruelling. Trying. The hardest work she, or any of the others had done, in her opinion. Long hours. Days of feeling inadequate—for her—and pushing through. Days of working with each other then, to become...the widow. Days too, of finishing the rest—the scenery, the costumes, the pay, the playbills, the advertising, the music—which had left them all exhausted, yet lit by the same fire.

And of course, an exhausting game of hide-and-seek this afternoon—William now held the coin, and Ruth found she did not mourn its loss as much as she'd thought she would, though she did mourn her wish to have Artemis there.

All followed by a most dreadful, most excruciating final rehearsal.

As it should be.

There had been incredible magic too.

A reminder of *why* she did this. A reminder of what she had in her life—love, creativity, fun—even though yes, of course, her heart still smarted something terrible. She learned to use it, though. Learned to go places with her performance she'd never dared to before. Realising that it had never been her lack of anything—depth, maturity, experience—which had prevented her from taking the lead, but instead, merely that old friend, *fear.*

That fear of relinquishing all of myself, in a way I'd not dreamt I could.

This week had left her feeling both renewed, and hopeful, determined to build that future she knew she wanted—a future built on her father's legacy, but not merely *his*—and also…still uncertain. Though it was in large part everyone's lot in life—to feel uncertain about the future—she also felt as if tonight…would hold so much more of an ending in its beginning than she could rightly comprehend. As though, she had to wait until the curtain fell tonight, to be able to glimpse more of what lay ahead. It really was the queerest feeling.

Though I won't let it stop me.

'Ten minutes, Ruth,' Fanny whispered in her ear meaningfully, before striding onstage to meet the others.

Ruth nodded as she did, and followed a few steps behind, taking in breath after breath.

Glittering, excited gazes, and meaningful looks met her as she joined the circle on the desolate moors they'd created, and she smiled, her mending broken heart, somehow full to the brim. Love, pouring out of the little cracks, only to return eventually, she knew, to mend everything back up.

In time.

As with everything.

Holding out her arms, she grasped St John's and William's hands, as the circle they created—including Dempsey— linked together. Inhaling together, they closed their eyes. The chattering, and electricity of the audience flowed through them, yet the calm which reigned where they were grounded them as they breathed together until they held the same rhythm without even thinking. Warmth and energy flowed through the circle, enforcing the bonds they already shared. Uniting, and strengthening them, to a degree which Ruth might've felt was unbearable—had she not needed every ounce of their friendship, and support.

After a long moment, they began opening their eyes, the settledness of the circle having relaxed, and prepared them for what came next.

'Perhaps I will curse us with what I'm about to say,' Ruth told them quietly. 'Only, as much as I enjoy our traditional recitation of the Bard, I have some new words I'd like to share with you this evening. I think, they would make a good new ritual for us.'

Some looked wary, but all nodded in agreement.

Locking eyes with Thomas, a smile on her face, she began.

'You'll forgive me, paraphrasing slightly, Thomas.' She winked, and he quirked his head in questioning, until she continued. 'We are people of the stage,' she declared, and Thomas nodded, shaking his head in amusement. 'Descended from a long line of travelling artists, and fireside storytellers. We are the minstrels, the saltimbanques, the clowns and the storytellers of every age. We have been run from towns, and thrown in gaol for practising our craft unlawfully. We have been called rogues, vagabonds, thieves. We have starved, and sweat, and we have bled to make people laugh, and cry. There is no doom for artists such as we, merely the truth and wonder of *theatre*!'

Hands tightened around hers, and around the circle, as heads nodded, and smiles grew broader.

'Thank you,' she added, before it was time to break apart, and begin. 'Thank you, all of you. There are…well, I am not the writer here, so I say simply thank you. You know, I'm sure, what you've given me. What this means to me. *Merde*, my friends.'

A chorus of *merdes* echoed gently, as they held fast once more, before breaking apart, and taking their places.

Typically, a speech would be made before they began, but Ruth had opted not to, considering everyone onstage, backstage, and in the audience, knew precisely what they were here to see. So instead, she took her own place beside Helen in the wings.

The lights in the house flickered, and dimmed, as did those onstage.

Thunder. Lightning.

The curtain rises.

Chapter Twenty-Nine

Artemis wasn't entirely sure what she'd been thinking, other than perhaps it would be much easier, getting into the theatre that night. Only, she'd not been counting on her own blasted success and notoriety—*and you sought more, you vapid creature*—which meant the queues to see the show were absolute madness, and barely what looked like a third of the crowd waiting outside eventually made it in before those guarding the doors finally cried *sold out!*

Of course, seeing as the crowd was there to see *her* play, she might've just made her presence known, and bustled her way through them, and in, but then she risked people noticing her arrival and presence, and it getting back to Ruth, and... that wasn't what Artemis wanted. First, Artemis needed to speak to her. Tell her...everything in her heart.

Oh, and beg forgiveness.

Though that, I will do until my dying day.

So yes, getting into the theatre was proving to be a chore she hadn't expected, and one she didn't feel properly equipped to handle after the rather long day she'd had. Telling Kit she couldn't be his new in-house dramatist—which he took surprisingly well after she spent a good half an hour explaining the reasons why. As she'd always suspected, but never truly realised until then, the man was quite the romantic, and in the end, they found their way to new terms. Then, she'd packed up her things again—which granted, she hadn't really *un*packed yet.

That should've been a sign in itself, Artemis Goode.

Finding the coach to Tunbridge Wells—which she discovered only left this afternoon, and which would get her here only just in time. She'd considered trying to find another option for travel, but then decided to keep with the reliable service she knew. Besides, the time would give *her* time to prepare her speech. Apology.

Begging. Grovelling.

Which it had, of sorts. She had the general gist of things, unfortunately her talents as a writer apparently didn't extend quite so far as to crafting the most important speech of her life.

Annoyingly.

Now, here she was, desperate to get inside, and find a place to wait for the show to end—at this point, she didn't quite care whether she saw a wink of it so long as she got to Ruth somehow. Without being spotted, or announcing her presence to the wrong person.

This is Ruth's night. I won't spoil it, or discountenance her before it's over.

Come now, Artemis, think!

Stage door. Of course.

Unfortunately, though she managed to find her way there unseen, she realised it too was guarded by a mighty crowd, already waiting for her eventual exit.

The irony. Almost amusing...

She could risk it—risk those waiting for her not actually knowing what she looked like—but also, she *couldn't* risk it. Frustrated, but determined, her heart beating with renewed purpose—and yes, fear that despite whatever she managed to say to Ruth, there would be nothing but a tragedy's ending waiting for her tonight—she went to the nearby hotel, found a boy, and paid him to fetch someone from the theatre.

He was gone long enough for Artemis to doubt whether she'd ever make it in, and to think about how, really, she wouldn't blame Ruth in any way for rejecting her in the end, considering how she'd treated her, and hurt her, but then finally he returned, one of the apprentices in tow.

Oscar, my little saviour.

Luckily for her, he seemed to bear her no ill will—and she didn't doubt he'd heard the grim details of her *leaving* business—and, clever boy that he was, he'd brought with him an old wig, cap, cape, and glasses, which would do just the trick to ensure no one recognised her. Donning it all, and following Oscar back to the stage door, Artemis couldn't help chuckling. It was a slightly hysterical chuckle, admittedly, given all her pent-up apprehension, though mainly it was the feeling of having gone from *tragedy* to *farce* in less than a minute.

Once just inside—their passage smooth, and without issue—she felt she could finally breathe again.

'I can't have anyone see me, Oscar,' she reminded him quietly.

'I know, Mistress.' He grinned. 'But you want to see the show? Ruthie's playing the widow!'

There was no stopping the rush of pride, and joy, in her heart, nor the giant smile which broke out on her face at that.

'Yes, Oscar, if you've a way for me to watch without being seen, I would.'

'Wait here then. I'll be quick. Can't be having you in that dress and those shoes, Mistress.' He nodded, a mischievous glint in his eyes.

Oh, dear.

What have I got myself into?

It turned out what Artemis had got herself into, once she was sporting trousers and barefoot, was the Heavens—well, the stage tower, but she liked to think of it as the Elizabethans did. Oscar led her up and about the miniature labyrinth of bridges high above the stage, and found her a spot on a section of the seemingly rickety—but very secure—boards where apparently no one came during this show, nor could even spot her.

Also from where she had an, if not exceptional, then rather good view of the stage.

She'd missed the first few scenes, though she'd heard them as she climbed up into the darkness, and even just hearing them… Hearing Ruth's voice rise up to those Heavens she now sat in… It had captivated her—and not solely because she was in love with the woman.

All of them, down there…there was something in their voices, something special, and arresting. Powerful, beyond anything she'd known in a long time.

And that was before she even began *watching* them.

It was like the very first time watching her words come to life, only magnified, a thousandfold. It was cathartic, in every way possible.

Writing it, even rehearsing it…she'd found it cathartic, but not been able to see the full picture in a sense. She'd not seen the entirety of her own story, and Ruth's—for their love story was neatly woven in there too, consciously, and unconsciously—not seen her redemption, her own learning of the lessons she wrote about, nor expelled everything which needed to be from her heart and soul. But sitting there, high up…she did.

She felt, as she had before, the friends who had told her their story, live, and then, turn into wisps of…something else, and dissolve into the ether. Except this time, those friends, those voices, had been…her past selves. It was as if she was shedding layer after layer of dead skin, like a snake, renewing itself. Until she was well, and truly, ready to begin again.

Complete.

Well, almost, but for one thing.

And that one thing… Ruth… She was as Artemis had always believed she could be. Fierce, magnetic, heart-wrenching, and funny. She kept the audience wrapped around her finger, kept them gasping, and groaning, and sighing, and crying, and laughing—including Artemis, of course. She gave absolutely *everything* of herself away to them, and Artemis was so proud of her… So happy for her, for she could feel, even from her perch, all that went into Ruth's performance.

The heartbreak she'd caused. The grief over the loss of her father. Her love of her family, her inherent exuberance and hunger for life. Her doubts, her fears, her passion. All of it, all Ruth was, laid bare in a way not many could.

It was the most beautiful thing Artemis had ever seen.

Revelatory. Exceptional.

And over far too quickly.

Indeed, the main portion of the evening passed in the blink of an eye—and not solely because the play itself wasn't exceptionally long. Before she knew it, the finale music for *The Widow* was playing, and the audience was roaring, leaping to their feet from what Artemis could hear.

Refraining from clapping herself lest she attract someone's eye, she did consider remaining hidden until it was *all* over—until they'd performed *The Thief*, and everyone was changed, the audience was gone, and she could find Ruth alone—but in truth, she couldn't…wait any longer. And if she waited until it was all over, they would surely go feast together as was their tradition, and interrupting *that* somehow felt more of an intrusion than trying to catch her…

In her moment of triumph.

Only, I need to know whether I stand a chance or not.

My heart cannot take this waiting any longer, and perhaps I've just long enough to catch a moment with Ruth before they continue the evening…

So, carefully, and quietly, whilst the audience contin-

ued to whistle, and applaud—and began to call for Artemis Goode, which unfortunately she could see even from
where she was, was beginning to distress Ruth—Artemis
clambered down, ignoring the questioning, and somewhat
accusatory stares of those she met along the way, all the way
down to the wings.

It was only Fanny where she stood—the rest were onstage
taking their bows—and the formidable stage manager raised
a brow, shooting her a look which said: *hurt her again and
you'll not survive.* Artemis nodded, and stepped to the edge
of the wings, her eyes affixed on Ruth.

Glowing, gorgeous, happy, and scintillating Ruth.

Silently calling her; silently begging for another chance.

Please, my love.

Chapter Thirty

Was there a word for feeling more alive than ever before? A word, which defined this feeling of being so full to the brim with life, your body couldn't possibly withstand it? Hold everything in? And yet… At the same time, feeling an insistent tug on your heart? The bittersweet edge of immeasurable joy and accomplishment? Exhilaration laced with sorrow.

Perhaps the Germans have a word for it. They apparently have words for everything.

Ruth had done excellent shows before.

Ruth had given excellent performances before.

But tonight…was something else entirely.

As she stood there, taking bow after bow, Thomas's and Montague's hands in hers, looking out into the wild and ecstatic audience, she felt both more present in her body, in this moment in time, and yet also as if she weren't quite fully here, but instead, floating about inside herself. She felt wrung out, exhausted by all she'd given, and buzzing with life, and pride. In herself, yes, but also in the others. Together, they'd produced something which was…

The best she'd ever been part of. Every single one of them—even the young apprentices flying the painted scenes up and down or making thunder crash and snow fall—had given everything they had in them tonight. There was a true fear inside her that they could never reach such heights ever again—let alone finish the evening and do *The Thief* proper justice—but then that was part of the magic, wasn't it? You gifted something to the world once, and gifted them something new the very next night, or even the very next moment.

Ephemeral beauty—with an everlasting connection.

However, yes, there was a bittersweetness to tonight. She missed Artemis sorely, and despite…all which had passed between them, she wished she was here. To share this moment she'd helped create with them.

Something else had happened whilst she played tonight, pouring all of herself into the role she now saw and accepted *had* been written for her.

Well, firstly, she saw, and accepted that very fact, which was something rather incredible. Secondly, she realised, or rather, released all she'd still been holding onto. She'd thought she had this week, and so she had in some ways.

Tonight however, was the culmination of that journey.

The journey of making peace with her father, and recognising his fallibility. Recognising that it had no bearing on the love they'd had for each other, and that, in the end, seeing him as only a man, did not diminish his impact in her life.

The journey of pushing away fear, and seizing a new chapter in her life.

The journey of accepting herself, and loving herself. Of hearing what Artemis had said to her, and that she'd been unable to truly accept.

I am not second best.

Even as she left me, she sought to preserve us both from repeating the sins of those who hurt us. Killian, Father…

She sought to protect me from the life she had led, and saw better than I did, that all I need is here.

Her choice was her own, and true to her heart.

Love is accepting the other as they are, not demanding they become who would be best for us.

As her mother had in many ways expected her father to become someone new, who *she* needed him to be. Ruth…

would never ask Artemis to give up on her dreams, her truest self, for her, just as Artemis hadn't asked her to.

I did tell her once, that I would never force a choice on her she didn't wish to make, yet that is what I might've done.

And that isn't love.

Not that I still feel I know anything of it, beyond how it makes my heart beat stronger.

So yes, this evening had been so much more for her than *just another performance.*

And the bittersweetness in her heart, for being unable to share this with Artemis, in no way diminished the rest.

However, when the audience began clamouring for Artemis Goode to come onstage Ruth did begin to feel a new lance of apprehension, for she knew she'd have to find some excuse to assuage them.

I thought I had more time to come up with one, the evening isn't over yet...

Or you simply tell them the truth.

They would be disappointed, surely, still, they would... have enjoyed the play nonetheless, and she doubted anyone would *walk out* because Artemis wasn't here. Well, no more than the usual few who sometimes left after the evening's main offering.

Ruth was just preparing to settle them so she could advise that Mistress Goode would not be joining them this evening, when the gentle rush of whispering caught her ear, and then Thomas squeezed her hand, and gestured to the wings stage right.

It cannot be...

Yet, it was.

Artemis Goode, standing there in the shadows of the wings, looking slightly odd, barefoot, in her underthings and trousers, but also looking like the most welcome sight on earth.

She's here.

Don't get carried away, she instructed her heart nonetheless, telling herself that it didn't rightly matter if Artemis was smiling like an angel—*beaming, really*—or that there was pride, and yet hesitancy in her eyes. There could be a great many explanations as to why she was here.

So go find out which it is, Ruth told herself, her heart not taking the instruction to not get carried away.

'Hold off on *The Thief*, and keep them busy,' Ruth told Thomas, as she ducked out of the line, and towards the wings.

'I think a jig is in order before we continue!' he called loudly behind her, and she laughed to herself, expelling some of her…trepidation.

Thomas's suggestion appeared to thankfully excite and distract the audience, and Ruth came to stand before Artemis as the others gathered their instruments and began dancing.

Why can't I breathe properly? she wondered, as they stood there, just…gazing into each other's eyes, devouring the sight of one another, as though they'd not seen each other for millennia.

'What are you doing here?' Ruth managed to get out, her whole body begging her to just reach out, and touch Artemis, kiss her, love her, until…for ever.

Only I cannot until I know why she's here.

Please be here for why I wish you're here.

'To tell you I've been completely stupid,' Artemis said simply, so much regret, and hope in her eyes that Ruth felt the flames of the latter ignite mightily again within her. 'I didn't want to ruin your night, but I couldn't stay away any longer. I couldn't wait a moment longer to tell you I'm sorry. So very sorry for leaving as I did, and not being able to see… There is no success, no soul, without you. All I want, all I need, *ever*, is right here. You, them,' she laughed, gesturing at the happy band onstage, as though it were the most incredible thing, that she should need a family too. 'This place. Or another. I'll go wherever you go. Really it's just you, and them. You…it seems so boring and derivative to say you changed me, Ruth,' she continued, shaking her head as her eyes teared up, and meanwhile Ruth was *truly* fitting to burst now. *Complete.* 'I tried to come up with all sorts of beautiful things to say, but that's the truth. You reminded me who I was, and showed me… What it means to be alive. What it means to love, truly. Desperately, achingly, yes, but also simply. Without demand. I want to make plans with you. I want to find a way we can both achieve our dreams. I'm terrified out of my mind, but I know… I have faith that together, we could build something, *be* something, extraordinary. I know I hurt you deeply, and I'll understand if you cannot forgive me, still, I hope…you can.'

Taking a deep breath, Artemis fell silent, fear in her eyes for what Ruth would say next.

'I never want you to give up your dreams, or any part of yourself, for me,' Ruth told her, and relief poured out of Artemis, right before she took Ruth's face in her hands, nodding almost maniacally. 'Not to borrow your words, but you changed me too. Held a mirror up to me, and challenged me to truly see myself, and what was possible. You taught me to conquer my fear, and step out of the shadows, seize what I truly want, and you've given me love. As for forgiving you… I already did. You had to be true to yourself, and you saved us both from repeating the sins of the past. Whatever comes next, however, we build it together. We make choices together, and learn how to do…*this*, together. That's the deal.'

'Yes.'

'Yes.'

Then, to seal their deal, a kiss.

Finally.

They clung to each other, desperately, all the emotion from

tonight, the past days, the past weeks, pouring out. The love, the healing, the desperation, the passion, the hope, the fear, the pride…all of it. It was messy, and clumsy, and still, perhaps the most beautiful kiss they'd shared, for every promise, and possibility held within it.

And then, breathless, Ruth broke away, grabbed Artemis's hand, and dragged her onstage. They joined the jig to the renewed and ecstatic acclaim from the audience, Artemis occasionally taking a bow, but never releasing Ruth's hand for a second.

Standing, dancing, just *being* there, onstage, Ruth felt that feeling again, of being alive without end. Boundlessly full of life, love, and hope.

And this time, there was no bittersweetness.

Only magic.

Epilogue

⟨⟨⟨⟨~⟩⟩⟩⟩

Tunbridge Wells, November 1832

A storm raged outside. Thick droplets of water poured down the diamond-paned windows as wind howled around them, fanning the already roaring fire. Scissors snipped through paper with a satisfying click, and Artemis smiled to herself. The incongruity of the similarity between this day, and that which had brought Ruth into her life, thoroughly amusing.

Reassuring too, in its symmetry; unbelievable in that as well, as though she herself had written the play which brought them to this moment.

Which she had—though that wasn't entirely how she meant it.

It wasn't her doing today, the cutting, and there would be no feeding the fire with newspaper confetti. The article Ruth was currently carefully extracting—she knew what it was because Ruth had woken her by shoving the paper in her face whilst she blearily tried to make out words rather than a mere blur—would end up in the memory book they'd begun together. It was an article celebrating *The Devil Jack or A Soldier's Return*, Artemis's new *triumphant coup* at *The Adelaide*, following her *exceptional* and *reviving* adaptation of *The Canterbury Tales*.

Both of which she'd written for the most part here, in Tunbridge Wells, whilst *The Widow* and *The Thief* enjoyed remarkable runs at both *Connell's Castle*—paying off Ruth's debts—and *The Agora*; part of those new terms she'd negotiated with Kit.

She'd gone up to London a few times, to see how rehearsals for *Canterbury* progressed, or to play with *The Adelaide*'s company—which didn't feel like a betrayal, but instead, a growing of her circle. Ruth had come up with her on those days she didn't have to perform *The Widow* to sold-out houses of people come from all over the country—and beyond—and though they'd not had inordinate amounts of time to explore and discover the city together, they had managed…a lot. Seeing shows, visiting Artemis's old haunts, meeting friends old and new, just…letting Ruth experience the city.

It had been wonderful—and not least because in some way, Artemis felt as if she'd…been granted a chance to make one of Ruth's dreams come true.

As she makes mine come true every day.

The Widow's run had not only enabled Ruth to pay off her debts, but ensured the company and theatre were safe for another year. Though it also meant they didn't *need* to tour, and fulfil any winter or spring engagements, they decided to nonetheless, as those venues which had shown Ruth and her father loyalty, deserved it in turn, and Ruth had promised them *The Widow* and *The Thief*. So together with the company, and the venues, they had settled on a month-long break—which was nearly over—to rest, and…plan.

So far, said plan was…to continue in some fashion as they had thus far. In the winter, Artemis would write plays, which Kit would produce at *The Adelaide*. In the summer, she would write pieces for Ruth to produce at *Connell's Castle*—and tour in the winter if they decided to continue with that—pieces, which would also be performed as part of *The Agora's* summer season, since reform was still slow to be passed into law, even if it was something which most already recognised as a *done thing*. Their success, the novelty of Artemis's return might wear off in time—whether or not her plays were good—but they would deal with such a problem if and when it came.

They also had vague plans to expand their theatrical operation in Kent, with the investment that not only Artemis had made in the company, but others too—including Dempsey—making them all partners now. And as partners, they'd decided they should quite like to find ways to support and attract new talent, beyond offering apprenticeships. A school for dramatists, or a theatrical library; a countrywide search for actors, musicians, and artists, even opening a new venue elsewhere… So many exciting ideas were being floated about, and though they hadn't quite decided which to pursue just yet, Artemis felt confident that in time, they would build something incredible.

Beyond what we already have.

Which was, in the plainest terms, to her, the home she'd never dreamt of, yet somehow found. She and Ruth had stayed at the theatre—in their respective rooms, though naturally, they did share more often than not—for the duration of the summer season, whilst they learned how to cohabitate, and settled into their relationship.

Neither cared to rush anything, not afraid of risking their hearts, just of bruising them on the path to the future. They made plans for the next few years, but words like *for ever* weren't thrown about, even if Artemis knew they both had a feeling this was *for ever* for both of them. It helped to… lessen the pressure whilst they learned to build the relationship they wanted, but hadn't expected.

One of trust, complicity, partnership, and also, individuality. Where neither was subsumed by the other, and where each person remained…their own person.

In Artemis's opinion—and Ruth's, for they discussed it often enough—it was going rather splendidly, actually. So splendidly, that they'd agreed to spend their month's respite in Artemis's cottage. Montague took over the top room in the theatre—Ruth didn't like leaving it unattended—and he found himself in need of a new home just as she was looking to engage a tenant for the winter, not that he'd yet shared why.

In time, as with all things.

Cohabitation in the cottage was going as well as could be expected. Naturally, there were heated discussions over dishes left unwashed, and using the other's hairbrush, but together, they muddled through.

And Artemis discovered that you could, in fact, find a home in other people. That in truth, it was the only place to find it. Whether at the cottage, or at the theatre, there was a settledness between them—all of them—and a warmth which couldn't be replicated.

A home full of love, that is what we've found.

Creativity too. Fun, play, of course. Intellectual exchanges, heated debates about new works or philosophy or even politics. More often than not, half the company if not all was here, with them, wandering in and out, as if they owned the place.

Once, Artemis would've minded. Recalling her grumpy, hermit of a self, she chuckled.

Yes, I don't think I would've enjoyed it, relished it, as I do now...

Which reminds me...

She had a play to finish. The others would be arriving soon for a Sunday roast which Ruth was currently preparing between sessions of article-cutting. The delicious scents were beginning to torture Artemis, as was—*as ever*—Ruth's presence nearby.

However I must finish, if I want them to read this later, and share their thoughts.

Indeed.

Personally, she thought this one had some promise, and that they, and eventually Kit, would enjoy it. It was a tale of love and woe as she preferred, about a runaway orphan finding home with a group of travelling players in the Middle Ages, whilst they brought mystery plays to forgotten corners of the realm, ravaged by war and desperation. It was ambitious, certainly, but then Kit had given her free rein of his theatre.

Though it is missing something...

The company will tell me, and help me fix it, whatever it is.

They were good at that, and always keen to help her—whether or not it was a play they would in time perform, or not.

'How goes it?' Ruth asked, her hands sliding over Artemis's shoulders, massaging gently before she leaned down to kiss her cheek.

'Nearly there.' She smiled, turning to capture those lips which she would never tire of.

Not in this lifetime, or the next, I think...

Artemis didn't settle for a quick kiss either. In need of inspiration, she let herself delve into Ruth for quite a while, until Ruth's hands gripped her tighter, and she could feel they were both becoming *too* heated considering what they still had to do before the others' arrival. Reluctantly she pulled away, licking her lips, as she took a moment to centre herself in the grey depths which would never cease to do so.

Just as she would never cease to have her breath taken away by this woman—in every way possible.

Thief that she is, stealing my heart, my breath, and my brush.

Temptress who makes my blood come alive, and goddess, who brought magic into my life.

'Perhaps you'd better be *all finished* soon.' Ruth grinned slyly, raising a brow. 'I'm going to check on my roast, prepare some vegetables, and then, we should have some time before the others arrive.'

'Well if that isn't an incentive...'

Ruth's smile grew, and Artemis leaned up to steal another

kiss, but her love was too quick, scampering off to the kitchen before she could, giggling all the way.

As I said.

Temptress.

It worked, however.

By the time Ruth had finished her work, Artemis had hers.

As she scrawled the last words on the bottom of the page, and rose to go make good use of what time they had before their home was invaded by the rest of the company, and everyone piled into every nook and cranny, and laughed, and sang, and read by firelight, Artemis smiled.

They were simple words, yet powerful ones. Words which somehow fit the moment, even if this, the great story of their lives, wasn't nearly over, only still beginning; at least so she hoped, for in the end, one could never truly know what God, or the gods, or life had in store.

They fit, and yet, as there had always been in Ruth, there remained so many possibilities within their finite yet immeasurable scope.

Fin.

Curtain Falls.

* * * * *

If you enjoyed this story, make sure to read
Lotte R. James's latest romances

A Lady on the Edge of Ruin
The Viscount's Daring Miss

And why not check out her Gentlemen of Mystery miniseries?

The Housekeeper of Thornhallow Hall
The Marquess of Yew Park House
The Gentleman of Holly Street

CONNELL'S CASTLE, TUNBRIDGE WELLS

This present Friday, July 6, 1832, and FOR A FULL SEASON
Will be presented a new play by
ARTEMIS GOODE
"THE WIDOW OF WINDSWEPT MOOR"
A most amusing but dramatic tale of love and betrayal in
three acts.

The Widow... Miss Ruth Connell
The Maid... Miss Helen Featherton
The Lord... Mr Montague Worthing
The Butler... Mr William Klein
The Valet... Mr Thomas Jennings
The Groundskeeper... Mr St John Roches
The Stranger... Mr Laurie DuMont
All Other Roles... Various Apprentices
Produced and Managed by Miss Ruth Connell
Music by Mr Montague Worthing and Mr St John Roches
Scenery and effects by Mr Guy Ashton with gracious
assistance from Mr Grant Dempsey
Costumes by Ms Rose Claremont

"THE WIDOW OF WINDSWEPT MOOR"
SYNOPSIS

The widow flees her home with her maid, seeking refuge and salvation from her deceased husband's debts at his brother's home. Becoming a governess to his young son, she soon finds herself tempted by the tempestuous man, even as it feels a betrayal to her husband's memory. The groundskeeper seeks to warn her off the lord, and her maid helps her keep far from him, still, the widow finds herself evermore enticed by the lord's quiet kindness and passion. In his home, she finds love, family, and a new life—at least until her husband reappears, having faked his own death, helped by the widow's maid. He demands payment for his debts, and the lord accepts, so that he and his love can live their lives in peace.

Delightful musical interludes and finale to complete this entertaining tale of woe and redemption.

To conclude the evening, Ms Goode's new Farce

THE THIEF & THE CLOWN